The Penance Drummer

The Penance Drummer

stories by
Lois Braun

TURNSTONE PRESS

The Penance Drummer
copyright © Lois Braun 2007

Turnstone Press
Artspace Building
018-100 Arthur Street
Winnipeg, MB
R3B 1H3 Canada
www.TurnstonePress.com

All rights reserved. No part of this book may be reproduced or transmitted in any form or by any means—graphic, electronic or mechanical—without the prior written permission of the publisher. Any request to photocopy any part of this book shall be directed in writing to Access Copyright (formerly Cancopy, the Canadian Copyright Licensing Agency), Toronto.

Turnstone Press gratefully acknowledges the assistance of the Canada Council for the Arts, the Manitoba Arts Council, the Government of Canada through the Book Publishing Industry Development Program, and the Government of Manitoba through the Department of Culture, Heritage and Tourism, Arts Branch, for our publishing activities.

Cover design: Doowah Design
Interior design: Sharon Caseburg
Printed and bound in Canada by Friesens for Turnstone Press.

In the story "Broken Angels," the botanical references are from an April 1967 issue of *Native Manitoba Plants in Bog, Bush, and Prairie*, by Hector Macdonald, published by the Manitoba Department of Agriculture.

Library and Archives Canada Cataloguing in Publication

Braun, Lois, 1949-
  The penance drummer / Lois Braun.

ISBN 978-0-88801-327-9

  I. Title.

PS8553.R36P45 2007   C813'.54   C2007-901881-5

CONTENTS

Bill's Girls / 3

The Penance Drummer / 17

The Half-Town Folly / 37

Goldie / 57

Assassins / 89

Broken Angels / 121

Sturgis / 143

A Private Paradise / 165

Laundry Day / 185

Rape Flower Tea House / 215

The Penance Drummer

BILL'S GIRLS

Green they flew, through air the colour of delphiniums in old village gardens. When they landed, they made hollow sounds on the broad metal and reminded Bill of shotgun fire heard at a great distance. The first apple, though, struck the back of the convertible, and Bill didn't know what had hit him. Then several pelted the hood and, after a thunderstruck moment, Bill saw they were apples—hard, shiny, green. "What the Sam Hill—" he wanted to say to her, but of course she wasn't there.

He slowed the Plymouth down—he hadn't been going very fast, had been just idling along, actually—but the fruit kept flying, bonking the side of the car, then the trunk; one long lob smacked him on the back of his head. "What the—?"

The car came to a stop. Bill turned off the ignition. Beside the road was the shelter belt of an abandoned farm—spruce, willow, maple. Skin flashed through the foliage. The glistening whites of eyes. Scattered. His attackers had been many, as he had suspected. His gaze followed their movements. It was like watching birds in a forest.

The engine ticked as it cooled in a midsummer breeze blowing off a mustard field. Bill turned his ear toward the trees and waited for children's voices. It didn't take long. Someone always had to have a last laugh. There it was: a long, high-pitched guffaw that startled a blackbird from its perch. The bird fluttered from treetop to treetop.

Bill half-stood in the car and checked the hood for dents. Today was the first day he'd had the convertible out since she'd gone. Today was the first day he'd taken a drive for pleasure since she'd gone. They'd never been pelted with apples before. Now that he was alone, he'd become a mark: *Look at the guy with his top down. . . .*

He opened the car door and planted his feet on the road. The soles of his shoes scraped the gravel. No dents that he could see. All was quiet now in the bush beside the road.

The farm had belonged to a family of Erdriches. Bill remembered Hermann Erdrich, a bachelor, the last of the farming Erdriches. He was in a nursing home in town. Others of his lineage had moved to cities, although one sister, he recalled, had married a local. The old farmhouse, hidden behind the shelter belt, in which Hermann had lived, had been barely inhabitable when someone had finally come and hauled the old fella to the home. Bill knew about the house because he'd seen it between the spruce trees in winter when he and Marion chanced by.

The apple throwers were probably hiding in the decrepit house. As he idled up to the weedy driveway, he tried to recall the local Erdrich sister. Bits of her popped out of his brain cells: short, shy, glasses, sweet smile.

A widow.

Ever since Marion had died, Bill was dismayed to find himself sizing up widows. He couldn't help it. The day after the funeral, his mind had flitted among the four widows who'd been there, like that blackbird, looking for a place to roost. And when he sat in his armchair, images of widows he knew passed between him and the television set, a whole parade of them. So he'd brought the picture of Marion—the one taken on Blossom Weekend at the orchard of the experimental farm in Morden—from the sideboard in the dining room to the armchair and held it while watching *MASH* reruns. It didn't help much; the parade went on and on. But he felt he was doing the right thing, holding the photo in his lap.

The Erdrich sister faded as Bill passed the trees only to find that the farmhouse had disappeared. No buildings whatsoever remained on the property. The heirs had either sold the farm or given permission to the renters to clean up the place, get rid of vermin. Bill got out of the car anyway. His presence might scare the children out of throwing apples at passing vehicles. He was certain they were watching him from the bushes. The grass had been cut, cut long; swaths of it lay in an orderly pattern all around him.

The Plymouth was red. Marion had been blonde. They'd gone well together. In the last years she'd tinted her hair a paler version of blonde to hide the grey. "They call this *champagne*," she'd told him when she'd first come home with it. He'd squirmed at the idea of his wife covering up her blonde-going-grey with dye. But when she called it *champagne*, it seemed all right after all. And when they tested the new look in the red convertible, Bill was relieved to find that the effect was better than ever. Even in the hospital, someone made sure her hair was nice. He wondered who. Who came in and washed it and applied the mysterious chemicals and put in the curlers? The whole time she was there, she hadn't had a bad hair day, unless you counted the flatness at the back of her head. And though illness had used up all her plumpness and sucked the peaches-and-cream from her cheeks, the mortician had restored her glamour. In her casket, Marion had looked like a movie star.

For his birthday the first year they were married, she'd given him a telephone moulded from red plastic in the shape of a convertible. After a while, they went back to a more traditional phone, but when they told him she was dying, he found the sports-car phone in the basement pantry and reconnected it. Mornings when he called her—or later, the nurses' station, or the doctors—he talked on the sports-car phone. Marion didn't know. Bill didn't take the real car out of the garage the whole time she was sick. He drove the Dodge.

Walking past the house site, Bill found the apple trees, about six of them, surrounded by unmown grass and nettles and Russian thistle. They were close to the rows of trees that bordered the road. The children must have seen him coming and gathered up their little arsenal in a hurry.

Every year Marion and Bill went to the Morden Experimental Farm in late spring to admire acres and acres of blossoms. They picnicked among the spreading fruit trees. Consulting the brochures the experimental farm provided, they planted three apple trees in their own backyard. She'd make jelly, she said. But she never had. Why not? He hadn't asked.

He could detect no sounds or movements in the underbrush now, but there were other thickets on the yard for the brats to hide in.

As Bill wandered back to his car, he gazed across the field behind the yard to the neighbouring farm, and it all became clear: that was the Sawatzky farm. Their boy had taken over the place when he'd married. Bill had seen him in the Co-op with a bunch of kids—girls, if his memory served him right. Blonde girls, hanging onto the grocery cart, running on ahead, dropping the wrong items into it. But they couldn't have crossed the field that fast. It didn't matter. Bill decided to visit the Sawatzkys. Drive past, anyway. "Check it out," Marion would say on their rides in the country.

This, too, had been a village once. Over the years, most of the buildings and yards had been razed for farmland. Dozens of such villages squatted at intersections of gravel roads all around the larger town. Bill's parents had once lived in such a village. His grandparents had tended a yard full of hollyhocks and delphiniums and peonies.

The Sawatzky place was cluttered with toys and tricycles. New shutters decorated the sagging, white, one-and-a-half-storey house. Petunias reached out from yellow boxes beneath the windows. "It's nice to see someone cares," Marion would have said. She often said that on their drives in the country. White and yellow. The effect was so cheerful, Bill turned into the driveway. No children were in sight. A goat trotted from behind the barn and glanced longingly at the fenced-in garden next to the house. Not many people had goats around here.

Bill hadn't thought about whether he would knock on the door. He really just wanted to look. To absorb the atmosphere of family that hung heavy in the sweet, humid air.

But he'd scarcely pushed the car door shut behind him when the screen door on the side of the cottage opened wide. A woman with a triangle of cloth tied over her hair stood poised there, her bare arm stretched along the door to hold it open. She smiled.

She's not afraid, Bill thought. In the city the door would be locked and stay that way until you flashed a photo ID. It was the convertible. No one feared a red convertible driven by an old man. The woman passed her free hand across her forehead. "Hello," Bill called before he went closer.

The smile broadened. She'd like a ride, thought Bill. She's been waiting for someone to take her away from her canning, or her bread-baking, and whisk her away in a convertible. She would untie the flowered scarf and let the wind cool her fair skin and flow through her hair. Mrs. Sawatzky had short, dark hair, unlike her daughters.

"I know you well," Bill said, meaning her people, and he swatted the air as if swatting away unfamiliarity. "Your husband is Jake. His dad used to come into my store all the time." Bill stopped near the woman. She kept smiling and stepped off the doorsill. They both looked into the yard. "I had a hardware store in town. When your husband was a boy, he always wanted his dad to buy him something. We didn't carry toys in those days. They do now. One time his dad bought him a door hinge. Jakie wanted that door hinge. So his dad bought it for him. I always wondered what he did with it, wondered if he grew up to be handy." Bill looked at the woman. "I don't suppose you call him Jakie any more."

The woman shook her head.

"And you're from the Schmidts," Bill went on. "They farmed around here. Still do?"

The woman nodded.

"I guess Jake isn't home."

Again the woman shook her head. But then she said, "Nice car." She spoke unclearly. "I have a Jakie in the house. He'd like to see it."

She seemed to have to work hard to make her words succinct. Cleft palate, thought Bill. "Sure, sure, bring him out," he said. Of course the girls would leave their little brother behind. While Mrs. Sawatzky fetched the boy, Bill glanced about, expecting to see the apple throwers peeking around the corner of some building or other.

Jakie was about five. He was dark like his mother. He approached the convertible as if it were a bull that might charge any minute. "Get in, sit behind the wheel," Bill urged from the doorway.

"My husband will be home soon," said the woman.

Bill grinned and nodded. He knew what farmers were like. There was no telling when Jake Sawatzky would return. It could be minutes or hours.

"I have lemonade. Come in."

She opened the screen door again and walked through, expecting Bill to follow. He did follow her, and thought, she hasn't even asked my name. What would her husband think, finding his wife entertaining a stranger in the house? What am I doing here? What excuse will I give Jake if he comes in?

Bill said, "The house looks good."

Answering an earlier question, the woman flung over her shoulder, "My husband made the shutters. Real ones. They open and close."

He learned how to use a hinge, thought Bill.

They passed through a lean-to pantry that smelled of

muskmelon even though muskmelons weren't in season. "I know you well," he repeated, to make it all right that he was entering her kitchen. "I'm Willie Wiebe."

Bill caught his breath. Why had he said *Willie*? He hadn't been a Willie since he and Marion had wed.

Mrs. Sawatzky nodded but didn't volunteer her Christian name. The kitchen was white. Fruit decals on the middle of each cupboard door comforted Bill somehow—twigged memories of some other, earlier, kitchen he'd been in; on the counter in straight rows sat sealer jars of bright green pickles. The square table—a solid one of wood—was covered with a plastic tablecloth. Spread on top of it were several white tea towels, carpeted with yellowish floury noodles, hand-cut, crinkly. They reminded Bill of blow-ups he'd seen in biology books of the micro-organisms living in pond water.

Mrs. Sawatzky took hold of the corners of tea towels at one end of the table and folded them over and over in one direction, clearing a space on one half of the table. "They're dry," she said.

Bill sat down on a painted chair, which had a fruit decal on its back. The pears and peaches and cherries had been nearly rubbed away by Jake's sweaty shirts. A decal on one of the other chair-backs looked as if someone had taken a sharp tool to it and tried to scratch it off.

Jakie padded back into the kitchen in bare feet. The boy gazed at his mother pouring lemonade into glasses with a pattern of orange slices on their sides. How like her he was! She handed him his drink first, and he took it and carried it back into the lean-to. A short time later Bill heard the rattle of toy trucks and imitation engine sounds made by a young human voice. Bill crossed his legs and ran his thumb through the condensation forming on the lemonade glass.

They talked about their families, mostly about her family. Not her and Jake's children, but about the line of Schmidts she came from. Bill liked to hear about families, even ones he didn't know well, or didn't know at all. Liked to hear about the odd occupations people went into, the exotic places some of them moved to, the marital snags, the feuds, the estrangements; about diseases, hideous disfigurements, tragic deaths. And the ironies a good family storyteller recognized and imparted in the telling. Bill had discovered over the years that deep, dark family secrets people wouldn't share with their friends were easily revealed to near-strangers sitting uninvited in their kitchens. He couldn't always decipher the words of this particular woman in this particular kitchen. When he missed a word, he'd squint his eyes and turn his ear towards her, and she learned quickly to repeat a phrase when she saw that signal. Of himself and his ancestry, he said little.

Mrs. Sawatzky went to tighten the rings on the pickle jars. Then she said, "Who is your wife?"

"My wife was Marion Krueger. She died last month."

The woman gasped. "Cancer?"

Bill nodded. "You know the Kruegers. They lived on the north side of town in that very big, tall house that burned down one winter. You wouldn't have been born yet, but everyone knows the story. The Kruegers had eight adopted children. Six of them and the mother died in the fire. Marion and her adopted brother and the father lived. You've heard this?"

"Sure, sure...."

"Mr. Krueger took the surviving children to live with him in Bolivia after the fire, because he couldn't stand our winters after that, had a fear of stoves and furnaces for the rest of his life. When Marion was nearly full-grown, he died in Bolivia, drowned in a flash flood. Then his sister and her husband brought the children back here to live with them. When Marion finished school, she moved to the city. She worked in a bank and didn't marry until we met each other at a school reunion. We both married late."

That was his wife's story. He had prized Marion for her story. He finished it off. "A man who was afraid of fire died in the water."

The woman shook her head in disbelief. "Do you have children?"

"No," said Bill. "We were married only ten years when she died. Too late for children. But—" Should he tell? "I called her sometimes from home—when she was in the hospital—on a telephone shaped like a sports car. Do you think that was all right?"

She tightened the rings over and over again, lost in thought, a sad look on her face.

Bill watched her slender arm flexing at the jar rings. Love filled him as though he had drunk it in with the lemonade. It didn't matter that she wasn't a widow, that she had a husband and a pack of bratty girls, that her voice often wound up in her nose, making her words incoherent. It didn't matter that she wasn't blonde, or that her care for him was only politeness. He loved her with all his soul.

"I think that was all right," she said. But she might have thought he was asking if it was all right that he called Marion from home sometimes instead of going to see her.

She went to the window. He pictured how it would appear from the outside, the yellow shutters framing her face and the bright bit of scarf. What did she see when she gazed out that window? The strong trunks of the twin cottonwoods on the front lawn? Or did her imagination summon up tropical butterflies and carriages drawn by white unicorns? Marion could remember the butterflies in Bolivia. Spoke of them often. Tried to draw them, but always gave up in frustration. And she had collected unicorns—posters, figurines, stickers, decals.

In their wedding vows, she'd said, "I love you with all my soul."

"Would you—" Bill began. "Perhaps little Jakie would like to—"

The woman turned from the window and put her hand to her throat.

A ghost appeared in the doorway. Shimmering in a frame of sunlight from a south-facing window in the lean-to pantry. A fair-haired girl dressed in a pale yellow shift. Behind her, other blondes, ghosts, some taller, one shorter. Four of them, fresh from apple throwing. They made no noise. Bill could see them, but their mother could not. Her eyes were on the man sitting at her table. Her hand was still at her throat.

Then the front child stepped into the room. The mother dropped her hand to her side. "These are my other children," she said.

They lined up in the doorway as innocent as angels.

Bill nodded. "I know you very well," he said to the girls. But, he thought, these girls have nerve, coming in here all devil-may-care, knowing I'm sitting right here. Take after the Sawatzky side for sure. Yes, I know you very well.

Suddenly one of the children spied the noodles partially enfolded in the towels. She rushed to the table, and then all four girls fell on the noodles, laughing, stuffing them as fast as they could into their mouths. Mrs. Sawatzky pushed her daughters away. "Girls! Girls! Here—have these." She reached into a cupboard and pulled out a packet of soda crackers. The tall girl snatched the packet and dangled it above the heads of her sisters. From a crock, their mother produced fresh dills. In a moment they were gone. They reminded Bill of the baby swallows in the nest above his garage door.

"I don't think I'll wait for Jake," Bill said to the woman. He leaned forward in his chair. "Thank you for the drink."

"Just a minute." She left the room. Bill could hear her tread on wooden steps. He listened to the children whispering and giggling in another room. They think I've told their mother on them, he thought. They think they're going to catch it when I leave.

Mrs. Sawatzky returned. In her hand was a small mason jar. "For you." She held it out to him.

Bill stared at the jewel-red colour.

"Apple jelly. Made last fall."

"Apple jelly? You made?"

She nodded.

"Your own apples?"

She gestured in the direction of the Erdrich farm. "From the neighbour. No one uses them."

As Bill passed through the lean-to, he held the jar up to the south-facing window. The jelly glowed in the sun like a giant, mystic ruby. "Thank you, thank you," he said, and he knew he would never open the jar, would never eat from it.

Little Jakie sat playing with his trucks and tractors in the lean-to. Bill paused at the screen door. Then he turned to the woman. "Would you like to go for a ride? All of you." He swept his arm towards the car as though ushering her to a coach drawn by matching unicorns.

But the woman laughed. She covered her mouth with one hand and pointed with the other. Her boy covered his mouth with one hand and pointed with the other and giggled in his childish way. Bill followed the pointing fingers to the goat standing on the hood of his red convertible.

The Penance Drummer

A capsule of despair," was how Archer summed up his early experiences as a bus rider. "Especially in November in the sleet and gloom and wind." He had hated buses since taking them to work dark winter mornings when he was a young man, a long time ago. "Everyone is miserable on a bus early in the morning," he would tell Sylvia when the topic came up. "Going to their dead-end jobs. And the whole thing stinking like a hibernating bear." Sylvia, too, had ridden buses in her day, and didn't remember the smell. Nevertheless, they decided to take a bus to the James Bay section of the city. They had not tried the bus before, at least not here. Not together, anyway.

Syl and Archer Roethke were in the middle of the fourth day of their holiday on Vancouver Island. They'd been to Victoria before, many times. The pub at the James Bay Inn featured blues bands Saturday afternoons. Syl and Archer had been there before, too, but they usually had a rental car to tour around in. This time they were delaying renting the car as long as possible. No sense paying for it if they didn't need it. The JBI wasn't far at all, but Syl's knees were bothering her, and she'd first suggested a taxi. "Let's just walk up the street and flag one down." Archer had agreed. Though more preoccupied than normal, he was also more agreeable. Polite. Accommodating.

Because a chasm had opened between them, deeper, more deadly than a disagreement about transportation.

They weren't staying in the kind of hotel that taxis frequented. The Web site had called it a "boutique hotel"—overheated, not enough closet space, clumsy furniture arrangements, desk clerks in a permanent state of bewilderment. Their room, however, had its good points: a quaint, deep bathtub; large windows that could be flung open if Sylvia decided to smoke, or to let in the bracing night air; and the location suited the Roethkes, being downtown among the shops and buskers.

The night before, while in their room above the street, Syl and Archer had heard musical notes from some uncommon instrument just below their windows. For about twenty minutes, as they prepared to go out for dinner at their favourite restaurant, they heard single notes being played now and then, as though someone were tuning up. At last, joyful music erupted, African-sounding, on instruments Syl and Archer had heard before but couldn't name. They rushed out of their room, coats half on, down two flights of stairs, into the lobby and then the street.

A crowd had already gathered around the band, a band that might have been a family: an older man and woman, perhaps in their mid-fifties, Syl and Archer's age, wearing embroidered tunics; two younger women; a boy in his teens. The players were stationed at what looked like giant wooden xylophones. Marimbas, Archer told Sylvia. At the back of the formation, the mother stood on a long bench behind the tallest instrument. With her legs apart, she reached the keys with large mallets. The music was loud and rhythmic, with simple melodic lines and harmonies, which, though repetitious, were nevertheless catchy. Syl was consumed by the music, but Archer, after three songs (Zimbabwean, the boy told the audience), tossed a five-dollar bill into the basket, where many five-dollar bills were piling up, and gently led Sylvia into the alley towards their café.

"Well, you know where this leaves your drummer," said Syl as their footsteps echoed on the cobblestones. Your penance drummer.

He'd stationed himself at a street corner near the hotel the first night they'd been in the city, this drummer. Syl and Archer had passed him on their way into the hotel, and he'd been there again the next afternoon. And this morning again. He was a sad-looking man with youthful hair but pale, cracked skin and a certain creakiness in the way he moved. He might have lived a hard life in a short time, or he might have been an older man with good hair. His drum kit rode around in a wooden cart he pulled to the street from wherever he'd spent the night. Once he was set up, he sat down and played the drums lethargically and steadily for hours with his eyes closed. While Sylvia finished her unpacking that first evening, Archer had gone back out to the street to listen.

She found him sitting on a bench under a tree. At first, she, too, had found the constant beat soothing. As they were leaving, Archer tossed some money into the drummer's empty, upturned hat.

But the next afternoon, while Syl was trying to nap, the drummer's music became tedious, and he'd added a cowbell, which prevented her from sleeping. When she looked out the window, she saw Archer on the bench. She called to him and waved, as though that would make the noise stop. Archer waved back and came inside, but first threw more money into the drummer's hat. And the following morning, walking back from breakfast on the waterfront, they'd passed him on a different street, and Archer had thrown more coins into the crumpled fedora in front of the bass drum.

"Why do you keep giving that man money?" Sylvia had burst out when they were out of earshot. "He's become tiresome."

"I don't know. It's as if he's waiting for something and measuring out his time in drumbeats. I'm just supporting his vigil."

At dinner, in the bistro that offered little light other than candles burning on each table, Syl and Archer avoided each other's eyes. But not because of the drummer.

The cuisine at the bistro had changed since last time. It was Thai now, something they seldom ate back home. They ordered several dishes to share, and focused their conversation on the flavours. Sylvia said she would try to conjure them up in her own kitchen. "Although I don't have a clue where I'd find edamame beans."

This afternoon, on their way to the bus stop a block up from the hotel, Sylvia pulled up short at a window displaying blown glass. Archer did not notice that she was no longer at his side and kept walking. She turned away from the window and watched him proceed up the street for those few seconds he thought she was still there. (Did he walk differently from how he would have if he'd been alone?)

I thought you were beside me, Archer. I carried on as though you were. But you weren't with me, were you?

Sylvia liked the way Archer looked. Today he was wearing his brown leather jacket and his suede cap. He was a tall man who'd always walked a little stooped at the shoulders. He moved in a casual, lanky way with his hands in the pockets of his jeans and the toes of his Wallabies pointed straight forward with each step. His gaze was usually directed at the sidewalk, though she was often surprised at how much he saw despite that. Something about the way Archer walked usually comforted Sylvia. But this time she could only wonder whether another woman had noticed those same things about him. Whether someone else had felt the comfort of his gait.

He glanced at the emptiness beside him and stopped and turned slowly. He waited. And as Sylvia started towards him to catch up, he looked at her eyes and she at his.

It had happened the day before their vacation began. Sylvia had left the house to take the cat to the neighbour's. She hadn't meant to sneak back into the house, but for some reason, Archer was not aware that she was there. He was in his study. She heard his voice in conversation; he was on the phone. The words were unintelligible, but he was not speaking the way he did to his siblings or friends—hearty, loud enough for Sylvia to hear wherever she was in the house. Instead, his voice was muffled, as though his back were towards the study door, which wasn't his usual position. Sylvia worried that someone was sick or dead. She hung up her coat beside the front door, flung off her boots, and, after smoothing her hair and the front of her shirt, approached the room on sock feet.

Archer was behind his desk, standing, facing the window with his back to her. There were no lights on in the room, and as Sylvia paused in the doorway, her physical presence caused a change in the atmosphere that Archer sensed immediately, even though he wasn't facing her. He might have seen her reflection in the window, or the hall light behind her casting her shadow on the draperies. He placed the telephone receiver gingerly into its cradle without saying goodbye.

"Who was that?" Syl had asked. "It sounded serious."

And then he had turned, not all the way, and even though she couldn't see his face clearly in the half-light, she saw that his eyes were glistening.

He looked down at some papers on his desk.

"What's wrong?"

"What do you mean? Nothing. Just a customer. Not happy that I'll be gone for two weeks." The papers crackled in nervous hands.

But those were tears she'd seen shining in the soft light from the hallway. "Are you all right?" she had said, or wanted to say. Later, she could not recall if she had said it. He turned away from her and coughed just then, and would not meet her gaze.

Sylvia felt her own hand clutching her throat. When she lowered her hand, it hung by her side in a fist. She went to the bedroom to resume packing. It wasn't until much later that Archer thought to ask her about how things had gone with the cat. They were together in the kitchen. But their world had changed.

The bus driver told them he didn't go past the James Bay Inn, but a man getting on ahead of Syl and Archer, a man with one arm in a cast, said the bus travelled within a couple of blocks of the pub. They sat at the front near the helpful passenger and watched for landmarks, their bodies nestled together.

As they drove, the driver appeared to be having a quiet conversation with someone. "Who's he talking to?" Sylvia whispered after they'd gone a few blocks. "He isn't wearing a head-set."

"Must be a speaker phone or something."

"But then we'd hear someone talking to him, wouldn't we?"

Archer shrugged. "Maybe he's in a play and he's practising his lines."

Sylvia focused on the bus driver's profile. He was a tall African man with sleek skin and finely chiselled features. His head was bare, but his hair fit him like a smooth, tight cap. She scanned the area around his seat for a manuscript, but saw none. She whispered, "Should I ask him?"

"Mind your own business, Syl. He might be schizophrenic."

"Would a schizophrenic be allowed to drive a bus? What if he got angry with the voices in his head?"

"We all get angry with the voices in our heads."

What was that supposed to mean?

"Get off at the next stop and go that way," said the helpful passenger, gesturing with his good arm. He himself remained in his seat.

Syl and Archer swayed towards the front door of the bus. As they disembarked, Sylvia turned and waved to the driver. He saluted back but his expression remained passive. "Well, that was fun," she murmured as they crossed the street.

The pub was further from the bus stop than expected. By taking the bus, Syl and Archer had really saved themselves only about four blocks of walking, they noted wryly as they meandered up the street. They moved slowly because of Sylvia's knees. But they might have gone slowly, regardless. The community of James Bay was mainly residential, Victorian in flavour, with gingerbread houses painted in pastel yellows and blues. Streets were narrow. Cherry trees posed along the boulevards like ballerinas frozen in a graceful dance. Yards were small, but crowded with hedges and shrubs and flowering plants with dark green, thick-fleshed foliage. Many of the houses advertised bed-and-breakfast accommodations or rooms to let. Small apartment blocks had been transformed into quaint inns. Syl and Archer paused now and then to look more closely at a window, or an ornate moulding, or the roses, still blooming in autumn. Archer especially liked to look at plants. Back home, he tended a sprawling prairie garden.

A youngish man going the other way was coming towards them on the sidewalk. "I'll ask him if there's a closer bus stop, for when we go back," said Sylvia.

The man was clearly trying to avoid them as he drew nearer.

"I always like to know where I'm going and where I'm coming from," she whispered to her husband.

Sylvia often wondered where her spontaneity had gone. Archer never spoke to her about it, but she knew he wasn't a willing victim of her overplanning. In the company of their friends, he referred to her as his tour guide.

"Excuse me, would you happen to know if we can catch a downtown bus on this street?"

The man wore a jaunty fedora and had a tattoo of a fern on the side of his neck. But his expression was stony. He glanced at Sylvia through small, round glasses. "No." He continued on.

Sylvia smiled at the back of his head and said, "That's all right—I'm sure we'll find someone who can help us."

The man stopped and turned. "I mean, no, you won't catch one on this street." His voice was brittle, his eyes wide, nearly angry. "You have to go to the next street." He took one hand out of his pocket and pointed.

"Thank you," called Sylvia. To Archer she said, "Well, excuse me for living. Why didn't he just say that right away?"

"I wonder what the tattoo was all about," said Archer. "That ferny thing."

"Some anti-social miscreant who lives in the woods and doesn't know how to behave in the big city, apparently."

"Don't take it so seriously."

"What should I take seriously, Archer? What's worth taking seriously in this life? Maybe we should talk about that."

But Sylvia still didn't look at Archer when she asked the question. He bent over a silver rose and retreated into silence.

When they arrived at the pub, it was nearly empty. Live bands now performed only one Saturday a month, the bartender told them, and today wasn't the one. Syl and Archer stayed anyway and ordered beer. Out of habit, they sat side by side at a table, near the back, facing the vacant space where the bands usually set up. The sights and sounds of past performances haunted their rambling thoughts. But try as they might, they couldn't summon live musicians to the stage, and made do with piped-in jazz. Two men squared off at the pool table in one corner of the room. The sharp crack of billiard balls colliding cut through the lazy Saturday.

However, a woman in her thirties came into the pub and sat at a table between them and the stage, half facing them. She removed her coat and ordered a late lunch. While she waited for her food, she opened a thick hard-cover book and read and sipped on a gin and tonic.

Archer used to drink gin and tonics, Syl recalled.

They stared at the woman. Her fair hair was tousled in a sexy, sleepy sort of way. She wore makeup, peach-coloured lipstick, and was slightly tanned. She paid no attention to the few patrons around her. But Syl began to think about Archer's lover. Was she like this young woman? Perhaps this was, in fact, the very lover he'd been talking to on the telephone the night before they'd left. He'd tried to blow her off, and she'd followed him to Victoria. A stalker. Out of the corner of her eye, Sylvia could see her husband studying the woman. So this probably wasn't her. But maybe she was his type, his type in mistresses. Syl thought she herself had been something like this woman at that age. She touched her own greying hair.

Archer leaned towards Sylvia and whispered, "What's she reading?"

"The book is probably a prop," Sylvia replied. "I doubt if she even knows how to read."

The bartender brought the woman her order: battered fish and French fries. The woman tucked in without taking her eyes off the page. She ate both the fish and the fries with her fingers.

"She'll ruin that book!" Sylvia hissed. "I can't believe anyone would eat greasy halibut and handle an expensive book!"

"Perhaps we've got her flustered with our gawking," suggested Archer. "Perhaps the book isn't expensive. Perhaps she bought it at a garage sale."

"Of course, you would defend her!"

Archer tilted his head at Sylvia and frowned.

"Does she remind you of anyone?" said Sylvia, louder now.

Archer's expression turned blank and stony, like that of the tattooed man on the street. "No. No one."

Sylvia's gaze fell into the bottom of her beer glass.

She felt a hand. His fingers were tight around her sharp-boned wrist. When her eyes met his, they had changed again, now hard and hypnotic, penetrating hers like lasers. He said in a low voice, "No one. No. One."

The woman reading looked up from her book. Instead of investigating the drama unfolding in front of her, she held up her nearly empty glass and peered at it as though wondering where the contents had disappeared to. A waiter ambled over to her and asked if she wanted another. She nodded and continued to massacre the halibut.

"Lush," whispered Syl.

Archer leaned back in his chair and turned to watch the men playing pool. But Syl could see that he wasn't really focused on the game. "All right. All right," she said. Of course it wasn't all right at all. But Archer had shut down for the moment, and they'd have to make another start. "What should we do next?"

Archer shrugged. "You're in charge."

But he had taken a journey of his own some time in the past year. Without Sylvia. Without his tour guide. She rummaged around in her floppy, worn, leather handbag for lipstick. The purse had accompanied them on many excursions over the past decade or so. If she dug deep enough, she might unearth artefacts from places like Alaska, New Orleans, Prague, London: matchbooks, subway tokens, ticket stubs, foreign coins, phone numbers jotted onto the torn corners of tourist maps.

And yet Syl could not recall ever noticing remnants or signs of her husband's latest adventure. No strange telephone numbers or stir-sticks from bars she'd never heard of when she checked the pockets of his laundry.

Suddenly Sylvia smelled jasmine. The fish-eating woman stood before her. Archer noticed her at the same time. Syl couldn't help but glance at the woman's fingers, to see if they were still shiny with cooking fat.

"I've decided I'd like some vinegar," the woman said. She peered at something on Syl and Archer's table. A cruet hid behind the salt and pepper shakers and the sugar dispenser. "I knew there was something not quite right about the chips," she continued. "I'm nearly done, but I noticed the vinegar on your table, and I just had to have some." She smiled.

Sylvia handed her the cruet and flashed a dangerous smile back. "It's malt," she hissed. Then, after the woman had sidled away, "Did you notice her scent, Archer?"

"I couldn't miss it, could I?" He pulled his wallet from his pocket.

"There's something sinister about the combination of halibut and jasmine, or perhaps something pathetic. It would be tragic to mistake her for pathetic, and then, when it's too late, find out she was evil."

Archer slapped some bills onto the table and stood up. He headed for the exit without giving the fish-eating woman another glance. Sylvia paused at her table and bent down. "I couldn't help but notice the very large book you're reading while you're having your lunch," she said. "Must be a real page-turner."

"Not really." The woman dabbed her now vinegary and oily fingers on a crushed serviette. She turned the cover of the book towards Sylvia. "Textbook. I'm in pre-med, trapped in my apartment for days, cramming for exams. Decided it was time for a change of scenery."

Sylvia straightened up. "Well, I hope you're enjoying the vinegar." She followed Archer to the door.

When they'd set out earlier, the sky had been a drab greyish white. Now the streets were wet. Late-day sun poked through the weave of the cherry leaves and lit up raindrops on the pavement. Syl and Archer saw that the heavy clouds had passed, but more were on the way.

"Time to find that bus," said Archer.

They started up a narrow street that ran perpendicular to the one they were on. It turned out not to be a straight street, but an S-shaped one that curved around cockeyed backyards and small parking lots. No one was about; the shower had rinsed away people and noise.

Syl and Arch arrived at the next cross street, which appeared to be a main thoroughfare. About a block away, they saw a bus-stop sign on the opposite side of the street and, without crossing, walked in that direction. But as they approached it, before they even had crossed the street, they read the sign: DOWNTOWN PASSENGERS MUST WAIT FOR BUS ON OPPOSITE SIDE OF STREET.

Archer spread his arms and said, "Wouldn't that be right where we're standing?"

"There's no bus stop anywhere on this side," Sylvia replied.

They both stared at the sign and mouthed the words as though trying to break a code. Finally Archer read it out loud. "What could it mean?"

Behind them loomed a high-class, high-rise condominium. "We'll have to assume we're in the right place and will be eventually picked up and whisked away by a bus," said Sylvia.

They stood rooted to their spots for several minutes without talking.

Then Syl and Arch spoke at the same time. Sylvia said, "Amazing how deserted this street is on a Saturday afternoon." And Archer said, "I don't like the looks of those clouds."

More silence. Sylvia began to pace.

At last a series of vehicles streamed by, heading downtown. At the end of the series was a city bus. It squealed to a halt at the bus stop across the street. "Isn't that bus going downtown?" Archer cried in exasperation. When it had moved off again, Syl and Archer saw two teenaged girls running along the sidewalk, tittering.

"Excuse me!" shouted Sylvia. "EXCUSE ME!" But they didn't even turn around. "Thank you!" Sylvia hurled after them.

More minutes passed. Archer said, "Do you know what idiots we are, standing here on the curb, staring at that sign? The people in this building watching out their windows must be dialing the police by now."

They studied the condominium and concluded it was a seniors' complex; the word *Golden* was in its name, and two rickety women stared out at them from the glass lobby. Between the sidewalk and the building was a well-tended garden—exotic-looking ornamentals, a fishpond, meandering paths. Archer asked, "Would you like to live here with me some day?"

"We couldn't afford it," Sylvia answered without thinking. But no sooner had she spoken than she remembered that they weren't the old Syl and Archer any more. The continuum of his life with her had been interrupted without her realizing it. For how long? Would Sylvia ever know? *Would you like to live here with me some day?* Not, *Would you like to live here some day?* It was a proposal. He wanted to grab on again.

They heard another surge of traffic approaching, this time on their side of the street, and gazed with hope at the cars drawing near. But no one stopped, there was no bus in the group.

This time Sylvia read the sign out loud. "What could it possibly mean?"

"I think I felt a drop," mumbled Archer.

"What?"

"A drop! There's another! It's raining!"

"Those ladies will think we're hitchhikers," Sylvia mused. "Or traffic planners."

"Then we'd have clipboards, or electronic thingamajigs."

More raindrops fell. Footsteps crept along the condominium walkway. A man peered at them from around the juniper bush. "He looks frightened," whispered Sylvia. "Let's not scare the old people. Smile."

The man stepped out from behind the bush. He was thin and elderly, his skin like onion peel. "Can I help you?" His voice was strong and kind.

"I hope you can," said Archer. "That sign over there says we should wait here for the downtown bus, but we haven't seen a bus, and it wouldn't really make sense for it to stop here anyway, because it would be going in the wrong direction, wouldn't it?"

The man gazed at the sign and shook his head. He appeared to be confused and didn't respond right away. "No," he said finally, "no bus stops in front of this place that I know of. But then, I don't ever use the bus myself. It's a conundrum, isn't it?"

"We don't live here and we don't use the bus, either," Sylvia put in.

His face brightened. "It's over there you want to catch the bus downtown, beyond that Russian olive."

Just a little further along, further than their impatient pacing had taken them, a silver-leafed tree drooped over the fence of a neighbouring front yard. Syl and Archer had noticed the tree earlier, but hadn't suspected it of concealing a secret. They marched up the sidewalk.

Even before they were past the tree, they could see that another street met the one they were on, and on that street, quite near the intersection, was the bus stop they'd been seeking. Not only a bus stop, but a sign announcing its connection with downtown, and a bus shelter.

Sylvia waved to the old man, and Archer shouted a thank you. To Sylvia he said, "We are idiots."

"Babes in woods," she muttered back. "A condo conundrum. Look, it's even got a bus shack. Isn't that what you called them, when you were a sad, young labourer?"

The spitting had turned to drizzle and they were grateful for the roof. But the shelter was narrow and shallow and scarcely kept the rain off their heads.

They sat down on the aluminum bench and leaned back to avoid the wet. Sylvia pressed up against Archer as though that would keep them drier. "It's a pretty tree," she said, gazing out at the Russian olive.

"We stood there, rooted to the spot," said Archer, "just like the tree."

"But we didn't search very hard. Why didn't we?"

"Frozen in a mindset."

"It should be coming soon. Certainly no bus came out of here while we were waiting."

And so they sat together, huddled under a skimpy roof, trusting the public transport to save them and carry them away from James Bay. And while they waited in mutual silence, Sylvia created the story about Archer's affair. She imagined it so vividly, she believed that Archer was telling it to her.

It was that client I told you about a few months ago—the lady with the Volvo and the trench coat and the big gold handbag. Remember? I told you she was a bit of a riddle, you used the word "eccentric" when I described her to you. One day she brought me lemon squares she'd made. You know what a pushover I am when it comes to home baking. We ate lemon squares and drank my horrible coffee in the office one afternoon. Everything she said was funny. I think I told you how funny she was. Then she came the next week again, and the week after. I was long done with her portfolio. Each time, she brought a different pastry—blueberry pie, chocolate eclairs, raspberry tarts—and eventually we had to face the fact that we were on the verge of physical intimacy. We kissed a few times; I won't try to deny it.

(Here the sequence of Sylvia's thoughts was interrupted briefly with images of lips and cheeks smeared with intense blues and reds and chocolatey browns.)

But we kept putting off—putting off—making love. We never left the office. And then one day—

(—she ripped open her trenchcoat to reveal a crimson teddy and tiny creampuffs nestled in all her crevices.)

I told her not to come back. I told her never to bring me home baking again. I told her I loved you and I wanted to stay married to you. When you walked into the den the other day, she had just called to make one last effort to win me. She was crying on the phone. Finally I just hung up. It's over.

But when Syl stole a glance at her husband's impassive face there on the bus-stop bench, she saw a wistfulness and a sadness in the outer corners of his eyes that made her ashamed of her fairy tale. It was over, no doubt, but Archer was grieving, and she would have to grieve with him, whether she wanted to or not. Eventually he would tell her everything.

"Aaah," Archer breathed as a bus appeared in the distance.

"At last," said Sylvia.

The driver was the same man. As before, Syl and Archer sat near the front of the bus; the driver was still mumbling to himself.

After a while, Sylvia asked Archer, "Why didn't we walk back? I could easily have done it."

"We wanted to believe in that bus, didn't we?" Archer replied. "Apparently we desperately needed to believe in the bus."

"And in the tattooed man."

Later, they would laugh about their vigil at the phantom bus stop. "What idiots we must have looked," one or the other would say at unlikely moments over dinner, or in the car, or while sitting on the patio late at night. "I guess you had to be there," was how their unamused friends responded.

The ride downtown took mere minutes. When they trudged along the avenue to the hotel, the penance drummer was nowhere to be seen or heard. They didn't stumble across him again for the rest of their stay, as though he, too, had finally found the right bus.

Archer continued sitting on sidewalk benches, listening to

other lonesome musicians, tossing coins into other empty hats. From the open window of their room, Sylvia watched her husband on the street below. Songs drifted up to her like memories.

THE HALF-TOWN FOLLY

With Fitz and Dooker in the back seat of the Fairlane, Willis had left the city before sunrise. At dawn the snow on the fields was deep blue. Not only the snow, but the sky, the very air itself. And as they'd cruised along the highway in the old Ford that Fitz had dug up somewhere for the job, Willis had found the colour pleasing. It felt to him like the colour of freedom.

Willis seldom leaves the city. None of them do, although Fitz has been hauled away on the prison van more than once. Willis can't remember the last time he himself has taken an excursion out of town.

Now the morning sun has cleared those rows of trees over there—evergreens and some sort of leafless trees with pointy branches—and, just like that, jewels have popped out of the snow. Alone in the car, parked at the side of a lonesome road,

Willis looks around him and realizes that he'd forgotten about diamonds after a fresh snowfall, about the peacefulness of open fields in winter. He's glad Fitz and Dooker have finally left. He was nervous enough without being trapped with them while they'd waited for the bank to open. He hated their chattering and farting and dirty language, and the stench of their Cameos. Fitz had miscalculated how long it would take to drive here. He had visited the town a few weeks earlier to size up the job. And yet, today they had arrived too early. All three of them had to sit in the car for more than half an hour, hoping the Fairlane wouldn't attract attention.

Willis kills the engine and takes off his toque. He'll be warm enough now without the heater. In the rear-view mirror, he can see the hamlet behind him, a clump of low buildings and scrubby, naked trees. And he can still make out the tiny figures of Fitz and Dooker, black against the snowy landscape, retreating into the town. To his right, about a mile off, is the highway, already busy with semi trucks heading for the American border.

Willis doesn't know why he's here. He tells himself he's taking care of his little brother. Dooker does stupid things. This time he's attached himself to an old school buddy who makes a living as a small-time crook. Fitz is a wild man, jittery and noisy and unpredictable, as though high on meth, probably high on meth. He takes crazy risks and sometimes they pay off. Dooker eats it all up. When they first told Willis about their scheme, offered him a piece of the action, Willis was so disturbed he considered drugging his brother, tying him up, and hauling him off to some hiding place for a few weeks. Fitz might have looked for new accomplices. But Willis is scared of drugs, and doesn't know how to get them anyway. Also,

Dooker is a lot bigger than he is. Willis would never be able to keep him tied up for very long. Roz might have stopped his brother. But Roz is the best thing that's happened to Dooker in a long time, and Willis was afraid to tell her what Dooker was planning.

"It's a cakewalk," Dooker had assured Willis. (*Cakewalk* must have been Fitz's word because Willis had never heard Dooker use the expression before.) "It's just this itty-bitty little bank in this itty-bitty little village. Two people in the whole place. Cakewalk."

Fitz had met a guy in the joint who told him about some hick town somewhere near the border that had a bank. "A credit union," Fitz said. He pronounced it "credit *onion*" as a joke, which was weird in itself, because Willis can remember when little Dooker—Dougie back then—was just learning to read and they came across a sign that said *Credit Union*, and how Dooker had said exactly that: *credit onion*. "It's somewhere south of here," Fitz had told them over beers at the River City Bar. "I'm not sure how to say the name of the burg, but the con told me it's German for Half-Town. What kinda idiots would live in a place called Half-Town, I ask myself."

"Halfwits!" Dooker had crowed over his pint.

"With half the amount of money," Willis had pointed out.

"Aw," Fitz had scoffed, "it's an easy job with very little investment, worth the effort, I says to myself."

"You can be our driver," Dooker said to Willis. "Won't have to get your hands dirty at all."

"'Course, you'll get a smaller cut," put in Fitz.

"Still, it's extra dough," said Dooker.

Later, Willis said to his brother, "Hey, man, what about Roz? What's gonna happen when you're nabbed for this and end up in the clink? Think she'll stick around? Think she'll stick around if she finds out you're even considering a bank heist?"

Dooker shrugged. "If you tell her, I'll have to kill you, bro." Then he'd laughed. "Lighten up, man."

In the end, Willis had to go along. He couldn't stop his brother from robbing the bank, but neither would he let the bastard get caught.

His concern for his brother isn't his only motive. It's that other one he wrestles with in the beat-up Ford parked at the side of the lonesome road just outside Half-Town: Willis needs the extra dough. He wants the money so he can leave his mom, leave Dooker, leave the crummy city he's spent his whole life in so far. Willis wants to buy an RV and a purebred German shepherd dog and travel all over North America. He particularly wants to see the Epcot Center in Florida. His journey will begin here, on a gravel road on a flat winter plain. He wishes he could just scoop up those diamonds lying in the snow and shower Fitz and Dooker and his mom and himself with wealth, set them right, save them all.

Willis has forgotten his watch and doesn't trust the dashboard clock. He's about to turn the key in the ignition so he can catch the time on the radio, when a vehicle emerges from behind the trees. It's a school bus, trundling along a road perpendicular to the one Willis is parked on.

"Just go on by, go on by," Willis mutters.

But the bus slows down, makes a wide yellow turn, and comes his way. It straddles the narrow roadway. Willis wonders if he'll need to squinch further onto the shoulder to let it pass. Obviously, there'd be school buses sneaking around. Typical of Fitz not to cover all the angles. It dawns on Willis that this whole caper is a very bad idea. At least the licence plates are fake, that's one thing Dooker has assured him. To hide his face, Willis leans over and rummages through the glove compartment. He finds it stuffed with fast-food coupons, ketchup packets, a pair of wraparound sunglasses, parking tickets, plastic baggies with specks of weed still clinging to the inside.

The bus crosses a small bridge that spans a creek between Half-Town and the intersection and lumbers towards the Ford. Willis hears the bus engine gearing down. He slips on the sunglasses and pulls his toque back on, way down over his ears. At the last minute he forces his dentures out of his mouth and hides them under one thigh.

When he straightens up, Willis is surprised to see a fresh young woman wearing a fat, padded vest and a big smile strolling across the road to his window. He rolls it down.

"Hey there," she sings into the cold morning. Her breath flows like magic vapour from her lips. Willis can almost see her words written in the air.

He raises two fingers and salutes.

"Everything okay?" she chirps. "I have a two-way in the bus if you need help."

Willis shakes his head. "Just pulled off the highway for a nap."

"Okay then." The woman laughs. "Sorry for disturbing your sleep."

He smiles, so she can see his toothless gums. She heads for the bus left idling in the middle of the road. But he notices her casting a quizzical glance at the highway a mile in the distance.

The bus continues on towards the village. Willis doesn't dare look at it as it passes with only inches to spare, but he is aware of pink faces and toques, and is reminded of the toy wooden bus with the wooden-headed passengers Roz's kids play with. He cranks up the window.

His teeth are biting into his butt. He adds them to the jumble in the glove compartment and decides he'd better keep the toque and glasses on his head.

"Someone's gonna spot us," he'd warned Dooker. "Everybody in a small town notices a strange car. What are you gonna do with it after?"

"Fitz's got a pal with a garage out in the boonies somewhere," Dooker had replied. "We're headin' there right after. Don't worry, they can't trace the Ford back to us."

"Look, it'll take five minutes for the cops to connect the car to the crime. Highway patrol will spot us just like that."

"You worry too much. Fitz has the blueprint all worked out. And hey, we're all gonna let our facial hair grow out before the job. Don't shave, bro."

Willis had started the beard growing a little late and wasn't much good at it anyway. His efforts had produced only a sparse frizzle.

As the bus lumbers off, Willis says out loud, "We are so screwed." He turns on the radio and half expects to hear a bulletin about a robbery in progress at the Half-Town Credit Onion. In the mirror he has become a toothless, scruffy, bearded man with a pilled Canadiens toque covering his ears and eyebrows, and black shades reflecting the glare of the snow. Willis smiles at himself. Who's the halfwit now?

A Boler. All he needs, really, is a Boler, one of those tiny egg-like trailers he sometimes sees being pulled along the highway. Willis watched a show about them on TV once. Bolers were classics from the sixties and seventies. He has no idea how much one would cost nowadays, but he was drawn to the weirdness and the simplicity of them. One guy interviewed on the show said they'd originally been meant to be septic tanks, but when that hadn't worked out, the company had furnished them and put wheels on them, and sold them as campers. Willis doesn't know if he believes that, but the story stokes his desire to own one. The trailer has everything he needs: a dinette, a kitchen, and bunk beds for himself and his dog. He doesn't require a very big cut of the bank heist to afford a second-hand Boler.

He's barely recovered from the encounter with the bus lady when another vehicle appears, this one in his rear-view mirror, coming from the village. This time it's a sedan, and it, too, slows down as it nears the Ford at the side of the road.

Willis glances around in despair. *The middle of nowhere*, Fitz had repeated over and over again. But there are farms everywhere, big farms. Why else would there be a bank here?

The flashy, black sedan parks on the shoulder in front of the Fairlane. Willis closes his eyes. "Screwed, screwed, screwed," he whispers as he hears the crunch of footsteps approaching.

The man is about sixty, tanned, good-looking. He has on a black formal coat and a dark blue scarf around his neck. His hair is sleek and shiny like his car. When Willis rolls down the window, the man grabs onto the edge of it with leather gloves and bends down. Willis smells Listerine and cologne.

Either the mayor or some goddamn drug kingpin, Willis thinks as he nods politely to the man's greeting.

"You in trouble, fella?" the man says in a loud, friendly tone.

"No, not at all. I'm on a road trip, and I was coming up from the States, thought I'd pull off the highway and tour around a little in this lovely neighbourhood, and then I got kinda sleepy, so...."

"Ah," says the man. He twists his head. "Hear that?"

Willis listens. Off in the distance, perhaps on the other side of the spruce row, engines are whining, moving across the fields.

"Snowmobilers around here meet at the store in town for coffee every morning. Good coffee. Maybe that'll help you."

"Oh, hey, thanks. Yeah, maybe I'll do that."

The man gives Willis a leathered thumbs-up. Willis gives him a thumbs-up back and smiles. He likes the way the man's eyes flicker at the sight of pink gums.

Earlier, in the milky morning light, the men had taken a swing through Half-Town. That's how Willis knows that the one and only store is right across the street from the credit union. Everything had been quiet then. Nobody had expected the store to be busy first thing on a Tuesday morning. Nobody had known they served coffee to snowmobilers there. And the store had windows along the front. Willis doesn't understand how Fitz could have missed that, and all those machines parked out front, when he'd cased the job. He'd been here in the morning then, too, to find out what time the manager opened up the bank. Of course, he couldn't have known that the gathering of snowmobilers was a daily event.

Who is to blame for this fiasco? Willis could put it all on the lamebrained Fitz. Bruce Fitzgerald hasn't learned a thing from his frequent incarcerations, not even how to be a better crook. Dooker is to blame for being such an easy dupe and for dragging Willis into it. Willis could even blame their mother, nearly seventy, who is now probably having her first smoke of the day. He pictures her fragile, arthritic body stooped inside a baggy nightdress faintly dotted with the centres of flowers whose pale petals have long faded to nothing. He pictures her knobby, lotioned fingers sorting through the bracelets and necklaces she keeps in a collection of trashy jewellery boxes.

Willis barely remembers his father. The boys were still young when he stumbled on a curb and fell and smashed his head on the concrete. By chance, while doing errands downtown on Saturday morning, he'd become entangled in the crowds watching a gay pride parade. His mother didn't hold the gays responsible for her husband's demise, but has harboured a contempt for parades ever since. She hitched up with various surrogate husbands after his death, but none had been fathers, and she had long ago given up on men. Except for her sons.

Though Willis doesn't make much at his job, it fell upon him to sustain her two habits: jewellery and spa treatments. She's suggested often enough that they live together, to free up rent money. But, for Willis, that would mean giving up his life, what there is of it. What very little there is of it. He's never found a Roz, he's never owned a home. All he needs is enough money so he can put some in his mom's account and buy the Boler and one of those dogs his friend Tony breeds on his farm out near Teulon. Willis figures there's almost enough in his savings to last him a year. And maybe he won't come back, maybe he'll like it down there in Florida, or somewhere in Canada, the Okanagan, perhaps. He can't quite picture the Okanagan, the way he can picture Florida because it's on TV all the time. But Willis has heard a lot about it. Dooker can take care of their mother. He wouldn't, though, not properly. The health authority would have to take over. It could work.

So Willis needs this cash, and his mother is partly at fault. Only, things aren't looking good; he's been made by a couple of locals already, not to mention the bus load of kiddies. Suddenly he's cold. He fires up the engine for warmth.

It's taking too long. By now they should have locked the manager and the teller in the vault the way they'd planned, and be on their way out of town. Twenty minutes, max, Fitz had said. But Willis has already faced the fact that Fitz knows nothing. Willis debates taking another swing through the village; there's no reason for him to sit on the outskirts any more, now that half the population has had a conversation with him. But he decides to stick to the plan, ill-laid though it may be.

The radio is playing music from the fifties, songs about girls and love and breakups. Willis goes back in his mind to the early morning journey, the conversation the three men had had as they cruised towards Half-Town in the dark blue dawn.

Fitz, as always, brought up the topic of women and sex. And they had started talking about their most memorable close encounters. Fitz had surprised them by using the word *unrequited*. Most of their stories went back to high school days, which, Willis believes, is where the sex life of men is always centred. After they'd exhausted that topic, things fell silent in the car for a few seconds.

And then Willis had said, "So what are we supposed to look for in chicks these days, anyway? You know, like, when you're in a mall or a bar—"

"Clubs," said Dooker. "They're called clubs, bro. That's where the chicks hang out. And what do you mean, *these days?* Nothin's changed, as far as I know."

"What I mean is, we're older," said Willis. "Shouldn't we be looking for something deeper now? When we see a bunch of girls—women—in *a club*, how do we know who to pick? It used to be easy—tits, legs, ass, whatever."

"Well, I guess I have learned something," said Dooker. "When two guys look at a girl's figure, they see different things. What I like and what Fitz likes and what you like are all different. Fitz here likes big, soft, pillowy bums."

A ruckus broke out in the back seat, with Fitz giggling and babbling about body parts and pummelling Dooker, and Dooker laughing and fending off the assault.

But Willis continued. "It doesn't matter if it's a young girl or one of those *cougars*, those older, desperate ones. And it doesn't matter if you don't want to get serious. The fact remains, a man our age should start looking for a woman who'll keep you good company, someone who has a big soft pillow of goodness inside her." A sliver of sun glowed behind the black trunks of trees that formed the shelter belt at the edge of the field. "What I think is, when you've got a choice beween two women in a bar, pay attention to the one who's tagging along, the girl who's a little less. She's more likely to be gentle and true."

Dooker snorted. "And what've you got to show for that philosophy?"

It was true, Willis had never had a long-term relationship with any woman except his mother. But his idea had only recently arrived. He'd wasted his time on the alpha girls too long. "The sexy one won't be as trustworthy. The other girl will be easier," he said. "She'll be easier all round. Relieved to get attention, proud to get attention before her friend. She'll be steadier, more loyal, spiritually deeper in the long run."

"*Spiritually!*" Fitz had spat through his Tim Horton's coffee.

"She's the one I'd go for every time," Willis concluded.

"Well, I guess if spiritual is what you want in a chick," Fitz had said. "Most of us, all we want is a piece of ass."

Willis means to find a girl when he's set free, when he hits the road and heads for Epcot. Maybe he'll find her out there, at Disney World, or maybe some other place. The lesser girl.

Willis relaxes. The sun and the songs are making him drowsy. He puts his head back and closes his eyes for a few minutes.

But something makes him open them again. And he catches a flash coming off the highway. On the same road as the bus had been, but from the other direction, a car is approaching the intersection in front of Willis, driving pretty fast. It slows down, and he can see it's a cruiser car, with the RCMP crest on the door.

Willis holds his breath, praying the car will continue on, turn the other way at the crossroads. But no, it swings towards him and creeps up. Even if he drives by, Willis is thinking, the Mountie's presence in the town will fowl up Fitz and Dooker's blueprint big time.

"Shit!" Willis utters through his gums. He leans back in his seat, closes his eyes, and opens his mouth slightly, as though sleeping.

He flinches at the slam of the cop-car door, stiffens at the knock on the window.

The Mountie isn't wearing a hat. Willis takes that as a good sign. "Good morning," he mumbles in a sleepy voice.

The cop is young and beefy, well-shorn and shaved. Willis is bracing himself to be asked for his driver's licence. Instead, the cop says, "Everything all right, sir?" He sounds friendly, but his face is blank.

"Oh, yeah, I'm fine. I was down in the States, and was just on my way back to the city for a meeting. I've been driving all night from—"

Willis searches his brain for the name of a North Dakota city from where he could logically have spent all night driving, and blurts out the only one that comes to mind. "—Fargo."

Willis went to Fargo once, a long time ago. He remembers taking his mother there for a weekend.

"And I was so darned tired, I figured I'd get off the highway and get myself some coffee. But that place back there—" he gestures with his thumb, "—wasn't open yet, so I decided to take a nap instead." Willis feels rather proud of this touch of detail he's added to his story.

The Mountie's expression remains blank. "Well, it's open now, sir. And you don't want to miss that meeting."

"Okay," Willis answers enthusiastically. He curls his hands around the steering wheel.

The Mountie returns to his cruiser. To Willis's relief, the car executes a U-turn on the narrow roadway and heads back in the direction it came from, away from Half-Town.

But Willis knows he's being watched in the Mountie's rearview mirror. He has no choice but to point the Ford towards Half-Town and step on the accelerator. He makes the U-turn, though not as skillfully as the cop.

As he inches towards town, he thinks about Fargo. And he tries to recall the trip he and his mom took down there that summer. She wanted to buy jewellery. They stayed in a hotel that advertised a new spa. But it turned out to be, in her words, *just a hokey little spa, just a sauna, really, and one attendant to do everything.* He remembers that because she still mentions it occasionally. Willis remembers her manicure and the loads of baubles they did not declare at customs on the way home.

On the way home. And that's when Willis realizes that Fargo is only about three hours away. Because he remembers that after checking out of their hotel, they ate lunch at a Mexican café, and then when they arrived at his mom's apartment, she'd asked him if he wanted to stick around for supper, but he'd said no, he was still full from lunch.

He had just told the cop that he'd driven all night from Fargo. Why hadn't he said he'd started out early from Fargo, or just that he was driving up from Fargo, period? But no, he'd said he was so darned tired from driving all night.

Willis doesn't know for sure if the cop took down his licence number and punched it into his computer. What would come up? Where had Fitz found the fake plates?

And now he must decide whether or not to enter the town.

The car pokes along towards the cluster of small, squat buildings. Willis expects to find Fitz and Dooker sneaking around somewhere with a bag of loot. But the place is dead. By now, the cruiser car is out of sight. A snow-covered lane with one set of tire tracks imprinted in the white leads off the road at the edge of the settlement and appears to circumvent the town. Willis decides to follow it instead of the main street. From this lane, he can scope the situation.

Willis guides the car along the soft track, taking a turn that sets it parallel to the main street. On one side are the backs of the properties that front the main drag. On the other side are the fronts of a row of homes. Some of the yards are small, like regular city lots. But some are the size of farmyards, with the houses situated far back. Willis keeps mostly on the lookout for the store and the credit union across from it. He sees no activity in the bank, but, yes, there they are: half a dozen or so snowmobiles parked in front of the store.

No wonder Fitz and Dooker are late—they're trapped inside the bank by the watchful snowmobilers. Willis follows the lane to the far side of the village, where it ends at a crossroad, and he has to drive either away from town, or into it. He turns around and heads back up the lane.

But this time he doesn't keep his eye on the main street, doesn't peer between the buildings for signs of his doomed comrades.

Because, as he passes one of the tidy farms, something else catches his attention. It's a bright spot of colour against the silver of a faded wooden granary. It isn't even the colour that snags him, though, it's the shape. No mistaking the shape. The bottom half of the Boler has been painted orange, and the top half white. Giant purple flowers with black centres are scattered randomly around the body. Willis slows nearly to a stop. He kills the radio.

Someone steps out onto the side porch of the nearby house. A woman descends into the snow and begins to cross the yard. Under one arm is what looks to Willis like a stack of record albums. She is wearing a skirt and high boots and a parka. The hood is down on her shoulders, the fur trim framing her face. She is young, perhaps twenty or so, with straight, pale hair, pink lips, and bright eyes, though she is not quite beautiful.

As she walks, the woman notices the car. A stray breeze lays a wisp of hair across her cheekbone. She looks at Willis, not smiling exactly, but with a friendly expression. His first impulse is to put his teeth back in. He tries to keep the car on track as he fumbles in the glovebox with his right hand.

But underneath the new snow the track is icy and only a car-width wide. When he feels the Fairlane slipping off the edge, Willis cranks the wheel and guns the engine. The car fishtails, and the rear tires catch in a wad of soft, deep snow in the ditch.

The woman unlatches the door of the Boler and enters. Willis imagines that she is inviting him in. He imagines what it would be like in there with her, snuggled into a corner of the dinette, sipping morning coffee and studying maps of North America strewn on the arborite table, the dog at their feet.

But he is stuck in the snow, and he doesn't want to get out of the car, in case he's being watched, and there's no shovel in the trunk anyway, he's quite sure.

But he knows how to rock a car in deep snow, and begins the process of gearing back and forth between REVERSE and DRIVE, with just the right amount of pressure on the accelerator. He's pretty sure he's snagged the attention of everyone in the neighbourhood, and the last thing Willis needs is another do-gooder offering to help.

While he's working at it, the woman, empty-handed now, steps out of the trailer and secures the door. She glances at the Ford, but then continues to the farmhouse without looking back again. And then she's gone, leaving only the prints of her tall brown boots in the dense snow. The lesser girl.

Willis has to free himself as fast as he can. He rocks the car back and forth, back and forth, and is almost ready to surrender to whichever idle farmer shows up to help, when, with one last surge, the car slithers back onto the road, as though a strong hand has pushed it out of the snow. Willis checks the mirror, half expecting to see some burly peasant in overalls waving a strong, thick-fingered hand at him through the rear window. But no one is there.

As though afraid to lose momentum, Willis keeps a steady foot on the pedal as he makes for the bend in the lane and the rendezvous spot on the road beyond. He glances in the mirror to catch a last glimpse of the Boler. He can see the edge of the silver-grey granary. The Boler does not come into view.

And as Willis turns the corner to get back to the main road, his heart takes a tumble. The first thing that occurs to him is that he will probably never see that particular girl or that particular Boler again. For those few minutes that he'd been floundering in the snowdrift, they'd become part of his life. He'd go back and make an offer on the camper, and meet the girl, and maybe something would develop between them. But now that he's around the bend, he isn't sure either of them were real. And if even if they were, he's more nervous than ever about the success of this Half-Town job, pictures his own glum face in the window of the prison van.

The second thing is that there are two helmets gliding along above the grade of the main road. Two men on snowmobiles are driving on the edge of the field on the other side of the road, away from the town. They are driving very slowly, which Willis finds unusual, are now passing the spot on the shoulder where he had parked earlier that morning, light-years ago, it now seems.

Willis twists his body and, with great care, backs up to a place on the lane where the car will be less noticeable.

The snowmobilers pause at the small bridge between Half-Town and the intersection. They are there only for the briefest of moments. Then they turn around and head back towards the village, only full speed now, standing bent over on their machines like jockeys in a horse race.

As soon as Willis calculates it's safe, he hurries the Ford to the bridge and pulls over just before it. From the shoulder he can plainly see two sets of footprints in the snow. They lead under the bridge. Willis gazes across the diamond-studded prairie. There is no one in sight, no buses or big sedans or cruiser cars.

He rolls down the window. His voice explodes into the silent and flawless fields so gently tucked in beneath their snowy quilt. "Get in, get in!" he shouts.

Willis imagines the whole town springing to life, its inhabitants bursting out of their doorways with toques and guns, the posse of coffee-drinking snowmobilers descending upon the Ford like a pack of demon wolves.

But all that happens is that Fitz and Dooker, dressed in those ridiculous black coats, scramble up from beneath the bridge. Their balaclavas are still pulled down over their faces. Beards had not really been necessary. The men fling themselves into the car. Willis floors it, his tires spinning in the icy tracks.

As they speed away, for a moment, everything inside the Fairlane is quiet. Fitz and Dooker appear, for once, to be speechless. Dooker is in the front passenger seat. He peels off his disguise. Willis doesn't dare look at him. Dooker runs his hand over his face to wipe away the sweat and snot.

Then all hell breaks loose. Fitz and Dooker are enraged that Willis didn't keep his post. They call him every dirty name they can think of. Above the tops of their voices, Willis demands the directions to the hideout where they're supposed to drop the car. But they harangue him relentlessly. Through their tirade, Willis mocks them for leaving footprints in fresh snow, suggests they might have laid low behind some building in town instead. He finally subdues them by telling them he had been looking for them, fearing something had gone wrong, and that they were lucky he hadn't been waiting for them on the road, what with those snowmobilers on their tails. If he'd been there, the cops would now have a full description of the car. As far as he can tell, none of the snowmobilers saw the getaway vehicle. By the time the Mounties have interviewed the witnesses, he and Fitz and Dooker will be long gone, the old Ford concealed in some shed in the boonies. Of course, all kinds of things could still go wrong.

"What took so damn long?" Willis asks once things have died down.

Fitz is quiet. Dooker explains. The pension cheques came in the mail Monday. But the bank is closed Mondays, so first thing Tuesday morning, all the seniors came to deposit their cheques. Between the time that the three of them had taken that swing through town, and the time that Fitz and Dooker had arrived at the credit union, a line of old people had formed outside the front door. Fitz and Dooker, instead of pushing their way in when the manager unlocked the back door, as planned, had waited until the bank cleared out. "We had to sit behind a dumpster out back until the place was empty," said Dooker. "And then we went in the front door."

"And all those guys across the street watching you through the window," mumbled Willis. "You should have just come back." He doesn't ask about the money. The old leather briefcase Fitz was carrying is beside him in the back seat. Willis can't tell if it has anything in it. Time for that later.

At the highway, where the semis have been rolling by all morning, Fitz finally gives Willis instructions to the hideout, and Willis drives as fast as he dares.

He won't tell them about the bus lady and the mayor and the Mountie. They'll just turn that against him somehow. He won't talk about how he needs to get free. And he isn't going to tell them about the Boler, about the not-quite-pretty girl he met, almost met, in Half-Town.

Because Willis is thinking now, among the diamonds sparkling in the bright, late-winter sun, that they might just get away with this, might just get back to the city a little richer than they were before.

And with his share of the take, his small cut, he'll lay his plans, and then return to Half-Town. There he will capture the Boler and the heart of the lesser girl. And even if they were only a dream, that Boler and that girl, Willis believes they are waiting for him somewhere.

GOLDIE

In the morning, they saw that the mouse-killing stick had moved. A straight-line wind had come upon them the evening before, after a day of rain. First the stormy skies had begun to clear, followed by fits and blusters of restless air. The sun was about to set brilliant red among purplish clouds when the hemming and hawing of the wind changed to a roar, a steady roar out of the west that lasted minutes. Leaves and willow shoots tumbled across the yard, birds shrieked in the sky.

A maple cracked in the tumult and toppled slowly.

And Calvin's mouse-killing stick, which usually lay beside the raspberry canes, leaped from the garden onto the lawn. It was a thick, sturdy limb from a dead poplar tree.

"Whenever I'm working in the garden, I see that dead branch lying there and I tell myself I'll take it to the burn barrel on my way out," Cissy had recently told her husband while washing up the breakfast things. "And then I forget, and the next thing you know, I'm here at the sink and staring at it through this window again."

"Why don't you march right out there and get it, then? Have done with it."

And Cissy had thought, my husband is so linear. She hadn't said it out loud then, though she had in the past. "I don't know," she replied. "I tell myself, next time. Deep in my subconscious, there's something preventing me."

"Like what?"

Cissy had tapped the side of her head. "Subconscious."

"Well, the stick is there for a purpose," Calvin had said. "Otherwise I would have removed it by now."

"What purpose is there for an old, dead stick?" Cissy had exclaimed.

"It's my mouse-killing stick. To kill the mice that try to live under the birdseed pails, and under those cranberry bushes."

Cissy grimaced. "Some people drown mice."

"But you still have to catch them first."

Cissy and Calvin Heppner lived in an old house in Gretna at the west edge of the village. Gretna was the bedroom community of a larger, nearby town in the middle of the prairie. Their property bordered a farmer's field and was at least four times the size of most city lots. The yard was broken up by flower beds and clusters of shrubs and trees. An enormous garden sprawled in one corner. Cissy poked around in it out of respect for Calvin. She took care of the lawns and the flower beds beside the house. He looked after everything else. Cissy tried to convince herself that he wanted it that way, that he accepted her disinterest in horticulture. But she still felt guilty, hence her occasional forays into the garden.

"There must be a better place for it than right there in the middle of the garden," she'd said that morning. "Put it against the house somewhere, behind the bushes."

"I suppose I could do that," Calvin had replied. And then they both forgot about it. The way they seemed to have forgotten about many things.

The home they'd bought two years ago lamented its lost grandeur. Once upon a time, the town had hustled and bustled with wealthy lumber importers and grain buyers and flour millers. The house had seen many owners in the hundred years that had passed since it had been built. Over time, various owners had begun restoration. But each starry-eyed resident had approached renovation with a different vision. The home had become, as Calvin put it, a camel. The arts-and-crafts exterior had come together nicely, but the interior had been disfigured again and again. Walls had been removed, walls had been added. Bay windows had been carved into the blueprint. Mouldings and baseboards had been changed. Wallpaper had been stripped, replaced, and stripped away again.

When the Heppners had moved from Vancouver to Gretna, returning to their prairie roots, they decided to gut the house and start from scratch. Being in their thirties, employed, and childless, they had money and time. What they did not have, they discovered, was momentum. Even the task-oriented Calvin, who usually set a clear path for himself early on and steadfastly followed it, had run out of steam. After the gutting, the plans clogged up with details. So Cissy and Calvin inhabited a large, draughty, hollow space, on floorboards daubed here and there with colourful rugs. A fold of wallpaper dangled from the wall above Cissy's piano, the one and only panel left in the whole house. In the centre of the rawness, an original chandelier remained suspended from the ceiling where the dining room had once been, and would be again some day. Its crystals caught the sun peeping through uncurtained windowpanes in the evenings and cast rainbows onto the furniture. The kitchen cabinets had been denuded of their finish and hardware, but at least there were cabinets. It was here that Cissy had created a cozy corner beside a window with a small, rustic farmhouse table and a collection of lamps and candles. Plants in colourful pots sat on the deep windowsill. It was the best spot in the house. The Heppners spent the most time together at that table. It was where the little entertaining they did took place. The only enclosed spaces on the main floor were a few closets, a bathroom with troublesome plumbing, and the master bedroom.

The basement had cracks and mice and cobwebs. The Heppners seldom ventured down the treacherous stairwell.

Cissy sometimes regretted leaving the ocean. "This place is like the Sleeping Beauty castle," Cissy would complain to her mother in Winnipeg, her sisters in Calgary, her brother in Brandon. "We just can't seem to make any headway. Calvin and I are under some sort of evil spell, waiting for Prince and Princess Charming to come along and wake us up."

"You're obviously not ready," said one of her sisters. "It'll happen when it's supposed to happen."

Her brother advised them to seek help from an interior designer. "Have someone come out and draw up some plans, toss out a few ideas. That'll get your juices flowing again." Her brother's ideas were always expensive, which Cissy thought funny, since his own finances were a mess.

Her other sister was more interested in who had put the

curse on them in the first place, and what would break it. "You and Calvin should kiss everybody you meet," she giggled. "Somebody's bound to break the curse eventually."

"All you need is a boot in the rear," Cissy's mother told her. Dorothy Lange's husband had died when only in his fifties. She had remained a spirited, confident, straightforward woman who irritated her friends and family by having the occasional cigarette and going out on dates with men they didn't know. Calvin called her Dotty and took pleasure in baiting her outlandish side. Cissy wasn't anything like her.

Cissy's dreams extended beyond resuscitating the house and yard. She hoped to start a bed-and-breakfast business. The property behind them was a small, woodsy lot with a small, well-kept cottage occupied by a small, sad widow named Bessie Hample. Cissy had once taken a jar of freshly made chokecherry jelly to Mrs. Hample. The woman invited Cissy in. "It's perfect," Cissy reported back to her husband. "The two bedrooms are on either side of the living room, and the Hamples added a second bathroom because he was an invalid before he died." The Heppners told Bessie that if she ever decided to sell, they would buy her place for their B-and-B.

"Oh, isn't that something," the woman had said with no enthusiasm. "Bed-and-breakfast. Hmmm. Yeah, I'm pretty well ready to go, just waiting for a nice apartment to open up downtown."

Gretna had only one apartment block, and, being little more than a hamlet, could hardly claim to have a downtown.

Cissy was searching for an object around which to build a motif: a painting, a sculpture, some glorious antique, or even something as simple as a piece of pottery. She wanted a starting point.

Meanwhile, she and Calvin nurtured the widow Hample, neighbouring with her over the hedges when the opportunity arose. They had the impression that she was childless, but, in the coffee shop lately, had heard otherwise.

When Cissy went for coffee Saturday mornings at Kim's Korner, the women she was with called Bessie's mysterious daughter *wayward, a poor lost soul*. When Calvin went Saturday afternoons with the men, and came home with doughnut icing ghosting his upper lip, she was *a crack-whore, a cheap slut*. She had left home in her late teens, much to everyone's relief. No one remembered her name, and no one had seen her since.

More than a year had passed since the Heppners had made their offer to Mrs. Hample. They knew for a fact that apartments had come and gone. And yet she hadn't budged. She prowled around her woodsy yard with a long, sad face, plucking at her perennials and collecting deadfall. In the winter, the only sign of life they saw at the Hample home was smoke from the oil furnace curling out of the chimney.

"She's obviously under the same spell," Cissy had once whispered to Calvin as they watched her drifting around her garden in slow motion. "Must be this whole corner of town." They turned their gaze to the home next door. Stanley Redding lived alone in a tidy bungalow sporting new shingles, a new garage, and flower beds so orderly Cissy dismissed them as neurotic. "Not this whole corner, I guess," she amended.

The day following the straight-line wind, which had happened on a Sunday, Cissy and Calvin walked around their property after work. Aside from the one maple and the twigs strewn about, not much had changed. Most of the flowering plants had hung onto their blooms. What Cissy and Calvin had not noticed on their tour after the storm the previous evening was that the nest was gone. A pair of barn swallows had built it on the west side of the house, above the pantry window. The cup of mud had dissolved in the blast of rain, and the eggs were scattered in the grass beneath. Not only that, one parent seemed to be missing.

"Boy, that thing just missed her roof," Calvin said. He was looking at Mrs. Hample's. An elm tree that had already been half dead had split partway up the main trunk and crashed to the ground.

"We'll have to help her with that," Cissy murmured, wondering how the missing elm would affect the overall appearance of the potential B-and-B.

Fallen trees weren't all the wind had blown in.

Later that evening, Cissy took her rake and wheelbarrow and began to gather up the twigs. She moved the mouse-killing stick from the lawn and slid it under a cranberry bush. Calvin had gone to a town council meeting. "Tell Mrs. H I'll do her tree tomorrow," he'd said to Cissy before he left. I'll have to remember to tell him where I put the branch, she thought, and moved her wedding ring to her other hand as a reminder.

Mrs. Hample wasn't around. As Cissy backed her way toward the rear of the yard, raking, raking, raking, she suddenly smelled cigarette smoke on the humid air. She lifted her head and turned towards the Hample house.

And there she was. Not Bessie Hample, but a bent stick of a woman leaning on the back porch railing, smoking. She was so thin, and dressed so plainly, it was hard to identify her gender at first. Her hair looked somewhat feminine—straight, black, the ends trimmed, her bangs trimmed. She did not look at Cissy, but studied the prostrate elm, and smoked.

Cissy went closer. "Yeah, that was quite a wind," she began. "Were you here when it hit?"

The woman shook her head. Her face didn't change.

"Okay. Uh—tell Bessie my husband and I will clean up the tree tomorrow after work."

"I'll clean it up," the woman said in a low, taut voice.

Cissy ambled closer. The woman had a handsome face, masculine, almost gaunt, with high cheekbones. But her eyebrows were slender and arched, her lips fuller than a man's. If she smiled, her eyes would be beautiful, Cissy thought. The woman wore a grey suede jacket and grey jeans and black pointy-toed boots. The sight of those warm clothes made Cissy sweat.

"You'll need a chainsaw," said Cissy.

The woman flicked her cigarette butt onto the lawn and straightened up. Cissy was struck by how curveless she was. Could she possibly be the daughter? Difficult to tell her age. Despite her thinness, she didn't fit Cissy's image of a crackwhore, nor did she appear to be a poor lost soul.

"There's a saw around here somewhere," came the monotone reply.

Why wouldn't Bessie Hample have a chainsaw? Almost everyone in Gretna did. Just because she and Calvin hadn't ever seen her using it didn't mean her husband hadn't had one. Yet Cissy couldn't picture the sad-sack Bessie Hample assaulting her shrubbery with a power tool. "Have you used it before?" she asked the wraith.

The woman nodded, but it looked to Cissy like a lie.

"Well, I'm Cissy Heppner, and my husband is Calvin, and we'll be glad to help. Bessie knows us."

The woman nodded again, then slipped back inside the house through the screen door. A second later, Bessie's face materialized behind the screen. She waved. Cissy waved back. The face dissolved. Cissy went back to her raking.

As she worked, she remembered how Bessie had talked about the dog. Cissy and Calvin had been emptying bales of peat moss into their flower beds early last summer. A lone black Lab had frolicked across the lawn and out into the field beyond. Then Bessie had sauntered over, her arms akimbo as usual, pulling her cardigan tight around her thin breasts, as if to shut out evil spirits lurking in alien territory. "That's Thompsons' dog. You'll notice him around here from time to time. Gets away from 'em sometimes."

She'd started to go back, but then, in her slow, sad way, began her story. "Ed and I lived on a farm before we moved to town. We moved because he got sick, couldn't be a farmer any more, couldn't help take care of that big farmyard, either. So we bought this place.

"But we had a dog, a funny little black dog, part Dalmatian, named Ringo. Had only one eye, lost it in a fight with a tomcat. He was like most dogs, full of jumping beans and eager to please. But still he was just a farm dog. My husband didn't believe in pets, even though that's what Ringo wanted more than anything to be.

"When we put the farm up for sale, a woman stopped in and asked us if she could take Ringo. She and her husband had bought a place about five miles down the road from us a few years before that. And then the husband died. We'd seen her driving by on her way to town. And she'd seen Ringo running around our yard. Said she was old and alone and wanted company.

"We weren't quite sure what the lady wanted with a jumpy, one-eyed dog, but Ed was happy to be rid of him so easily. As far as I could tell, he never had a single regret about passing Ringo over.

"Shortly after that we moved here. But I'd often see Ringo riding in the truck with that lady. I even saw him with her in town once in winter. He was wearing a sweater and booties. I asked her how she got him to do that, and she told me she used to be an animal trainer for movies in Toronto.

"I couldn't believe it. She'd taught him all kinds of tricks, too. She said she loved him. And he loved her, I could tell. Now whenever I see his funny little face in the truck window, I think how lucky he is. How very lucky."

It was the longest speech Bessie Hample had ever made. Cissy and Calvin had listened and nodded, and smiled at the fortunes of the dog. But later, alone, Cissy had nearly wept over the yearning in the story. And she began to keep a lookout for the one-eyed Ringo.

And Cissy was quite certain there'd been no mention of a daughter in the tale of the dog. How long ago had the girl left home? How long had Bessie lived in the cottage? When had her husband died? Coffee shop questions.

Cissy puttered around the yard until dark, but Mrs. Hample did not leave her house that evening, nor did the scrawny woman. Once, through the foliage, Cissy did see a shiny black pickup truck speed away from Bessie's house. When Calvin returned home late, complaining as usual about the inefficient running of the meeting, he said, "She's not necessarily the daughter. Could be a friend, or a niece, or a church visitor; this town is overrun with church visitors."

"A church visitor?" snorted Cissy. "Would the church send someone who has the social skills of a turnip?"

"Your ring is on the wrong hand," said Calvin.

He noticed little things like that.

"What were you supposed to remember?"

"I forget," Cissy replied, and moved the ring to its usual location.

The next morning Calvin spotted the woman at the post office on his way to work. "I recognized her right away," he said. "She's the exact opposite of you."

That evening when the Heppners set forth to clean up their own fallen tree, they saw immediately that Bessie's had been taken care of. The only thing that remained was a stump.

Cissy and Calvin stood and stared. The evening was sweet and still. At that moment, no voices could be heard from neighbouring properties, no dogs barked, no wind blew, no engine sounds erupted from driveways or streets nearby. The chainsaw hung from Calvin's hand. Cissy stood with her arms akimbo like Bessie Hample.

"She must have been a busy little beaver today," Calvin said in a whisper.

"It wasn't her," Cissy replied. "Someone else came and did it. Probably the neat-freak from next door."

They stood there quite a while, hoping Bessie would come out through the screen door and explain.

But nothing happened. "They must be out celebrating," said Calvin. He reluctantly started up his chainsaw, slashing the stillness.

Cissy wondered, if the strange woman was her daughter, how Mrs. Hample felt about her being home. Would they be celebrating? Or did the girl spell trouble?

They didn't finish the maple that night. Just after they'd called it quits and were strolling towards the house, Bessie Hample emerged from the gloaming. Her pale countenance hovered ghost-like above the cotoneaster hedge that separated their yards. Cissy hurried over to her. Before she could even say hello, Bessie called, "I came to say goodbye!"

"What? Goodbye?" Had she found an apartment downtown at last?

"I'm going on a vacation."

"A vacation. Ah." Calvin sidled up.

"Yes, I'm going to Swift Current to see my cousin." Bessie's voice was a pitch higher than usual. "My daughter is driving me to the airport tomorrow."

"Your daughter," said Cissy. "So that is your daughter. You didn't tell us you had any children."

"That's my Goldie. Came for a visit. She'll be staying here while I'm away."

Goldie. Cissy pictured the birth of a yellow-haired child, so full of promise. "Where is she from, your daughter?"

"Well, she's from around here, of course," Bessie said with a lilt approaching merriment. "But she's been living up at Fort St. John." Her face clouded. She added, "Lately, anyway. Well, goodbye." She started to walk away.

"Have a nice time then," said Cissy.

"How long will you be gone, exactly?" called Calvin.

The words floated out of the dusk. "Oh, just a week. My cousin and I don't need much time to get into trouble."

"I think she laughed just then," Cissy breathed as they neared their back door. "Don't you think she laughed? She was almost giddy."

"I guess the girl makes her happy," Calvin said, his voice a little too loud in the calm evening. "We forgot to ask who cleaned up the tree."

The question was answered a few days later.

On Saturday morning, Cissy and Calvin loaded the maple debris onto the back of a half-ton they'd borrowed from a friend. They discussed the buying of a truck, the need, the expense. Bits of bark crept into Cissy's work gloves and behind her shirt collar. Exertion and the scratchiness of the bark on her wrists and neck made her perspire. She tried to wipe away the sweat by running the top of her forearm across her brow. Her other hand was unable to keep its grip on the large section of log Calvin was helping her carry. It fell to the ground with a *flump*.

"Geez, Cissy!"

They grabbed hold of the log again and heaved it onto the pile on the back of the half-ton. "Are you sure you don't want to use these pieces for the firepit?" she asked.

"I've already put some aside." Calvin nodded towards the back of the yard where he'd created a round pit and edged it with brickwork. That had been last summer's project. "Without a woodshed to keep it dry," he continued, "it doesn't pay to stockpile it."

"Weren't you going to build a woodshed this spring?"

"Yep. Hasn't happened yet, has it?"

Cissy flung a slender log with a little too much force. It banged against the side of the truck box. "Nothing happens around here," she said. "Except we've cleaned up this tree. That's it. All our other plans just...."

Calvin straightened up and leaned on the box. "You blaming me?"

"No. It's both of us equally. How come we can clean up this tree, but keep on living in a shell of a house?"

"You mean you haven't figured that out yet?" Calvin swatted at a mosquito.

"What do you mean?"

"First of all, we know we can't do the work inside ourselves, much as we don't want to admit it. That means hiring a project manager. So now we have to choose a project manager, plus make a basic design for the house, plus figure out how we're going to pay for it. You're thinking if we open a B-and-B, that'll help with the financing. But you don't want to start the B-and-B operation until you've got Hamples' place in your clutches." He gathered up an armful of branches. "Am I right?"

"*Clutches?*"

"You are kind of obsessed."

"It's my dream, Calvin," said Cissy, wounded.

"Well, maybe if you would settle for the four upstairs bedrooms, and then, if that's successful, annexing Bessie's place some time down the road, we could get a start."

"I need—" Cissy began. "Something. An inspiration. To form a theme around."

"Well, maybe you're not looking hard enough."

Cissy and Calvin continued their work in silence. As they raked up the last of the twigs with their glove-thick fingers, they heard a clatter starting up somewhere nearby.

"Whose chainsaw is that?" said Calvin.

"It's coming from over there," said Cissy. "Hamples'."

They walked around the grove of evergreens and perennials that separated them from the back of their property. They could see nobody in the Hamples' yard. But the sound seemed to come from the front of the house. "I think she's in the garage," said Calvin. Bessie Hample's garage was attached to the side of her house. The door faced the street at the front, invisible to the Heppners.

"I think you're right. What on earth is Goldie doing in there with a chainsaw?" Cissy shivered. "She scares me."

"How often have you seen her?"

"Just once. It was enough. She's never outside. Stays in the house like some kind of mole."

"Maybe she goes gallivanting at night," Calvin said.

They both climbed into the truck and took the remains of the hapless maple to the compost dump several miles out of town. When they returned, they could still hear the intermittant snoring of the saw.

"I'm going to go look." Calvin stripped off his gloves and dropped them on the ground.

"Wait!" Cissy touched his arm. "What if Bessie didn't make it to Swift Current? What if Goldie offed her for the inheritance? Maybe she's cutting up the body." The image of the lucky little dog wearing a sweater and booties flashed through Cissy's mind.

"Boy, she really must have done a number on you." Calvin slipped through the cotoneasters, trudged across Bessie Hample's lawn, and disappeared around the front of the cottage. But even before that, the noise stopped.

He was gone a long time. Cissy waited. Suddenly, she heard his voice behind her. She was startled and let out a small shriek.

"I came back up the side street there," he said.

"Did you see her?"

Calvin shook his head. "She was pulling down the garage door just as I got there. All I saw was two sexy bare legs in a pair of steel-toed boots."

"Skinny legs."

"I don't think she even saw me," Calvin went on. "But I didn't want to chance sneaking back across her yard, in case she went straight into the house and spotted me through a window. Anyway, there aren't any rivers of blood gushing down the driveway." He picked up his gloves. "Those legs had muscles."

"If she's here to stay, Bessie won't sell."

"No," said Calvin. "She probably won't."

After a week had passed, Goldie appeared in her mother's yard. Cissy and Calvin observed her pacing up and down the lawn with her head bent, as if looking for something she'd lost. Then Bessie came from the house and joined her daughter.

"She's home," mumbled Cissy.

The two women spoke quietly to each other for a few moments, then Goldie stuck a broken twig into the ground.

Before Cissy knew what was happening, Calvin strutted right over to the cotoneaster hedge, barged through it at a thin spot, and approached the two women. Cissy hung back.

She saw him take off his glove and reach out to shake Goldie's hand. Goldie allowed that, but slid her left hand behind her back, as though afraid of exposing both sides of herself at once. The three of them conversed too quietly for Cissy to hear.

When Calvin came back, he said to Cissy, "Mrs. Hample appears to be in one piece, after all. Not a scar on her. Got back from Swift Current just minutes ago."

Cissy laid a handful of twigs in the wheelbarrow. "What about Goldie?"

"Oh, she seemed all right," Calvin replied. "Yeah, standoffish, though."

The following Friday, Cissy's mother telephoned. She offered to come and spend the weekend with Cissy and

Calvin. *Cal*, she called him. Cissy had mixed feelings about her mother's visits. There was never a dull moment with Dorothy, who liked to look up her husband's friends and relatives in Gretna, with Cissy tagging along. But Dorothy Lange's over-sized personality sometimes wore her out. The other Lange children took after their mother; Cissy was more like her father.

Saturday morning, as Cissy and Dorothy stood in the backyard observing Calvin's gardens, Stanley Redding came strolling over in his bright green tennis shoes, pruning shears in hand. He had met Cissy's mother several times before. The two had hit it off, though Stanley was ten or fifteen years younger. They chattered away while Cissy slapped mosquitoes.

Stanley had just invited them to his house for Sunday brunch, when they saw Bessie Hample's head and shoulders above the hedges. Dorothy beckoned to her, and Bessie, arms akimbo, wandered over aimlessly, as if approaching a crowd of strangers. Goldie followed at a great distance, meandering in that same aimless way, stony-faced, defiant.

"Well, why don't you all come?" Stanley gushed. "Brunch tomorrow, eleven o'clock. Don't bring anything."

"Oh—all right," said Bessie with a frown. She glanced at her daughter. "I don't know if—"

Stanley began heading back to his yard. "See you all tomorrow!" he tossed over his shoulder with a wave of his manicured hand.

Goldie turned and went back through the bushes.

"Nice to see you again, Mrs. Lange," Bessie stammered, and followed her daughter.

Dorothy seemed to think nothing of the meeting on the back lawn, but Cissy was bewildered. Neither she nor Calvin had ever been inside Stanley Redding's house. Bessie and her mother had met a few times, but it wasn't like Bessie to make a point of coming to say hello. And would Goldie actually show up at a brunch?

"My, you're quite the little neighbour magnet, aren't you?" Cissy commented as she and her mother continued their tour.

"I don't know what you mean," Dorothy replied, bending over a pink rose. Her hair was dyed a reddish blonde, she wore wraparound sunglasses, a yellow-and-white-striped T-shirt with a deep V that revealed her cleavage and a seductive tan, and white cropped pants with a yellow flower embroidered on the rump.

Cissy laughed. "Neighbour magnet," she repeated.

Sunday morning at eleven sharp, Cissy and Calvin and Dorothy paraded through the tidy row of Lombardy poplars that formed a division between the Heppners' property and Stanley Redding's. Calvin, dressed in jeans and a white cotton shirt, led the procession. Dorothy came last, stepping cautiously in slender-heeled sandals, and still blowing on her freshly lacquered nails. Cissy couldn't decide whether to keep up with her husband or wait for her mother. She hovered in the middle. Her morning had been taken up with three changes of outfits and she was tired. The black, beaded peasant dress she'd ended up in hadn't seen the light of day for years. "Oh, my," was all her mother had said about it, peering at Cissy over a bottle of nail polish.

Bessie was already settled in a luxurious bamboo chair on Stanley's deck with a glass of champagne in her hand. Goldie sat at the patio table, sipping beer from a tall glass. Bessie chirped a greeting as Dorothy Lange and the Heppners mounted the deck stairs. Her daughter pulled a pack of cigarettes from the sleeve of her black T-shirt and remained silent.

"Oh, we're all here!" gushed Stanley as he stepped out onto the deck. "Let me get you your drinks!"

Bessie was chattier than usual. Everyone except Goldie was in a jovial mood. To Cissy, it seemed as though the patio, the pleasant weather, the costumes, the champagne, were creating a brief enchantment; the event had a dreamlike quality, with Goldie playing the role of the sorceress lurking at the edge of the festivities.

As the platters and baskets flowed around and across the glass-topped table, Cissy learned many things: Stanley had settled in Gretna as a draft dodger in the sixties; Bessie's Jewish mother had escaped the Nazis with her German husband; someone in town was hoping to establish a small museum about Gretna's history; Dorothy claimed to "just love history!"; Goldie had completed a course in welding; Stanley owned a cat that was never allowed out, because Stanley suspected that his previous pet had been poisoned. One time Cissy observed Stanley patting Goldie's arm in a reassuring way. Another time she saw Goldie smile at him. He seemed to know Bessie and Goldie in a way that the Heppners did not.

It occurred to Cissy after a while that everyone was drinking a lot of champagne. Even Goldie had given in. Yet she, unlike the others, did not become merrier as the afternoon wore on.

When, after the meal, the conversation turned to travel, Dorothy Lange said, "My daughter is hoping to run a bed-and-breakfast some day."

"Here?" said Stanley. "Wouldn't that be simply marvellous! I'd be happy to provide the breakfast part sometimes. I'm a fierce amateur chef!"

Cissy's mother pointed in the general direction of the Hample house. "She wants to—"

"—put in a koi pool over there, at the back of our yard," Cissy interrupted. She sensed Calvin frowning at her.

"And, of course, we have a lot to do in the house," she continued. "It'll be quite a while before—"

Goldie rose from her chair. Mumbling something that might have been "Thanks, Stan," she fled from the deck and headed for her mother's house.

Stanley looked concerned. Bessie seemed to think nothing of it. The topic of B-and-Bs went on a bit longer. Bessie related her experiences in Swift Current, which revolved mostly around hunting for antiques in neighbouring towns. "I found myself a nice string of pearls," she crowed. "Not necessarily real ones, but pretty."

Cissy couldn't help but wonder on what occasion Bessie would wear pearls.

Eventually the conversation lagged. The Heppners, with Dorothy again bringing up the rear, made their departure.

"I'll need a good nap before I drive back," said Dorothy as they entered the house. "You know," she added with a yawn, "you should ask Stanley to remodel your place. He'd do a bang-up job."

That night, Calvin and Cissy built a blaze in Calvin's splendid firepit. They roasted wieners and marshmallows. The maple logs disintegrated into smoke and ash and vapour. Calvin complained that the hotdogs didn't taste quite right and worried about food poisoning.

For several evenings following, the chainsawing continued in the Hample garage. The Heppners heard short outbursts of it when they puttered in the yard. "We forgot to ask them at the brunch what was going on in their garage," said Cissy one evening.

"Too drunk," Calvin replied.

"Do you think that's why Goldie bolted off Stan's deck like that?"

"No," said Calvin, "I was talking about us."

They watched their barn swallow wheeling above the lawn. The female had not returned. Calvin said, "His mate must have been killed somehow."

Cissy tried to imagine how the female had died. Perhaps the swallow had been hunting for food when the storm hit. In her panic she might have flown into the path of a vehicle tearing along a Gretna street. Goldie drove fast; Cissy and Calvin had observed her speeding up the side street more than once.

The bereft male landed on the railing of the back porch, which had been the favoured perch of both birds since arriving at the Heppner house in late spring. "It's probably too late for him to find a new wife," said Cissy. "There aren't any other swallows around here. Most people don't want the mess." She nodded towards Stanley's house. "He was washing those mud nests off his siding all spring."

At the moment, Stanley was nowhere to be seen.

One Sunday in early July, Calvin and his friend, Mike, decided to go fishing at the Red River. Cissy roamed around the house and stared at the walls. The remodelling deadlines she and Calvin had established had all long past. What her husband had said was true—Cissy was putting too many eggs in Mrs. Hample's basket.

She paused at the piano and ran her knuckles along the black keys at the bottom of the keyboard. Without much thought, she grabbed hold of the wallpaper panel dangling there and tugged hard. With a sharp gasp it came loose, all the way down to the baseboard. Cissy flung up her arms in a gesture of triumph, liberating the entire strip from behind the piano. She dropped it onto the floor. Thunder sounded in the tranquil morning, not unlike the low, rumbling sounds her knuckles had made only seconds earlier.

The wallpaper was decorated with ferns and palm trees. So suitable for a prairie home, Cissy had scoffed when they'd first looked at the house.

The lawn needed cutting. A brief drizzle of rain the previous afternoon had dampened it, but the grass would be dry by now. Perhaps she could mow part of it before this next rain came. It might not rain at all. At first, Cissy thought she'd leave the wallpaper where it lay. Then, worrying that it would lie there for weeks or even months, she rolled it up and set it on a windowsill in the back porch.

The thunder was a little louder now. Before she cut the grass, Cissy always made sure there were no bits of deadfall strewn about. When she neared the edge of the garden, and had just flung a large scrap of bark into the firepit, some movement caught her attention. She whirled around to find Goldie Hample already very close to her. The stone face had darkened like the skies.

"You scared me!" Cissy blurted. Thunder. Closer.

"I want to talk to you."

It wouldn't be a friendly chat.

"You seem upset," Cissy replied. "What's wrong?"

Goldie's grey sweatshirt was streaked with red. Her eyes flashed. "It's about what you're doing to us." Goldie took a step closer to Cissy. A cold fragment of wet hit Cissy's cheek, which could have been a small raindrop, or spittle from Goldie Hample's cold mouth.

"Doing to—you?"

"Trying to steal our house from us!" Goldie stepped closer yet.

Our house? *Us?* Cissy moved back. In her mind she tried to locate the mouse-killing stick, in case she needed it to fend off the irate Goldie Hample. A peal of thunder, very near now. The muscles in Cissy's face twitched.

"We're not trying to steal it. Did your mother tell you that?" Cissy tried to sound nonchalant. Goldie was either drunk or high on something else.

"She won't sell it to you!" The woman was shouting now, above the thunder.

Then Cissy remembered she'd moved the stick. It was several feet away, underneath the cranberry shrub, where lurked, according to Calvin, a family of dangerous mice. She was defenceless.

"We didn't know—" Cissy began. "We didn't know you had an interest in the house. Your mother told us she was planning to move."

"My mother says what people want to hear! Don't you know that?"

"Well, no. . . ."

"My mother's a friggin' doormat!" Goldie screamed.

A distant roar now, the same one they'd heard about a month ago, of a wind moving across the flat land in a straight line.

Cissy whirled towards the sound. "You'd better get inside!" she yelled. "This could be a dangerous storm." She ran for the back door.

"It's not that I don't love her, don't you think that!" Goldie yelled after her.

From inside the porch, Cissy peered through the screen door. Goldie caught the full blast of the storm. Her hair whipped back and she staggered. Then came the rain. Cissy saw Goldie's mouth open and close with surprise, and perhaps fear. Goldie turned and, propelled by the monstrous wind, made it to her own porch. Through the grove of swaying evergreens, Cissy could just glimpse Goldie struggling with the door of Bessie's house. The door had to be opened into the wind. And as the evergreens bent before the blast, Cissy caught a glimpse of something else in Bessie Hample's backyard: a giant, gleaming, red fish, pointing to the sky.

The sound of the wind became unbearable. Cissy hurried to the dreaded stairwell that led to the dungeon. There she and Calvin had taken cover last time, also on a Sunday, when the first tornado-like wind had come upon them.

Calvin wasn't here now. He and Mike were standing on the riverbank, casting their lines into a gentle flow of water. The sun was probably shining, dancing on gentle ripples. This storm would most likely miss them. He would come home to what kind of devastation this time? Was this a real tornado?

By the light of a 40-watt bulb, Cissy descended to the bottom step and sat down. She watched for mice, and thought of Goldie. Had she made it into the house? What had brought on that burst of wrath? But Cissy's mind was mostly occupied with the image of the fish, a sudden magnificent sculpture in Bessie's meagre garden. Where had it come from? Where was Bessie?

The electricity cut out. Cissy sat in blackness. She rubbed her ankles and arms in case spiders were crawling there. Every once in a while, for reassurance she looked for the strip of daylight under the door at the top of the stairs.

Footsteps clunked across the kitchen floor. Cissy recalled Calvin's description of Goldie's legs and her steel-toed boots.

"Cissy?" The door opened. Natural light pierced the stairwell. The wind had stopped.

"Calvin! How come you're back?" She climbed up to him.

"We heard the weather warning on the way to the river. Mike's wife is terrified of storms. So we turned around and came home."

"Were you on the road in that wind?"

"We were parked in Mike's garage. He drove me here as soon as it let up."

"What do you mean, *Mike's* wife? What about me?" Cissy pouted.

They inspected the damage. The power was still out. Only a little rain had fallen. Two more trees were down, old maples again. One young evergreen was askew, leaning towards the east as if resigned to being kicked around by bully storms. A few poplar boughs lay scattered here and there. "More mouse-killing sticks for you," said Cissy. Stanley, too, was surveying his property. He was garbed in black rubber boots and a polo shirt tucked into Bermuda shorts. With gloved hands, he began picking up debris. Cissy and Calvin returned his gestures of dismay.

Cissy told Calvin about being confronted by Goldie, and about the apparition. They walked to the back of their yard.

There, in the centre of Bessie Hample's back lawn, stood the fish that pointed skyward like a rocket, a salmon, they thought, about four feet tall. It had been carved out of a tree trunk, but not the short stump of the elm, which was off to the edge of the lawn. The salmon's mouth was agape, as though the fish were reaching for a morsel of food. Its fins were fully flexed, and its tail was curled beneath it. The base for the sculpture was part of the tree trunk itself. Goldie had attached thick wrought-iron feet for extra stability.

"That's what she was doing with the chainsaw," said Calvin. The fish had been sanded to a smooth finish and painted. As the sun slipped out of the passing clouds, it glistened a luminous red.

"It's beautiful," said Cissy. "It has human eyes, *her* eyes, come to think of it."

"Amazing," said Calvin. "She must have worked on that thing day and night. Look how it's been honed and detailed."

"Bessie said Goldie lived in Fort St. John," said Cissy. "She must have learned it there. Who would have suspected Crack-Whore Goldie of being an artist?"

Calvin began to pick up branches. But Cissy stared at the fish. The scales glimmered on its sensuous body. She wished Goldie would emerge from her lair so Cissy could tell her how much she admired the salmon, and so they could mend their differences.

Most of all, Cissy wished the sculpture belonged to her. A small, childish part of her still hoped that wishes could come true.

Cissy remained slouched beside the wheelbarrow. "She called her mother a friggin' doormat and said she loved her."

Calvin shrugged. "Families. Complicated."

At supper, Cissy said loudly, "She won't let Bessie sell the house. She wants her to stay there forever, I suppose." Her voice echoed off distant walls.

Calvin glanced towards the piano. "Hey, you ripped down the wallpaper."

Cissy gazed at a strand of spaghetti dangling from her fork. "She's staked her claim with that stupid salmon, hasn't she?"

"Plan B then," said Calvin.

Cissy watched him wind his spaghetti. She sighed. What exactly was Plan B?

As the week went by, Cissy became more and more obsessed with Goldie's sculpture. She imagined it on the small lawn in front of her own house, perhaps in the centre of a flower patch. In bed at night, she plotted how to swindle it away from Bessie Hample. Cissy's mother merely said, "Get over it."

"Why don't you just ask Goldie to make you one?" said Calvin as he picked raspberries into a china bowl. "Or, better yet, make you something more suitable for the prairies? How about a gopher? You know how they stick up out of the grass when they stand on their hind legs beside the road."

But Cissy had really connected with the ocean when they'd lived on the coast. She wanted Goldie's fish. The name she'd chosen for their B-and-B business was *Between Two Seas*, or perhaps *Between Two C's*. It was unlikely that, if Goldie really was an artist, she would create two the same of anything.

"That poor barn swallow is still here," Cissy said. "He still expects his mate to return."

"I wonder if he'll stay until it's time to migrate," said Calvin.

One evening Cissy marched across her yard, right through the thin spot in the shrubbery, and mounted the steps of Bessie Hample's back porch. She knocked on the screen door. Bessie answered. Goldie wasn't home. And she would be returning to Fort St. John in a few days. "But she has a good job now," said Bessie. "With her new schedule and her salary, she'll be able to come home a lot more often."

Home. The house in Gretna wasn't really Goldie's home. Hadn't she been raised on that farm Bessie talked about? How long had Goldie lived in the house now inhabited by her mother and coveted by Cissy? But then, Gretna wasn't Cissy's home, either; she and Goldie were both transplants, like the fish.

Cissy returned to the tall, square, empty house. With her hands on her hips, she studied the gaping rooms: the parlour, with its seldom used fireplace, faced by a slightly lopsided futon; the dining room, decorated with the dusty but promising chandelier and Cissy's upright piano; the kitchen, where, despite the ugly cabinets, Cissy most liked to spend her free time, not cooking, but reading and dreaming and planning at the table by the window.

From inside the kitchen, Cissy heard a familiar sound: the chattering and squeaking voices of barn swallows. She reached the window just in time to see the lonely male fly up from his perch on the wood railing. He joined a flock of about ten swallows fluttering and soaring above the lawn. Cissy soon lost track of him in the little crowd of birds. But she could easily sense excitement in the flock. She ran into the yard and flung herself down onto the grass, where she lay on her back to watch the aerobatics overhead. Somewhere up there, among that band of rescuers, her sad little bird was frolicking with new-found friends. Cissy felt his joy, his relief. She smiled to herself. The swallows, as one, flew higher, and then drifted away on an invisible cloud of warm, rising air. They disappeared beyond the row of maples.

Would he come winging out of the sky next spring, with a new mate? What would have changed down below?

    A day later, Cissy stopped at the post office after work. A quiet, intense heat had settled on the prairie after the last big storm. Cissy looked forward to arriving home, throwing off her clothes, and taking a cool shower. The post office was a stately brick structure backed by sheltering trees. Its operators were a talkative widower and his shy daughter who lived in an apartment on the second floor. Their names were Biff and Elizabeth, but townspeople had nicknamed them Bizzy and Lizzy. As Cissy walked through the lobby to the bank of mailboxes, she paid little attention to the customer standing at the wicket, or to Bizzy's jabber on the other side. The Heppners' box held a neat stack of flyers and letters and magazines. One envelope was addressed in fluid handwriting to Cissy. She slit the flap with her mailbox key and studied the handwritten sheet inside. But she soon realized that the handwriting was fake. The message was just another form letter.

    Dear Cecilia, it began, *Have you reached a crossroads in your life? Do you need a secluded retreat surrounded by easy beauty and peaceful ministrations?* The letter advertised a week at the Enchantment Women's Resort *tucked secretly away in the mountains of central British Columbia.* Staying at the resort would help her *secure reacquaintance with her inner femininity.*

    Cissy tucked the bundle of mail under her arm and continued reading the letter as she made her way to the exit. *The Enchantment Resort offers a spa-like atmosphere and professional staff practising a variety of physical and spiritual therapies.*

    Cissy bumped into the person who'd been at the wicket and was now also leaving the post office. She looked up. Goldie, straight as a stick and clad in black, glared down at her with those dark, slitted eyes.

"Excuse me," Cissy mumbled.

"My mom told me you'd been by," Goldie said. "Quit hounding her about her house and I'll do one for you next time. It won't be free, though." She turned and opened the door. Before Cissy could reply, Goldie descended the post office steps to the sidewalk. Cissy shaded her eyes and watched the black-clothed figure stride away.

Cissy headed for her car, which was parked diagonally on the street. Out of the corner of her eye, she saw Goldie halt, and heard her voice once more: "I also do ice!"

On her way home, Cissy passed Goldie walking in that slightly hunched-over posture of hers. Cissy looked at her through the side window of the car and said out loud, "You know what, Miss I-Also-Do-Ice? I don't want it any more. Your mom's house or the damn fish!"

She didn't think Goldie could hear her from behind the glass.

At home, Cissy stood in the late afternoon light, among peonies and lilacs and honeysuckle, and let the sun soak into her skin. From where she was, Goldie's sculpture was not visible. The mouse-killing stick was back beside the raspberry canes, she noted. Calvin had found need for it some time in the past few weeks, and had laid it in the spot where he was used to finding it. Above it gleamed a ripe, dark red berry, the first one of the season.

"This is my own secluded retreat," Cissy said out loud. "And this is where I will find something inner. Something."

She plucked the raspberry from its thorny shoot and put it

between her lips. The frequent rains had sweetened the fruit. Its juices trickled across her tongue.

One morning Cissy and Calvin awoke to the sound of a dog yapping and whining. From their bedroom window, they could see the widow Hample smiling and throwing a stick. What they did not see then, but observed many times after that, was the little black dog Goldie had given her mother before she left. Throughout the summer, Bessie and the puppy cavorted around the giant salmon.

    Cissy remained under the Sleeping Beauty spell. Her dreams about the fish sculpture receded into the ocean she'd left behind. The Heppners became accustomed to their cavernous home, although Cissy did find a grand oak table to place beneath the chandelier. They seldom sat at it. Swallows nested again under the eaves of the house and raised two broods there each summer. Cissy was certain the male was her special one. There was really no way of knowing.

    Once in a while, Goldie showed up in Gretna, although she didn't stay long, and kept the Heppners at bay. Bessie Hample and the little black dog, on the other hand, lived happily enough. She called him Spunky and put boots on his feet when the weather was snowy.

ASSASSINS

In the dining room, the woman-talk is suspended. "What?" says Magda to the loud-breathing, windblown girl at the door.

Fronds of hair have come loose from Katy's ponytail. She corrals them behind her ears. "That bird," she begins, "that heron—"

Hearing a new voice, Pitty growls in that half-hearted way dogs do when they would rather not, but can't control their instincts.

Then Katy wishes she hadn't come to tell them. They don't care the way Isaac does about the drama unfolding in the ditch near the farmhouse. Katy stopped to check on the heron as she biked her way back from town. She stopped, not only to see the bird again, but because she wanted to think about the storekeeper's boy for a little while before re-entering the fray of aunts.

There they sit, in the same places as they always do. All three have inherited the handsome peasant features and the bosoms of their Polish grandmother. "The boobs of Amazons," Isaac calls them. "Capable of deflecting arrows and assholes." Magda and Claire like their bosoms well-bolstered, wear bras that lift their breasts and at the same time flatten them somewhat against their rib cages, so that they look like the armrests on luxurious sofas. But Tess, who is a middle child, has rebelled and wears no bra at all under her loose T-shirt. The breasts lie long and flaccid on her stomach, on the head of Pitty, who sleeps in her lap.

The three women sit at the bare table as they always do after the noon meal. Magda's dishes, thistle patterned like the fields and pastures, have been washed and put away. Leftover food has been loaded into two refrigerators. The placemats with autumn scenes have been removed. In a few hours, everything will come out again for the evening meal. But when Katy flung herself through the dining room door, the table reminded her of how she imagined a prairie pond in January to be—hard and white and clean.

Aunt Magda, whose house they are in, and Magda's sisters, Claire and Tess, are killing the hour or two between lunch cleanup and supper preparation. They sit at the big table, knitting the affairs of the world. The scene has been part of Katy's life ever since she can remember. The family tends to gather at Aunt Magda's because she has remained in the ancestral Suderman home, along with her younger brother, Isaac. Tess and Claire and Katy's mother, Annabel, moved to faraway cities after they married; their brother, Arthur, and his wife, Susie, are already dead. ("Art and Susie were unlucky all their lives," Magda often said. "To some people, them veering into the path of that semi truck looked like suicide. But we know it was just dumb, bad luck.") Three sisters, and sometimes their husbands, make the twice-yearly visits. When the uncles come along, they always do the same things, too: after lunch they escape to Isaac's workshop to while away part of the afternoon talking and smoking among the tools and nail kegs and mowers. Later, they go to town for beer and to pick up last-minute groceries. As the men settle into the car, the women shout things like "Whipping cream!" and "Marshmallows!" from the front door. The men seldom remember to bring everything. They never forget the beer.

And Katy's own father is never among them. Her parents separated when she was still in diapers. Katy sees her father occasionally, but he is quiet and distant, a lot older than her mother. Though Annabel had been attracted to his maturity, his education, and what she fancied as his mystique, she realized after the birth of their daughter that he was simply a shallow man with no imagination.

But the uncles haven't come this time, just the women. Annabel has returned to Ottawa early for a friend's wedding. Since she was a little girl, Katy has been spending the last few weeks of summer at the house of her dead grandparents, now inhabited by the two unmarried siblings, Magda and Isaac. Katy's cousins used to come, too, but they are all older. They don't visit very often any more.

Tess takes cigarettes out of her handbag. Claire, the oldest, smooths the skirt fabric on her thighs with the palms of her hands, and Magda gazes at Katy with a questioning frown.

"It's still there," Katy continues. "It hasn't moved for two days."

"Go tell Isaac," says Magda.

And when the word *Isaac* emerges into the air, so does the sweet aroma of his smoke. Tess has not yet lit her cigarette, and it's anyway nothing like Uncle Isaac's. Katy was there last summer when Isaac told Magda what the doctor said about an alternative therapy, and saw her aunt's lips tighten. Katy has seen those tight lips often during her stay. Isaac likes relating the story of that visit to the clinic, when he practically shouted at the doctor that he could no longer tolerate the side effects of the pills, and that they weren't doing any good. And Isaac likes to imitate the way the doctor spoke. "He talks like Gielgud—'for medicinal purposes, you understand. It's not a social crutch.'"

Isaac is good at impersonation. "You should have been an actor," Katy says when he recreates conversations he's had with colleagues or students at the high school, or anyone else—a neighbour, the ladies at the library, the cop who pulled him over for speeding. And he replies, "Everyone's either an actor or an imitator, Katy-did. Imitators lead shallow lives. Actors suffer."

Magda couldn't really forbid the new treatment. She couldn't secretly hope that this shameful therapy wouldn't work. So they agreed that as long as it wasn't too cold outside, he could smoke his reefers (Magda's word) out in the workshop. The plan worked until winter set in hard and cold as it does on the prairies. Then she allowed him to light up in the house, *but only upstairs*, with windows opened a crack and the bathroom fan on. And only until he'd winterized the workshop and installed a space heater. But as the months passed, Isaac became incapable of insulating the little outbuilding where he stored his tools, could no longer handle them with the necessary precision. He never talked about it, but Magda and Katy knew. Finally Magda announced that they would hire Billy Fielman to do the job.

Billy still hasn't started, and Isaac seldom goes into the workshop at all any more. Magda has become accustomed to the smouldering joints. She's convinced herself that as long as he smokes upstairs, visitors down below won't notice anything. The reality is quite different, and Magda has recently taken to cooking with powerful herbs she grows in her garden. At that very moment, a vigorous shrub of basil in a vase of water fills a corner of the kitchen counter.

The sharp stench of Tess's Cameos mingles with the sweeter aromas. Magda doesn't like Tess to smoke in the house, but can't very well expect otherwise, under the circumstances. Old Suderman himself had been a smoker. Tess gazes at her niece and says, "What about the heron, Katy?"

"I'll tell you later." Katy slides around the door jamb so that she is no longer in the room with the women, and lingers as they resume skating words across the empty white table.

But her own thoughts are on Robbie. When Katy was ten, her mother started allowing her to go to town on the old bike stored in Magda's garage. With a few coins in the pocket of her jeans, Katy often pedalled the mile and a half along the smoothed-out tire track of the gravel road to a convenience store at the edge of town. Robbie, the owner's son, worked there even then. For the past four years, she's been going to the store nearly every day during her holiday.

She's pretty sure she knows what the aunts are talking about: Clifton's bride. And so, before running up to Isaac, Katy lurks at the door.

"I can't possibly let them sleep in the same room," says Magda in the stiff voice that matches her lips when she's worried.

Tess says, "But if they're married, Mag? You can't put them in separate rooms!"

"They won't stay here at the house," drawls Claire. "They know we're all here, and there isn't space. They'll stay at the motel in town. Don't even think about it."

"Ooooh, at the motel. What could be worse—the whole town talking about it."

Two weeks earlier, Magda had received a call from Arthur's son. "Guess what, Auntie Mag—I'm married! We're coming to meet the family later this month. They'll all be there, right?" No one has seen Clifton for years.

"Put them in a tent out in the yard," giggles Claire.

"Besides, he may very well have married a *woman*," says Tess.

"HA! How would that work?" snaps Magda. "Five years ago he announced to the world that he was a homosexual, and now he's married to a woman?" Katy hears a hand slap the table. Pitty barks.

Clifton and his spouse are due to arrive in two days.

"It might be some sort of marriage of convenience," suggests Claire.

"How could a gay man marrying a woman be convenient in any way?"

"Something to do with his job? Politics?"

"Ah-HA! What IS his job?"

"Are you sure there weren't any clues in the conversation?" says Tess.

"Oh, I forgot," says Magda. "He did mention at one point, 'I hope it doesn't bother you that my spouse has a penis!'"

Pitty barks, and Katy, fleeing the dreaded word, slips away on sock feet. She ascends to the second floor two steps at a time.

"I suppose it's dying, then. Some things are too beautiful to live. Tigers. John Lennon. The world nurtures assassins to destroy them. Someone or something probably wounded it."

Isaac leans on the deep sill of the window, looking out. Classical music plays on the radio on the windowsill. His smoking room, the largest room in the house, is not normally the room he sleeps in. (No one calls it the smoking room except Katy, and only in the privacy of her mind.) But Magda has made Tess take his bedroom for the duration because it has a good mattress. He sleeps in the smoking room, on a daybed covered with a patchwork quilt. Mahogany bookcases flank the window. Books overflow the shelves. Katy often wonders if she will ever walk into that room and find them tidied up, the books culled and organized. His computer occupies a modern desk in a corner. But Abram Suderman's oak desk dominates. Isaac has kept the ancient gooseneck lamp, even though it's falling apart. Old Suderman's ink bottle and fountain pen remain fixtures on the desktop, shuffled among notebooks and paperbacks, and documents Isaac prints from the Internet. Leaning up against the desk is the hockey stick Isaac sometimes uses as a crutch to ease his walking. Three walls of the room are crowded with photos of rocky shorelines.

The window frames a vista of harvested fields, a sunlit sheen of wheat straw. Isaac sometimes calls Katy to the window and points out foxes and rabbits, cats and hawks, the occasional dog, as they hunt the rodent-rich stubble. Katy likes to run in the fields after they've been cleared, scaring up blackbirds, before the farmer who rents the Suderman land has a chance to plough. Racing across stubble next to the deep ditch between the field and the road is how Katy found the heron.

"He hasn't moved at all for days. He's sick."

"Injured," says Isaac. "Shot in the wing."

"If he'd been injured, he would have moved at least a little, wouldn't he? At least sort of flap around, try to escape when people come near?" Katy falls onto the daybed. "But he's been in the same spot, the same position for days, like a statue." One time as she cycled past, she saw a man and his little son get out of their truck and approach the heron. The ditch of water prevented them from walking right up to it. The boy waved his arms and shouted. The heron didn't move.

Isaac turns from the window and stutter-walks, hunched over, to the desk chair. As he does so, Katy is struck by his masculinity. She's never thought about him that way before. Magda's words seem to have seeped into her subconscious and into her perception of men. She sits up and closes her knees.

"Whatever is supposed to happen will happen," says Isaac. He picks up a magnifying glass and studies his fingernails. "Have you given it a name?"

"No. What should we call him?"

"Something grandly pretentious, I suppose. None of those cutesy names girls always seem to come up with."

Katy sneers. "I wouldn't."

"Macbeth, maybe, or Lear."

"Shouldn't we phone that man, that bird man you know? Wouldn't he come and get the heron and patch it up?"

"Maybe we should." Isaac frowns and swivels the chair, turning his attention again to the open window.

Katy lies back on the bed. She imagines Robbie lying there with her, holding her. But that image prompts her to sit up straight again. She's glad Isaac can't see the look of surprise on her face.

"I'm going out of my mind, Katy-did," Isaac murmurs. "Slowly. Going out of my mind."

Katy hugs herself. "What do you mean?" She waits for Sean Connery or Cary Grant to reply.

Isaac is very still. His back is turned to her. He says nothing. Katy fixes her gaze on the snapshot. It's been propped up there forever, against a fat volume called *Russian Stories*, a picture of Isaac in his younger days: he and a friend standing in front of the Harley, around the age of twenty. Both men wear dark leather jackets. The hem of Isaac's white t-shirt hangs below the bottom of his jacket. His hands are hidden in the pockets of his worn blue jeans, which have cuffs that rest on top of the brown workboots he calls his shit-kickers. (Those same boots still squat at the back of one of the coat closets downstairs.) In the photo, a breeze has blown Isaac's neatly cut hair back from his forehead. A pair of dark glasses conceals his eyes. But what intrigues Katy is his smile. Seldom seen these days, it's a charming grin, she realized one day on a previous visit, because one of his two front teeth protrudes just ever so slightly more than the other, giving him a mischievous look Katy has come to love. His eyes still flash and twinkle when he's in a teasing mood, or when Katy amuses him by something she says. But the photo has apparently caught Isaac at the last moment in his life before worry and illness and cynicism began to take root.

Isaac's straight brown hair has turned grey, "prematurely, like his grandfather's," according to Magda. It hangs about his face like shards of steel. His eyebrows, also grey, have thickened somewhat. The dense lenses of his rimless glasses distort his eyes. Katy rarely sees Isaac grin. But when he does, he looks, despite all the changes, like the young Isaac in the photograph. He still favours white T-shirts in summer.

"What are they talking about down there?"

Katy straightens her back. "Oh, they were talking about Clifton and—"

Isaac hoots so loud Katy's sure everyone in the house can hear it.

"Ah, yes—Clifton and his mysterious bride." Isaac rotates his chair and stares hard at Katy. The twinkle is there. "And what do you think of all that, Katy?"

"All what?"

"Two men married to each other coming to our respectable Christian home."

Katy searches for the right word. If she were with her friends, she would say *pretty weird*. But Isaac was a picky English teacher who has scorned her often enough for her choice of words. "Well—" she begins.

"Pretty weird, eh?" says Isaac.

"Well, they're not sure Clifton married a man...."

Isaac mumbles something that sounds like *fools*. He says, "I love Magda being in suspense, in moral limbo. She chews on dilemmas the way a sparrow chews on a sunflower seed. I mean, visibly *chews*. Watch her face, Katy. Watch her over the next few days while she waits for Clifton."

"They're thinking of putting him and his—whatever—wife—in a tent out in the yard somewhere." Katy's aunts, though each very different from the other, and often at an impasse, always become *they* between Katy and Isaac.

"We don't own a tent," says Isaac. "Can you imagine Magda going to the hardware store in town and asking the price of a tent? 'Basically what kind of tent we lookin' at here?'

the clerk will ask. 'Pup tent? two-man tent? canvas? nylon?' And Magda will say in her imperial snootiness: 'What we'd be lookin' at here, my good man, is your basic fag tent!'"

Katy can't help but laugh. But she feels uncomfortable at the same time—*fag* is one of those bigot words her mother lectures her against.

Isaac says, "Don't worry, Katy—I'm sure Clifton and his partner have something beautiful together. Magda worries more about her social status than she does about the Ten Commandments." Isaac closes his eyes. The magnifying glass tumbles out of his hand. A swallow flutters at the window, looking for spiders in the cobwebs; a vehicle pulls into the yard. Isaac notices neither.

Katy becomes alarmed. "Are you okay?" She adds a fake laugh to the end of the question.

He shakes his head.

Katy stands. "Should I call Magda?"

Again he shakes his head and looks steadily into Katy's eyes. "I'm losing my mind."

She's tempted to say, "We all are, Isaac. We all are." But instead she says, "Because of the medicine?" The topic of the pills and marijuana has always been off-limits for them.

"No."

Katy sits down and hugs herself again. Something is going bad here. She watches Isaac carefully.

"I've seen you taking the bike to town," he says unexpectedly.

Katy nods. His window faces the opposite direction, but he could have noticed her from some other window. And in thinking about that, Katy is suddenly aware of how seldom Isaac actually leaves the house. Has she seen him anywhere in the past few weeks other than up here, or in the dining room at meals?

He turns to her and stretches his arm across the desk. She is struck by the virility of that bare arm, and for the first time she wonders why he's never married, or had steady girlfriends. Of course, she asked her mother when she was a child how come Uncle Isaac didn't have a wife, like almost every other adult man she knew. But that had been a different kind of wondering. Today it's connected with romance and sex. Is it possible that he's like her cousin, Clifton?

Magda's voice at the bottom of the stairs startles her. "Ike!"

Katy's eyes dart from Isaac's arm to his face. When she visits the heron, it's hard to tell what the bird is focusing on. But Isaac is staring at her.

He says, "Katy, I need you to be a go-between."

"A go-between?"

"I need to get a letter to someone in town. You can be my messenger."

Magda calls again. "Ike! For goodness sake...."

Katy jiggles her feet and rubs her arm. Is Isaac really going crazy? Finally she says, "Can't you just phone, or e-mail?"

"Hmmm—e-mail. That would be a completely different message in itself, wouldn't it?" he replies.

"Ike, you there?" Magda calls again. And still Isaac does not call back to her.

It's all right for him not to respond; Magda is used to that. But it doesn't feel right to Katy to ignore her. She rises from the daybed and steps into the hall. "What, Auntie Magda?"

"Tell him Moses is here. Wants to take him out for coffee. He's sitting out on the driveway, waiting."

Katy runs into the bathroom across the hall from Isaac and looks out the window. There's her uncle's old buddy, Moses Schmidt. He shows up occasionally during Katy's holiday at the farm, but she can't remember when she's last seen him. He's leaning on his truck, puffing on a cigarillo. Smoke curls into the still air. His tall, wiry body suits his cowboy style. He and Isaac make an odd couple. Whenever Katy has observed them together, Isaac has done most of the talking. They were classmates and pals until Isaac went off to college, and then when he came back to his home town to teach, they didn't resume their friendship. Until Isaac got sick. He's told Katy more than once how Moses came roaring up the driveway one day in his Chevy. "'Came to kick you out of your self-pity, Spike. We're gonna drive up to Buffalo Bush and walk to the edge of the creek and gather wood for a fire and drink a six-pack. And there won't be one word of gloom and doom outta your mouth.'" Isaac always relates the story in a low, slow voice to impersonate the reticent Moses Schmidt.

Now there he is, waiting on the driveway, a patient man with a patient Chevy and a patient cigar.

How do two men make love?

"*Drawn from the water*," says Isaac when Katy returns to his room. "That's what the word *Moses* means." He pulls himself to his feet and lurches unsteadily towards the hall, leaving the hockey stick behind. "But Schmidt's as dry as an old bone."

Katy monitors his progress down the wooden stairs. It's several minutes before the sound of the engine revving up flows like thick lava through open windows.

Katy grasps a corner of the snapshot between her thumb and forefinger and turns it around. She's seen the writing on the back many times: the date, and, *Ike with his new motorcycle and his friend Moses S at the farm*, written in Grandpa Suderman's elegant hand.

Katy doesn't tell the aunts what Isaac said about losing his mind and go-betweens and messages. She hopes he won't speak of it again.

The next morning after breakfast, she goes to his room. "What do herons eat?" she queries. "I thought I'd take him some food so he won't starve while he—"

"While he heals."

"I guess."

"Maybe it's a she."

"How would I tell?"

"You couldn't, really."

Isaac has a large book in front of him on the desk. Katy suspects it's the Shakespeare book. He often studies the Shakespeare book. Today he seems to be making notes. He holds a pen, and a notebook lies open under the gooseneck lamp. He does not look at Katy. She gazes through the window at a sunlit panorama.

"Rosencrantz and Guildenstern," he mutters.

She moves a little nearer. "So what do I feed him, then, or her?"

Isaac sighs. "Water snakes. Fish. Grasshoppers." He glances up at her. "Want to go out to try and catch a water snake, Katy-did?"

"There's tons of grasshoppers. I try to squish them with the front tire of my bicycle when I ride on the roads."

"Tons. All around the heron, right?"

Now Katy sighs. "I guess." She slumps and turns and starts to leave the room.

"When do you go home?" Isaac says.

"Four days."

"Sit down, Katy." Isaac points to a straight-backed chair

Katy never sits in. But she follows his instructions nevertheless. He does this sometimes, shifts into teacher mode.

"Don't be surprised if the bird doesn't recover," he begins. "I've been trying to prepare you for that. He's weak. Most likely a fox or a dog will take him, might be happening as we speak."

Katy runs the scene through her mind's eye: the stoic heron watching with its deep, shiny eye the approach of the enemy, attempting to raise its wings to fly away, to fend off the snapping teeth. She wants to rush out and stand guard.

"It's the way things are," continues Isaac. "If you've learned anything in all the days and years you've spent here, it should be how nature works."

Now the assassination of things too beautiful to live has simply become the way of nature. Katy is frustrated. Isaac still hasn't phoned the man who fixes sick and injured birds. It's as if Isaac wants the heron to die.

"Katy, I need you to deliver a letter."

And now that again.

"You're frowning. I don't blame you. It's the request of a madman, you're thinking, and it may well be."

Katy feels his eyes burning into her. "Why can't you mail it?" she asks.

"Simple: I want information from you, certain facts. Her—situation. Her response. The expression on her face."

Her?

"Because, you see, she may never answer. And under certain conditions, I may even expect you to abort the mission."

Katy's mouth is dry. "All right," she replies. She would have to do it. Because who knew what next summer might bring?

"Can't deny the request of a dying man, can you?" The grin

is forming, there at the corners of his mouth. He adjusts the lamp. With a loud snap, a spark shoots out of the frayed cord.

That very afternoon finds Katy cycling to town. She scarcely notices the grasshoppers. Her feet are reluctant on the pedals. At the intersection of two roads, she veers from the straight course to town to check on the heron, and to waste time. "Ah," she breathes, "you're still here." She dismounts, hears the crackle of Isaac's envelope in her back pocket. Such a small sound it is, but she worries that it will startle the heron. "We're calling you Macbeth," she mouths to the statue just beyond the cattails, on the opposite bank of the ditch. "Or Lear." She tries to imitate her uncle's voice. The envelope is in her pocket. Isaac's instructions are in her head.

Katy can't tell if the heron has become thinner, or if he's changed in any way since she first found him there. To her, he looks the same as he did at the beginning. Isaac told her birds need to preen to keep their feathers healthy. Perhaps Macbeth does look a bit shabbier now. Perhaps the feathers have lost their gloss and fullness. She studies the landscape. No foxes or dogs in sight. But, for the first time, she sees that the heron and the cattails are mirrored in the water in the ditch, a glossy reflection of a tragedy. Katy will be sure to tell Isaac later. It's the sort of thing he likes to hear about.

She continues on toward town. The air is warm and damp. White clouds have billowed up on the horizon. Magda had warned Katy that a storm was on its way, come home quick. But Katy, scanning the distance as she pedals, sees nothing threatening.

The aunts decided that morning to make no decisions

regarding Clifton and his partner. Over breakfast, while Isaac hid behind yesterday's newspaper, the women had again plucked fretfully at the dilemma of the sleeping arrangements. Finally Claire said, "Let's just forget about it and follow Clifton's lead. Perhaps he'll solve the problem for us."

Magda wasn't entirely happy with that approach, you could tell. But Tess agreed, Isaac said nothing, and the subject was laid to rest. No doubt Magda is still mulling over it like a sparrow chewing on a sunflower seed. Katy herself has reached her own decision: she will spend only as much time with the family as politeness dictates. She doesn't want to be around when Clifton arrives; the sight of luggage being unloaded from the trunk of the car might start Magda fuming. Katy dreads that awkward moment at the end of the evening when someone has to make the first move regarding where Clifton and his partner will spend the night. Isaac will probably not come down to greet them. At some point they'll have to go up to see him, and that's where Katy will be, too: with Isaac in his smoking room. Isaac told her she will like Clifton, that he is by far the funniest and most well-adjusted of the lot.

The pedals of the bicycle turn even more slowly when Katy reaches the outskirts of town. She is in no hurry, after all. Why not visit Robbie first? That tickle between her hips. Happening more and more often when she thinks of boys, or smells male sweat. A hit of Robbie might boost her confidence.

The store is an old, wood-sided structure in need of paint. Two picture windows facing the street are cluttered with sale flyers and handmade signs. Robbie told Katy that his grandparents had run the store back in the days when it was one of only two in the whole town. They had lived for a time in a tiny apartment above. Robbie doesn't think he will run the store when his parents retire. Business isn't that good any more.

But he isn't at the store when Katy stops by. His father stands behind the counter, talking to another man in a friendly, gossipy sort of way. Katy is too shy to ask about Robbie. She buys a package of gum instead and sticks it in her pocket. The letter crackles again.

"I don't even know if she lives there any more," Isaac had said. "If some punk answers the door, or a hairy ape, skidaddle!"

The envelope he gave Katy looks as if it has been handled and shuffled about for a long time. No telling when he wrote the letter. He hasn't inscribed her name on the face of the envelope. Instead, he's drawn a map there. "X marks the spot," he'd whispered. Then, at the last minute, "Her name is Cora." Such an old-fashioned name. Katy pictures a skinny, spinsterish woman with a brooch at her throat and her hair in a bun. She can't imagine anyone naming a baby Cora nowadays. Isaac went all soft and daydreamy as he watched Katy stuff the letter somewhat carefully into her jeans pocket.

Katy has already memorized the map, has taken it out and studied it several times before heading for town, trying to coax the words out of the folded paper.

Small and square and white, the house sits back from the shady street, trying not to be noticed. A roofed porch runs the width of the house. The front door features one of those big oval, curtained windows, the very kind a Cora would have. The front lawn is somewhat parched. Flower plots look sparse and withered. But then, it is late August, and even Magda's regimented gardens are losing their vigour. Giant cottonwoods overarch the house. The roof is under repair but no workmen are in sight. A driveway comes off the street, ending in front of a garage towards the back of the property. Nothing moves, no one peers out at her through a windowpane.

Katy keeps moving on her bike. She does not want to call attention to herself. At the corner she makes a U-turn and pedals back along the street. Still no sign of life at the house. Instead of approaching it, or going back to the intersection, she cycles around the whole block, knowing that when she reaches Cora's house the next time, she will have to have worked up the nerve to ring the doorbell.

Blackbirds flutter in the spaces among the boulevard trees. They scold Katy with disorienting chatter that always reminds her of sticks colliding, breaking, striking concrete. The other sound, so much like the rumbling and rolling of trains on a track heard at a great distance, a sound that often reaches the Suderman farm on a still day, was today not the train, but thunder in the west. The birds land above her. Katy stops the bike. Gazing up, she can see the leafy canopy decorated with their sinister silhouettes, fluttering.

Cora.

The last time was the last time after all. I have little left to give except the certainty of misery. I could ask you for one more kiss, or to feel the brush of your eyelashes on my neck. I could ask for a glimpse of you through a small window or for a lock of your hair.

But that day, that last day. The air so blue, the river so white, with snow textured like ripples and waves, then the sudden storm that imprisoned us in the little fishing shack, we with the most fragile of fires to save fuel, but enough vodka and desire to keep our innards aflame.

And then I told you that it would be the last time, that I was ill and possibly slowly dying, and you ran out into the storm before I could catch you, but you couldn't get far and returned with tears frozen to your cheeks.

I remember the promises you made—tried to make (I smothered your words with my fingers and my words). I said goodbye. The wind died. We made our way across a transformed lakescape, scarcely speaking, and I said, "This is the last time." And you replied, "Never...." And I said, "Forever."

But then I went away, on my "farewell world tour," as I called it. Small world—got as far as St. John's. By the time I returned, the illness had taken a firm hold. I didn't want to see you. Or, I didn't want you to see me. I was thankful you didn't try.

My mind is starting to go now. Who knows when these episodes will consume me? If I were a wild animal, I would stand very still and wait for death. Old people curl up under a quilt and disengage. But no one will leave me alone. They keep asking me questions and expecting life from me! Thank you, dear Cora, for honouring my waning dignity.

I showed you the poem near the end of our affair. It wasn't finished, still isn't. What there is of it now I want you, and only you, to have—forever

>*vast*
>*sky and land*
> *fill us*

>*grey gauze of rain*

ASSASSINS

murky dawns and dusks
curtained with falling snow

in an early autumn southbreeze
a chorus of ditchgrasses
uttering asides
to a dialogue of ducks

the bark of a fox
from shadows
and owl voices
mingling with cottonwood

heron
wings up
legs dangling like broken sticks
                            lift-off

on a wintery morning
sundogs
guarding the brittle morning sun
breathing fire
                            skyward

in summer,
rainbows
beginning and ending
perfectly before my gaze
while the black-robed nimbus
beyond
continues a sorcerer's dance

*with thunderbolts
and kettledrums*

*blizzard chaos
sculpting warm caves/coves
for wild hearts
fluttering within furred
or feathered breasts*

*faithful moon
desolate
naked
in the midnight ballroom*

*sky and land
pierce the glass of our eyes
melt into our skin
fill us
lull us
cover us
mark our days
while*

By the time Katy turns onto the unpaved road that leads to the farm, the sorceror's dance and the thunderbolts and kettledrums have begun. Behind her, the west sky is black. She crouches over the handlebars and pedals for all her life. Halfway home, she feels rain stinging her arms and neck, and she imagines that the hairs on her scalp are standing on end, that she is being hounded by lightning, chased by the devil.

The sisters are quarrelling in the kitchen. Countertops are littered with pots and vegetables and slabs of beef. Katy has caught the women in the middle of a conflict over borscht. They pay no attention to her when she bursts through the door. She stands damply in the doorway, panting.

They've witnessed these cooking disagreements before, she and Isaac—culinary battles, he calls them, waged upon the backs of high horses. "We don't know if Clifton and his whatever like anise!" Magda barks at Claire. "You always put in way too much!"

"And you should add it only towards the end," adds Tess.

"Well, I never put dill in my borscht," says Claire. "I don't think Mother did, either."

"And I don't use carrots, and I know for sure that Mother didn't, either!" Tess pronounces, glaring at Magda.

You'd think they'd be concerned about me biking home in a lightning storm, thinks Katy. But then she realizes that, in the mood they're in, if they do see her there, she will be scolded by all of them for even heading out in bad weather. She begins to slide towards the staircase. She can't talk to Isaac just now. Perhaps he's napping.

Then, that sharp thumping from overhead, not thunder, although there is that as well, but Isaac pounding the floor of his room above with the hockey stick. He is awake. "Aw, shut up, Ike," Magda mutters without taking her eyes off the dill she's chopping. To her sisters, she says, "And I suppose you're going to pour vinegar into the soup at the end."

"AND Tobasco sauce!" crows Tess.

Katy is tempted to linger, to observe the final confrontation over the soup pot. But she's wet and confused, and yearns for a few hours of privacy in her bedroom, to dry out and reflect, maybe sleep.

The toilet in the upstairs bathroom flushes. If she runs up very quietly right now, she can be past his room and in hers before Isaac emerges. Her sneakers are already off. Up she flies, reaching her room around a bend in the hallway just as the latch clicks on the bathroom door. She shuts hers softly and hopes that the storm will mask the creaking and groaning of the wood floor as she tiptoes to the dresser. After replacing her wet shirt with a dry one, she stretches out on the bed.

Moments later, she hears Isaac call down the staircase, "Has anyone seen Katy?"

Muffled replies from below. Within seconds, Katy hears the floorboards outside her room. Shadows shift beneath the door. No knock comes, no whispering of her name. And soon the shadows move away. Light in the house dims. Katy turns her back to the door and closes her eyes.

Lightning snaps. Thunder crashes. The windows blur with rain. Katy stares at the fall of water down the panes. At one point, she hears a voice and sees Tess's head sticking through the half-opened door. "You okay?" she asks.

Katy nods.

"Not scared?"

"No," says Katy. "I kinda like it, actually."

"Good then." The door closes.

"Tess?" Katy calls.

The door swings open again. Her aunt enters the room along with the sound of Pitty's nails clicking on the floorboards. Tess sits on the edge of the bed.

"I was wondering some stuff about Uncle Isaac," Katy begins. She keeps her voice low because he is just on the other side of the wall, the closet wall. She hopes all the stuff crammed into it will muffle their voices.

"Ah. Such as...?"

"Well, did he ever have any girlfriends?"

Tess lifts Pitty onto the bed. She knows Katy doesn't mind. "I'm pretty sure he did. Apparently he had trouble keeping them. This is all filtered through Magda, you understand. But he's always been—intense, shall we say? Especially when he was young."

"Was there any special girlfriend?"

Tess shrugs. "I don't know. Not that I know of. But then, I didn't live here when he was a young man."

"And—did he ever live anywhere else besides here? Besides university?"

"Let me think." The dog nestles into the space between Katy and her mistress's hips. "He went away for the summers quite often, to different places. You really should ask him. Those pictures he's got hanging in his library—I think he took those in Newfoundland, come to think of it."

Katy thinks for a moment. Then, "Do you think he's okay? Does he seem to be getting sicker?" She can't bring herself to say *crazy*.

Tess strokes Pitty's ear. "Yes, he is getting sicker, as he and all of us knew he would. I've noticed that he talks less, seems preoccupied. His brain probably isn't as sharp as it used to be. And he can't see or hear as well as he used to, either. But—"

"But what?"

"I think it's really important that you not pity him." The dog lifts her head and whines. "Or be afraid of him. Keep stoking the fire. You know what I mean, Katy? Whatever intelligence and skills he still has, challenge them, build on them. He's embarrassed that he's being cared for by Magda, his sister, his opposite, and he's lumped the rest of us in with her. Except you. He loves having you here. He does not want you to feel sorry for him."

Katy wonders if she should tell about the letter.

"Gotta finish supper," Tess says as she gets up from the bed. "No telling what's all gone into that soup by now." She and Pitty disappear into the hall.

Katy drifts off as the thunder recedes. When she awakens, she can see rifts in the clouds, sunbeams piercing the rumpled sky. She swings out of bed. In a mirror on the wall above the dressing table, her face looks puckered and troubled. She forces herself to smile, feels the muscles of her cheeks stretch and loosen. She ruffles her hair with her fingers but doesn't brush it. Before leaving the bedroom, she runs the flat of her hand over the chenille bedspread, the way Magda would.

He is in his chair with his back to the doorway. Katy stands there, not making a sound. She wonders if he's asleep. Or dead. Some sort of sound forms in her throat. He turns the chair and faces her. His eyeglasses have been replaced by a pair of sunglasses, the same ones, Katy realizes, as in the photo. She can't help but glance at the picture, perched there against the *Russian Stories*. And she wonders what will happen to it once Isaac is gone, when Magda has her chance at last to clean up the mess of books.

"Ah," he says. Then, "Well?"

"Yeah," Katy replies. His regular glasses lie on the desk. She saunters over and picks them up and puts them on. The chaos on the desk swims, Isaac shimmers. She sits down on the daybed.

"Yeah?"

"Mm-hmmm."

"Didja—didja get the—the job done I asked ya?" he stammers. Jimmy Stewart.

Katy wags her head, trying to bring him into focus. "Yeah." Just a hint of the grin. "And?"

"I gave it to her."

The hint of grin freezes there.

Katy lets the glasses slide down her nose. She stares at her uncle over the tops of the lenses.

"Well."

"Yeah."

"Tell me more," he says.

"Such as?"

"How does she look, first."

"Beautiful. Long golden hair. Brown eyes. A sweet face."

"Aaaaah!"

"And she cried when she read it. Your p— letter."

"Cried!"

Katy nods. She feels like crying herself. But there is also a bubble of laughter in her gut. "She said, 'Thank you, thank you.' Several times. That's about it."

"Well."

"Of course, she asked about your health."

"What did you tell her?"

"I said you were managing okay."

"Good answer."

"I didn't mention you were going crazy." Katy lies back on the daybed. "Too bad about her leg, though."

"Her leg?"

"Happened after you knew her, I guess? Wooden leg. Or—what do you call them?"

"Prosthetic?"

"Uh-huh. Funny little chirp in the knee when she walks."

Then there it is: the grin, unfettered, made boyish and prankish by the oddball tooth and the dark glasses. The young man still lives somewhere inside the weakened body.

"Well done," he tells her.

The next morning, intense sun burns off the previous day's rain. A haze of humidity softens the countryside. Katy takes an early walk, before the others are ready for breakfast. With her time at the farm drawing to a close, she's spent a restless night and needs to savour her last days under the huge prairie sky. Her mother always insists she keep a camera with her on her farm holiday. Katy seldom thinks of using it, but grabbed it as she left her room.

When she returns a half hour later, the white table is still empty, and she hurries up the stairs to Isaac's room. His door is open. He is dressed but looks rumpled and disturbed. Katy calls it his mad-scientist look.

"What?" he says.

"He's gone."

"Finally." He notices the camera on a strap around her neck. "You were too late."

The ditchwater danced with the feather-light touch of insects dropping to its surface, spinning up again, landing somewhere else. The reflection of cattails rippled in the blue mirror. But where the graceful neck of the heron had been, and its head and beak, now was simply sky. Had it recovered and flown away? Had someone else called the man who repaired broken birds? Or had someone or something killed it, as Isaac had predicted? She will never know.

Isaac sits down on the bed to put on his socks.

"I thought I'd see feathers," Katy continues, "or even his whole body, somewhere around. But there's no sign. He disappeared. It's mysterious."

"God's spy," he mumbles.

From the doorway, Katy stares at the back of his tousled hair and remembers the poem, the chorus of ditchgrasses, the heron's legs dangling like broken sticks. She wants to say something to him about the poem, let him know how it filled her. She's not certain for whom he wrote it, probably not for her. But she will have the poem for the rest of her life, and wants to tell him so. But not now. Next time. Next time they will talk about the woman he gave up.

She says, "I wish I didn't have to go home."

After a moment, he nods his head. He does not look at her.

Katy had cycled past the cottage under the poplar trees a third time. As she began to cross the driveway where it launched from the curb, an approaching car slowed down and began a turn onto the driveway. Katy hurried across, then sat on her bike, one foot on a pedal, the other on the cement, and watched. She'd caught a glimpse of a man at the wheel of the car. He stopped the car in front of the closed garage doors. The driver's door opened. The man cradled a bulky paper bag that might have been filled with groceries or bottles of liquor. His hair was thinning and he wore wire-framed glasses. Something about him reminded her of Isaac, the protective curl of his body when he stood and walked.

As he headed for an entrance at the back of the house, he

turned and, seeing Katy was still there, waved and smiled. She hurried up the driveway on her bicycle and caught up with him at the back door. Out of the corner of her eye she noticed a yard filled with children's things: swing set, tricycle, sandbox. The man seemed too old to be a father. But neither was he a punk or a hairy ape.

"Hi," she ventured.

He seemed surprised. He shifted the paper bag from one arm to the other and put one hand on the doorknob. "What can I do for you?" His voice was heartier and friendlier than she'd expected.

"Uh—does Cora still live here?"

The man asked, "And who might you be?"

"Well, someone I know wants to find out about Cora."

The man pursed his lips. "I had to let her go. Quite a few years back."

"Let her go?" Katy repeated. "Where?"

"She didn't take to the grandkids. Sent her out to a dairy farm west of town. Probably not there any more."

Had Cora been a housekeeper? A maid? A babysitter? "Could you tell me which farm?" If it was close by, Isaac would want her to bike out there with the letter. Katy hoped it would be far, far away.

"She's probably dead by now, long gone."

"Dead?"

The man shifted the bag again; bottles clinked inside. "Look, I'm not sure why anyone would be interested in a mangy old mutt, even if she was still alive."

"Mutt?"

"Who sent you, anyway?"

Katy swallowed hard and backed her bike away. Without

meeting the man's eyes, she turned the bicycle and said, "Oh, just a kid who used to play with her. Sorry for bothering you."

She sped away and didn't stop until she reached the park near Robbie's store. It was there, under gathering clouds and sharp jolts of thunder, that she decided to open the envelope. Isaac had played a trick on her. All would be revealed in the letter.

Katy read it many times before the storm chased her home. She trembled with confusion and found herself shaking her head as she pored over the sheet of onion skin on which Isaac had penned the letter and the poem. She was unfamiliar with the feelings they drew from her, with the tears. But to whom had he actually written the letter? Had Isaac been in love before he found out about his illness? Or was this only a part of his elaborate prank? He'd obviously expected Katy to read the contents of the envelope once she'd found out who Cora was. What did he expect her to do next?

When she passed the little grocery store at the edge of town, Robbie was at the window, holding a pop can, his eyes cast upward at the seething cloudscape. She didn't wave, didn't care if he noticed her speeding by. What startled her was how young he looked, how like a boy, captured in that pose, in that window cluttered with words.

In the middle of supper, Magda, who is facing a window, jumps to her feet and nearly upsets her borscht. "Look at that fancy red car coming down the road. Has to be them."

Everyone abandons the bowls of soup arranged around the perimeter of the white pond. They cluster at the window. The car seems to be slowing down as it nears the driveway.

Sunlight glints off the red paint and the tinted windows. They cannot tell who is inside, even as the car approaches the house.

The sisters gabble with anticipation. Isaac whispers to Katy, "Now we'll see what has risen from the ashes of your heron."

She smiles. The doors swing open. Startled by the flash of the sun on sleek metal, blackbirds in the maple trees scatter.

BROKEN ANGELS

She lifted the stubby wings out first, one at a time. Before, their size and the texture of feathers carved into the cement had deceived her. Now she braced her knees against the fender and hefted each one from the depth of the trunk. Before, she'd placed the head face down, to avoid the accusing eyes of this cold and brittle angel. She laid it so in the grass again.

From the dry cracks of the cemetery lawn, crickets bleated a fearless tune. Della stepped into the beams of the car's headlights to face the rows of concrete and granite. Her shadow fell across several graves; she wanted to laugh at the shadow, to ridicule its false death, but couldn't bring herself to disturb the chorus of grave-dwelling insects.

A few days earlier, in the middle of the afternoon, the sisters had stood together in a patch of weeds beside Della's veranda. Della had the book. "'Sarsaparilla. Woodland. Common. From Spanish: *zarza*—bramble; *parilla*—vine; or perhaps from Dr. Parillo, who first made a tonic from its root.' What did they call it before Dr. Parillo came up with his bright idea?"

"Is there a picture?" Margaret clawed at the booklet with pomegranate-coloured nails.

"Just zarza, I guess." Della handed the book to her sister. "Parillo was some sort of snake-oil salesman, I bet. Selling tonic to the upper classes to cure their stomach aches."

Margaret held the page beside the plant growing at the foot of the veranda. She tried to match the picture to it. "Does it get nice flowers or anything?"

Della shrugged. "Read for yourself. He probably learned it from the peasants."

"'Small greenish flowers.' Learned what?"

"How to make the tonic."

"So?"

"I was just thinking about all those snake-oil salesmen through history who introduced the aristocracy to peasant lore and decked it out and put a high price on it." Della stroked the toothy leaves. "Why are you so interested in this weed?"

Margaret straightened up. "I just wondered if it would be something to transplant to Mom's grave. The leaves aren't poisonous, are they?"

"I don't think Mom will eat it, do you?"

"I mean, on your skin."

Della withdrew her hand. "I guess we'll find out soon enough. Remember in the old westerns how the eastern pantywaist always swaggered into the saloon and ordered a *sars'parilla?*"

"No," said Margaret, still gazing at the plant.

Della was aware that she and her sister did not share the same childhood memories.

"It doesn't say anything here about being poisonous," Margaret continued. "But it doesn't sound like it has a very pretty flower. I just like the tropical look of it. Isn't this Mom's book? How come you have it?"

Della shrugged again. "It just ended up here."

"Dad still has her collections of pressed plants," Margaret said. "I'm surprised he let you take this."

"She had dozens of books like this," Della replied. "If you're wanting to put flowers with meaning at Mom's grave, I'm sure you can do a lot better than a plant they make root beer out of."

The women moved on in the direction of the pond. A smooth layer of cloud hid the sky. Red paint on a row of granaries glowed against the grey. Everything of colour stood out. The pond was quiet. Even the red-winged blackbirds held their tongues. Della shivered. "It feels like a storm is brewing."

"Nothing in the weather forecast," said Margaret. "We don't really need any more rain right now, do we? Farmers trying to cut their grain." She bent over to examine the foliage at their feet. "I want to collect native plants. I don't want to go to the greenhouse and buy perennials they've shipped in from Brazil or Florida."

"There are native plants all over that graveyard. Aren't there?"

"It's mostly lawn. And it's a *cemetery*. "

It's a graveyard if you're going to fill it up with gnarly old weeds, thought Della. Out loud, she said, "You can't take pond plants. They only grow in a pondy habitat. Mom's grave isn't in a low spot, is it?"

"How long since you've been there, Del?"

Della looked away.

"You haven't been there since she was buried, have you? Since she died? Haven't even seen her headstone?"

Della and Margaret's parents, Helen and Herbert Loewen, were missionaries. They'd been working up north at a First Nations reserve for several months. Then Helen had drowned in the lake. Wes had tried to shield Della from the reality of the death by keeping the radios and TVs turned off. But she'd heard a news report on the radio at sunrise, before Wes was awake, two days later: 'Helen Loewen was walking at the edge of a steep slope with a group of children from the reserve,' said the reporter, 'when she lost her footing and plunged into God's Lake and drowned.'

Della's mother couldn't swim. It happened in spring when the currents were lively. The children hadn't been able to save her, though they said that when they left her, she'd been grasping for a handhold along the shore. By the time they'd summoned the adults, who were a quarter of a mile away, she'd disappeared. Her husband had been fishing with the elders at the time. When he returned, he found the entire reserve waiting for the missionary lady to walk out of the bush and say, "Here I am—I'm all right." Searchers found her body twenty-four hours later. Herbert Loewen wasn't in contact with his daughters while he waited for his wife to show up. He only told them when they finally found her: "She fell into God's Lake and drowned." That had been the beginning of Margaret's faith, and the end of Della's.

What had their mother been doing there with the children? Looking for wildflowers, they'd said. She'd loved botany, tried to identify the local plants wherever she went. The children took her along a trail, they said. She left the trail. They followed.

Margaret thought it appropriate to put wildflowers around their mother's grave. "To symbolize what she was searching for when she died. People will say, 'Now she's found it.'" Della thought it absurd.

Della's aversion to the cemetery was the fault of the monument next to their mother's grave. A child was buried there, a girl. The parents had chosen to erect a statue of an angel in her honour. "Oh, this is just like Margaret Laurence," Margaret had whispered before the closing prayer. Except that this angel was more like a female cherub in a long, flowing dress, a concrete cupid without a bow, mounted on a boxy pedestal. One of its hands was clenched into a fist, as though the angel were angry and out for revenge. It had those blank, staring eyes that statues always do. When Della had stood beside her sister at the gravesite the day of their mother's funeral, she hadn't been able to escape from the zombie angel's piercing, sightless eyes.

And it was facing the wrong way. Della might not have noticed if it hadn't been for Wes. At the cemetery turnoff, the highway deviated from its east-west path and snaked into an S-curve. Then the slender gravel road leading to the graveyard took a few meaningless curves of its own. It was easy to become disoriented. Wes was prone to spatial disorientation. While the pastor flung epithets into the prairie wind, Wes leaned towards Della and said, "The graves are wrong. Shouldn't they be facing east?"

Della, who had an unwavering sense of direction, had replied, "They are." She had slipped her arm around her husband, because she had already decided to give up Danny and try to relove Wes. Wes had then studied the horizon, the distant highway, the shape of the gravel road, and whispered back, "Oh yeah, I get it now."

Helen Loewen's grave and several others were on the west edge of the cemetery and looked east. The child's grave was one row over. The angel looked west, away from all the other graves, right at Della. Accusing her.

At the pond now, Della said to Margaret, "Just plant a peony like everyone else, or one of those shrubs whose leaves turn red in fall. It will look nice all year. Some wildflowers look like hell when they go to seed."

"I'll trim them back," sniffed Margaret. "I'll take care of them."

"Fine, fine.... Don't they call that *deadheading*?"

Margaret started back to her car. "You do the sarsaparilla. You seem to have so many sarsaparilla stories."

"What?"

"Dig up two of those sarsaparillas, take them to the cemetery, and plant them at the foot of the grave. Or maybe one on either side of the headstone. You decide."

"No. What if it turns out to be one of those ugly plants that gets burrs in fall?"

"I'm counting on you," Margaret replied. In the car, she blew her nose into a tissue plucked from a white leather handbag. "I think I'm allergic."

Della had told her mother a lie. Just before the Loewens had gone up north to do the missionary thing, Della had lied. Children often tell little white lies to their parents, to protect them from things they really don't need to know. And so it was with the lie Della had told just before her mother fell into God's Lake. A lie to protect. Except it hadn't been very little and it hadn't been white. Helen Loewen had asked her daughter if she was having an affair with Danny Spencer. Della had said no. Don't be silly. Of course not. Wouldn't do that to Wes. But she was, and she had.

Worse, her mother hadn't believed the lie. She'd died having lost trust in her own child, died realizing that one of her children was a common cheat. She herself, a born-again Christian, had been granted the ultimate reward: God had reached up and pulled her into his own lake to be with him. Maybe that was where Heaven was—at the bottom of that lake.

Margaret sped away in her Volkswagen. The driveway gravel crunched beneath its tires, stones spurted into the grass on the shoulders. She's so slow and methodical and cautious, thought Della, and yet she drives like a hellion, as though all day she bottles everything up and then releases it behind the wheel of her car. Della wondered if she should worry about Margaret's safety. But then she thought about the sarsaparilla. She clenched her teeth. She hadn't obeyed her older sister in the past, no need to start now.

Della picked up a sharp-edged rock from the driveway. "Is that creepy angel still there?" she yelled and threw the stone after the yellow Volkswagen, which had already turned onto the road.

After supper Della lingered at the table and thumbed through the plant book. Wes patted his left ear with the flat of his left hand and rubbed his stomach with his right. The hand on the stomach barely moved. It was something he often did when he was feeling thoughtful, or contented. "You getting into that stuff?" he asked.

He would be pleased if she were getting into that stuff. He had admired his mother-in-law's interest in horticulture. He didn't seem to be bothered that it had killed her.

Della had found the book in a box in the attic where she'd put the things her father had given her after the funeral. He'd gathered them up from his wife's dresser drawers.

"Not really," Della answered her husband.

The hand stopped moving on the khaki shirt.

"Maybe," she said then. "In a certain way. A different way."

Wes shuffled through the mail Della had left for him on the radiator, studied the headlines of the local weekly. "Listen to this: 'Vandalism escalates—police blame media.' What the heck does that mean?"

"I read it. The cops say the media are glorifying the dumb things those characters have been doing around town. You know, like stealing lawn ornaments off people's front yards."

Wes snorted and went out to start swathing the wheat.

Fairy bells, bishop's cap, golden glow, wake robin.... Why had they paid so little attention to something their mother loved so much? Those kids she'd walked with on her last day had probably known more about her hobby than her own daughters. "I'm looking for this," she might have told them, and showed them a picture of a blue wood aster or a frog orchid. But she'd never really shared her collections with anyone, seldom offered to sit down with her albums in her lap to talk about her passion. The plants she'd pressed and mounted were like another set of children to her, a separate family, one that didn't argue with her or disappoint her.

Della dialled her sister's number. "Margaret? This is me. I've changed my mind. It isn't sarsaparilla after all."

"Why?"

"Sarsaparilla is shorter. I think it might be agrimony."

"*Agrimony?*"

"*Agrimonia striata.* I'll know for sure when it blooms."

"I don't like that nearly as much."

"Agrimony might have nicer flowers. Anyway, does this let me off the hook? I have no stories about agrimony."

"No."

Della hung up the phone. But she sat beside it for a while, remembering all the times she and Danny had had long conversations in the evenings when Wes was working in the fields; how hard it had been for them to find places to meet on the bald prairie, where it was almost impossible to hide, where a car travelling down a country road could be spotted by any number of people, where the only woodsy hidey-holes were on farmyards. The uninhabited groves of oak and willow that did exist—beside creekbeds, for example—were frequented by legitimate lovers, teenagers who didn't much care who saw them. Still, Danny and Della did visit those lovers' lanes sometimes. They chose the ones miles away from their home territory, and went in the mornings when no one else would be there. Danny was a crop insurance adjuster. He knew where the secret places were. Della had a part-time job at the school board office. Rarely could they both disappear for a few hours at the same time.

Early in their relationship, Della's mother had seen them together. They'd been at a pig roast celebrating Greg and Leona Janssen's twenty-fifth wedding anniversary. Danny and Della hadn't actually started their affair yet; they were allowed to spend time together at the party, to enjoy each other's company in public. Yet the flirting had not escaped Helen Loewen's attention.

But that wasn't when she had asked the question. Wes had gone to a sugar beet show in the States, that time. The Loewens were in the States, too, at some kind of missionary jamboree, wouldn't be home till the next day. Margaret was working the four-to-midnight shift at the hospital. Della had felt deliciously and wickedly unfettered. She and Danny spent the day together in the city. As they pulled into her driveway at about ten o'clock, the headlights Danny had been watching in the rear-view mirror followed them. "It's not a truck," he'd reassured Della as they'd slinked down the driveway. Della tried to fabricate a story in her head for whoever it was in the car behind them.

"We came back a day early because of the terrible heat down there," Della's mother had explained. She'd pulled a package from the passenger seat of her Oldsmobile. "I brought you the gravy boat for your china set." Helen Loewen had started Della on the china pattern almost the day her daughter was born. "I couldn't wait to give it to you, so I told Herbert, I'm taking this to Del before another minute passes. Left him at the door with the luggage and came right over." She glanced at the red tail lights fading into the prairie night. "What were you doing with Danny Spencer? Where's Wes?"

Della fumbled with the tape on the lid of the square box. "Wes went to Crookston. We were invited to a barbecue tonight. Karla offered to pick me up." (It would be safe to involve others in the lie; her parents were leaving for God's Lake in a few days.) She unnested the gravy boat and tried to change the subject by gushing over every detail of the dish, though she had no interest in china.

"That wasn't Karla," said her mother. "Why didn't you take your car? Is there something wrong with it?"

"Nothing."

"You're home awfully early."

"I had a headache. Danny offered to drive me home. Did you travel in those clothes?"

Helen Loewen almost always wore shirtwaist dresses and high-heeled pumps and earrings. Della hardly ever put on anything other than a T-shirt and jeans. Her mother eventually learned to hold her tongue. "Oh well, I suppose a farmer's wife has to be practical," she'd sigh after giving Della the once-over. The only times Helen dressed down was when she was in the garden, or hunting for wildflowers in the bush. Margaret took after her mother.

Della lowered the gravy boat back into the tissue paper. Her mother waggled her fingers and said, "There's a special plate it sits in."

"I'll look at it later. I really do have a headache."

Her mother had gazed down the driveway again, even though Danny was long gone. After a few seconds, she'd looked hard at Della and said, "Are you having an affair with him?"

The lie had reduced her, in her mother's eyes and in her own. She wished she could have sucked it back in the minute it left her mouth, wished she could have confided in her mother the way daughters sometimes do. But how could a barefoot woman in cut-off jeans, a woman whose mouse-coloured hair hung slack along a plain face, who lived for the weekends when she could go to a barbecue party and slouch around and drink cheap red wine, how could someone like that confide in a woman who wore a white vinyl belt and matching pumps and confessed her faith in Jesus, in public, at least once a year?

Now Della longed to call Danny, to have one of those endless talks that left both her ears hot and sore from the pressure of the telephone receiver. He would like it if she called. But she'd told him she would not be doing that again. Instead, she sat on the porch with her mother's nature book.

Enchanter's nightshade. Woodland. Frequent. From Anglo-Saxon: shadow of night, referring to its narcotic qualities. Heart-shaped, toothed leaves.

The morning after Margaret came to the farm looking for plants, Della stood at the kitchen counter, staring at the ice cream pails full of plums. She'd just picked them from a wild tree near the pond. Every year she harvested the yellow plums and every year she wondered what to do with them. They usually ended up sitting on the basement floor for a few days before she came to a decision. She'd made jam once. Most of it was still in the pantry. A couple of times, she'd found someone else to take the plums, people who acted as though she'd given them gold. She'd mixed them with apples to make sauce, had created her own version of chutney (still in the pantry). People asked, why don't you make wine? One time she'd hauled the pails up from the basement and flung them back at the tree, along with the fruit flies.

The phone rang.

Della expected it to be Margaret, checking to see if she'd dug up the agrimony yet. "Hello?"

At the other end, the voice of a phantom: "Sorry, Del. I really do need to talk to Wes."

"He's already left the house." Danny knew their daily routine as well as they themselves.

"I could have dropped in after supper, but I thought it might be better if I called ahead."

"You just missed him. He's cutting the wheat."

Danny had warned her this would happen.

Della's eyes fell on the little carving of the fox. She still hadn't removed it from the shelf above the phone. It stood between a silk ivy plant layered with dust and a brass watering can she used to water the few live plants they had in the house. *It's beautiful, Danny. I'll keep near the phone so I can hold it while we talk....*

"I need to look at his soybean field again."

How are you? she wanted to whisper. *I miss you....* "He's working on the field right beside the soybeans."

It's better this way.

It's not right. You and I are right together.

It's better this way for everyone else. I have to think about my dad now. It's over, Danny.

"He's there now?"

"Yes."

Then Danny said, "It's as though you'd died. That's how I mourned."

Past tense.

Della hung up the phone and lifted her eyes again to the sculpture of the fox. Danny had brought it back with him from some sort of insurance conference at Waterton Park in Alberta. He'd given it to her the day they'd run off to the city together, the very day her mother had asked her The Question. Della had tucked the carving into the old leather handbag she'd taken with her. The wood was polished maple. The animal was graceful and elegant. And she had held it and stroked it during their phone calls after that, between his giving it to her and the death of her mother. Wes had probably gazed at it absent-mindedly while he spoke on the phone, probably wondered where it had come from. Why had she left it there on the shelf?

Because there was no place else to put it.

Had she mourned for Danny? Had she mourned for her mother, for that matter? What had she lost, exactly, in those two deaths?

The plums had not gone away while she was on the telephone. She looked up "wild plum" in the plant book. *Prunus nigra*. Nothing in its description helped her figure out what to do with the fruit.

The phone call, more than Margaret, was what led Della to the cemetery. That and restlessness. Two mornings later, it drizzled just enough to dampen the wheat. Wes told her he was going to drive out to Saskatoon to pick up a header he'd bought from some farmer there. He would come back the next day.

"Come with me," he said.

"I can't. I have to go back to work tomorrow, just for the morning, but everyone is supposed to be there. I can't miss."

Wes went alone to Saskatoon. They hadn't been separated overnight since Della had broken up with Danny. In those days, Wes's taking an overnight trip was cause for jubilation. This time the whole thing put Della out of sorts. By late afternoon of the first day, she was edgy and restless. She couldn't start anything, and paced inside and outside the house. On her outdoor pacing, she passed the mysterious plant growing beside the veranda. In a methodical, almost mechanical way, as though some magic word had been uttered, she changed into her old garden shoes, took a garbage bag from the pantry, found the spade and garden gloves in the tool shed. In seconds she'd uprooted the plants. Just before she left for the cemetery, Della reached up to the shelf above the phone and brought down the little fox. She squeezed it tightly in her hand for a moment. Then she dropped it into the plastic bag with the plants.

Town lay between her and the graveyard. When she turned off the driveway onto the gravel road, the profile of the village lay long and low and flat ahead of her. Contained in it were Danny, and Margaret, and her father, and Karla, her best friend. Della was glad to be separate from the town, liked the space farm life gave her. When she'd first started dating Wes, the solitude of his farm was one of the things that had drawn her to him. She decided not to drive through town, even though it meant going miles out of her way.

The sun came out. When Della arrived at the cemetery, she was pleased at how park-like it was, with its well-kept lawn and trees, and all the flowers.

With her weight on it, the spade made four cuts in the wet sod beside the headstone. Della had expected the excavating of the sod to be hard work. But the morning drizzle and previous rains had softened the ground. The job was easier than she'd thought it would be. When she'd finished the first hole, she dug the second, on the other side of the stone, always taking care to keep her back to the wrong-looking angel one row over. Avoiding the angel's eyes became an obsession as Della slogged at scooping up earth and shaping the holes with her spade. She wondered if they could have chosen a different location for their mother's grave. Della had had nothing to do with the details of Helen Loewen's burial. Herbert had been oddly clear-minded and calm in planning his wife's funeral. He'd probably even liked the idea of an angel watching over her grave.

Della dropped the agrimony plant into a hole and, with gloved hands, clawed and packed the loose, wormy soil around the root ball. Robins appeared. They kept a wary distance but eyed the fresh earth hungrily. "When I'm done," she said out loud. Her voice, sudden and sharp in the graveyard silence, startled the birds. They retreated, skimming across the lawn between the rows of headstones.

Before closing up the second hole, Della remembered the wood carving. She pulled it out of the trash bag and held it for a moment in the palm of her muddy glove. "Mom, I've tried to make it right," she whispered, but couldn't help giving the fox one last caress before dropping it into the hole.

Clutching the spade in one hand, she tamped the soil around the stems of the plants with her feet. The robins returned. She caught the flapping of their wings and the flash of their colour in the corner of one eye. In glancing at them, Della noticed for the first time the severed head on the ground one row over.

Her feet stuck to the mud at the root of the agrimony. A greyish-white ball of a head, on the ground, stared straight at her. And further away, also on the ground, two larger shapes. Della's gaze flew to the zombie angel. There she stood, wingless, headless, like an insect tortured by some nasty child.

The spade fell from Della's grasp. She'd been so intent on avoiding the angel that she might have missed something. The vandal might still be in the cemetery, hiding behind gravestones or trees, watching her. Probably more than one, probably a gang of vandals. But she saw and heard nothing of them, if they were still here.

How had they done it? Just taken a sledgehammer and pounded away? Finding courage in the camaraderie of the robins, Della approached the head and studied it. Both the front and back showed signs of a brutal attack. And yet, the angel's babyish nose was unharmed.

Della crouched down and touched the head, the cheek of the angel. 'Weird, evil little cherub,' was how she'd described it to Margaret, who'd scarcely noticed it at the funeral. And now, here it lay, ruined, pitiful, helpless. "Who would have thought," Della whispered, "that you could be toppled so easily?" She turned the head so that it faced straight up. But the hard, empty eyes disturbed her still. She turned it face down in the grass, and, as she did so, realized how horrified the family of the dead girl would be to find their monument desecrated. Della glanced at her watch. The police office in town would be closed by now, and this was hardly an emergency. She'd have to report it in the morning. *One partially fallen angel....*

Looking around first to see if any criminals were watching her from their hiding places, Della began to pack up the trunk of her car. She stowed the spade, the trash bag, and, almost without thinking, the head and wings of the angel, to deliver to the police. Couldn't leave them on the cemetery ground overnight—the vandals might return. She might have surprised them in the act; they could be waiting for her to leave before they broke off the arms, and then ran off with the loot. Before picking up the second wing, Della looked at the body of the angel still upright on its pedestal. "I can't protect you," she said.

On the way home, Della stopped at the police station, in case someone was still there. The door was locked. A sign gave an emergency number for her to call. She knew where the police chief lived, pictured herself pulling up on his driveway, opening the lid of her trunk, showing him the evidence. Would they dust the wings and head for fingerprints? She'd worn her gloves when she'd carried them, not thinking at all about fingerprints; the gloves just happened to still be on her hands.

I'll wait until morning, she decided.

But for the rest of the evening, the concrete angel weighed heavy on her mind. After the sun went down behind the sheet of cloud, night fell quickly. Della imagined the angel standing alone, more dead than ever on its square pedestal overlooking Helen Loewen's grave. Its head in the blackness of the trunk of the car cried out to be returned to its rightful place.

Della went to bed early, hoping that sleep would bring morning more quickly. But she felt agitated. And even though the day had been warm and humid, she found herself cold under the thin summer blanket.

I've tampered with a crime scene, she thought. Who knows what clues the police would have found in the way the head and wings had fallen? Mostly, though, it was the separation that plagued her. Why had she taken the head and wings? The police will think I'm crazy, bringing them home with me, she thought. The vandals hadn't been in the graveyard with her—they'd been long gone.

Disjointed memories and illusions intertwined in her half-sleep. At one point, she imagined the head and wings of the angel in the bed beside her, wrapped in the blanket the way Wes usually was.

Her life with her husband had been a lie during her affair with Danny. Or was the affair the lie? She'd lied to her mother about Danny, and that had bothered her more than deceiving Wes. Why?

Because she couldn't make it up to her. There would be no chance to become whole again.

She couldn't make it up to Danny, either, what she'd done to him.

But she still had a chance with her husband.

Della felt Wes hovering high above the bed, looking at her from a greater distance than usual. He was waiting for something, waiting for the old Della.

She thought about all the different Dellas there were, each living in someone else's mind. She'd lost her own definition of herself, just as though her head had been severed.

Wes had always been, and would always be, patient and true—it's just the kind of man he was. And now he was waiting for love to return.

Della sat up in bed. The clock said twelve-fifteen. She donned jeans and a T-shirt, and, on the way out the door, slipped into a fleece jacket of Wes's that always hung beside the porch door.

And that was how she ended up at the cemetery for the second time in one day, after not having been there for so long, this time in the dark, in the company of crickets and sleeping robins. She wore her gloves, not wanting to leave fingerprints.

After work the next day, instead of going to the police station, Della drove to Schmidt's Memorials at the north end of town. She described the desecration to the man at the desk, who smelled of cigarette smoke. A sign on the desk said he was a memorial consultant. To Della, he looked more like a construction worker.

"Someone already reported it," he told Della. "We've informed the authorities." He didn't know if the police had started an investigation—probably not, if the head and wings were still lying around. "It's the same ones as are doing all the other pranks around town, no doubt," he said. "Don't worry—we're on top of it. You a relative?"

When Wes returned from Saskatoon late the next evening, Della told him about the angel and her midnight visit to the graveyard. They joked about it. In the morning, Wes went to cut the wheat.

In the middle of September, Margaret phoned Della. "The plants are blooming! Strange, tiny, yellow flowers, dry, like straw flowers. They're really doing very well...."

Then, a week later: "You were right." Margaret's voice was low, harsh-sounding. "Those flowers have turned into burrs. You planted burrs at Mother's grave!"

"I...!"

"We have to pull them out. Right away. It's embarrassing."

"Why didn't you do it when you were there? When were you there?" For the first time it dawned on Della that Margaret must be visiting their mother's grave every week.

"I just got back!"

"Why didn't you pull them out?"

A pause. Then, "I wasn't dressed for it."

Of course she wasn't. "I put them in," said Della. "You take them out."

The sisters planted peonies together in the spring. Della wondered if the fox was still under the ground, or if it would have already rotted. Not yet, it wouldn't have. Coffins were dug up intact many years after they were buried sometimes, or so she believed. But, as she prepared the hole for the peony crown, she saw no sign of the carving. Perhaps Margaret had found it when she'd excavated the so-called agrimony. She hadn't mentioned it.

As it turned out, the unidentified burr-bearing plant was not quite done with the sisters. It had been in the earth beside Helen Loewen's headstone just long enough to establish a network of hair roots. And from these hair roots, eager young burr plants continued to shoot up every spring after that. It was all Margaret could do to keep them under control. She finally begged Wes to zap them with herbicide. Even then, one or two sprouts popped out of the ground every year.

"My cross to bear!" Margaret would sigh every June while sitting on the porch with Della, sipping lemonade.

"Not sarsaparilla, not agrimony," Della would reply as she twiddled with her drinking straw. The women had finally agreed on wild licorice. "It has a sort of burr seed pod," Della pointed out.

"It sounds nice," said Margaret. "Too bad Mother isn't here to tell us."

"If Mother were here, we wouldn't need to know," said Della. "'*Glycerrhiza lepidota*—frequent, perennial, sweet-tasting; root used for medicine.'"

A new angel stood where the old one had, whole and righteous and still accusing, and Della had the feeling, whenever she went to the graveyard and faced her accuser, that clenched in the angel's fist was Danny's wooden fox.

But Della was no longer afraid. She looked to the angel for forgiveness, and spoke to it about how her life was coming along. She knew that even if she remained faithful for the rest of her time on earth, she might never be quite whole again, never quite forgiven. Not here, not in this lifetime.

In the summers, Della drove to the cemetery every week, following the flat prairie roads and the long, curving driveway. She tended to her mother's grave and sat beside it in the grass. And always the robins were nearby, plucking worms from freshly dug earth.

STURGIS

"Man in the creek."

Fishin'.

"You know he can't be fishin'. There's no water in it."

There's water further up in the slough.

"Did I say there's a man in the slough? Which I can't see anyway from here." Liddy bent nearer the small window in front of her kitchen sink. She kept her hands in the soapsuds, swishing mason jars in a hot bath. "Look at him hunkerin' down and runnin' at the same time. You could get a real knot in your back doin' that too long."

Man runnin' in the creek hunkered over? What's he tryin' to get away from?

"He's hidin', all right." Liddy continued to watch the figure in the dry channel that cut across farmland about a quarter-mile from her trailer. Buffalo Creek, the locals called it. The signs on the bridges that crossed it called it Buffalo Channel. Parts of it had been dredged and widened to carry spring runoff to the river.

"He's gone out of sight now," said Liddy. "I don't see anybody else out there. Don't know what kind of game he's playin'." She slid a trayful of wet jars into the warm oven. A pot of sugar syrup simmered on the stove. "After I put up these raspberries, I'm gonna do the peas. I hate the idea of shelling those peas, though. Wish you could help me."

She spread the berries out in her mother's cast-iron bun pan and began to pick out stems and leaves. "This afternoon, if it doesn't get too hot, I might go look for arrowheads in the bush." The creek snaked past an oasis of scrubby oak everybody called Buff Bush, and beyond that was the slough where people fished sometimes, even though it was private property. The oak bush and slough had been a favourite hunting ground of ancient buffalo tribes. The fields around it were loaded with arrowheads.

You always say you're gonna go look for arrowheads, and all these years we've been here you still haven't done it. Besides, you shouldn't go out there with a man in the creek.

Liddy plucked at leaves and stems contaminating the pan of fruit and sighed. What kept her from searching for arrowheads was the prospect of not finding any. It seemed to her that you had to have a special talent for spotting those things, unlike the process of spotting ripe tomatoes under a mess of vines, or swollen pods on a pea plant. She was reluctant to find out if she had the gift or not. Still, picking up just one arrowhead that had not been touched by human hands for centuries would be thrilling.

After a while, Liddy went to the refrigerator and pulled a ring of farmer's sausage out of the freezer compartment. Then she wiped her hands on her apron front and walked over to the bay window at the end of the trailer. There she had a wider view of the landscape beyond the wildflower patch.

Can you see him?

She raised the Venetian blinds. "Nope. Guess he's gone."

How old would you say he was?

"Hard to tell."

Better wait a while before pickin' peas, anyway.

Liddy tightened the elastic holding her grey hair in a tail at the back of her neck and went to the oven. "Those jars are hot enough now."

She packed raspberries into brittle jars and poured the syrup over the fruit. The liquid turned brilliant pink. Liddy liked that part, the marrying of the clear syrup with the berry juice, and the way the pink deepened to garnet red. Twelve jars of raspberry preserve, one for each month, sat on the Arborite peninsula that separated the kitchen from the living room. Every year she made the same number. The first time she'd put them up in Gil's trailer, he had called them the twelve apostles, teased her when she dished them out for lunch: "So who's this now—Peter? James?"

Once she'd sealed the jars, cleaned them with a damp dishcloth, and washed up the syrup pot and the pans, about an hour had passed since she'd spotted the man in the creek. Another look out the bay window revealed nothing more about him. Between her place and Buff Bush to the south, all was still except for the blackbirds in the marsh plants. The trees on her own yard obscured the creek on the north side. He might be on his way back where he came from, or he might be in the bush. "Guess I'll go to get those peas now."

Outside the trailer, Liddy stepped over the garden hose she used to water the flower beds and removed a skirting panel. She found the basin she always used for picking vegetables. The basin was made of light aluminum and had been her mother's, as had many of the things in the trailer. Most she'd brought with her from the bungalow in town after her mother had died. Bulky items like the bun pans and the basin, pails and baskets, were stored under the trailer. Honeybees hummed in the poppy patch.

She'd picked the raspberries from the canes at the back of the garden early in the morning and had placed them under the air conditioner that roared in the hallway leading to the bedrooms. She'd taken a little rest in the living room and then had done some light housework before canning the fruit.

It was about ten o'clock when she started to pick the peas, but the day was already hot. "Labour of love, Mother always called pea pickin'. Remember that? 'Every pea we eat in winter is a diamond,' she'd say, 'for all the work that goes into getting them into your plate.' Remember?"

And I'd always say, 'Then string 'em into a necklace and wear 'em to the ball.' Gil loved the garden. He'd died in it. Liddy had found him curled up between the beets and the banana peppers, colder than cucumbers despite the warmth of the sun. The following summer she'd left the spot where he'd died fallow. But the vegetables overtook the plot of earth, twining into it, leafing over it, and thereafter she didn't bother. She still knew the exact spot where Gil had died. Or thought she knew the exact place. By now her memory may have shifted it this way or that by a few feet, what with the ever-changing pattern of the garden.

You should have worn your hat.

"Yep."

The sun beat down hard.

Liddy and her brothers had not been—were not—the marrying types. None of the four Hamm siblings had married, although no one could say for sure whether or not Ferris would have married if he hadn't died young. Ferris Hamm had been a hydro worker. He was accidentally electrocuted when he was thirty. Because of his good looks and the sexy horror of electrocution, several women claimed afterwards that they'd been his sweethearts. He might have married eventually. But his mother said more likely he was a love-'em-and-leave-'em kind of man, as her husband had been. Jim, the youngest, lived in Toronto. Liddy hadn't heard from him much since Gil had collapsed in the garden, but he wasn't hooked up with any woman, as far as she knew.

"This pan's almost full," she said. "I'll have to go get another one. Seems we have a bumper crop of peas here." She tossed more pods onto the growing pile. They made a comforting sound when they landed.

A lull in the buzzing of the cicadas caught her attention. Some fleeting glitch in the ambience was cautioning them to hide their noise, probably a sudden breeze wandering across the hot fields. "We're gonna have to decide about the offer," said Liddy. "We told them we'd let them know by the end of the month." Liddy straightened up and twisted her torso from side to side. "Can you picture a big, fancy, new house on the spot where your trailer's been standing all these years? They think this is just the prettiest farm. High ground and what a view of the prairie, they said. I always thought farms like this were a dime a dozen. What place doesn't have a view of the prairie around here? Anyway, we could get a fancy house of our own in town, for what they said they'd pay."

Gil did not reply, and she took it to mean he was against the idea.

Imagining the life of a young married couple on her and Gil's farm, the first married couple to make it their home since her grandparents had pioneered here, reminded Liddy that her brother Gil was the only man she'd ever really known. They'd never been intimate, of course, had never even shared their deeper feelings—at least, not when he'd been alive. Liddy had never had a boyfriend, let alone a husband. She had been kissed a few times in her teens. But nothing had come of those furtive pecks. For most of her life, Liddy had planned to have a baby. Always somewhere in the hazy future were children. She had no idea when exactly she'd realized that her time had passed.

Still, she knew the ways of a man, having lived with Gil for so long. Why hadn't Jim suggested, after Gil died, that she leave the trailer and the farm, that she'd be too lonely out here all by herself? She'd felt the physical loss of Gil more intensely than she'd missed her mother. But Jim had gone home the day after the funeral without saying a single word of sympathy to Liddy. He was afraid, she thought, afraid that she would ask him if she could live with him in Toronto, as though bunking up with brothers were some kind of habit she had.

Liddy stood in the garden and stretched her arms up to the sky. Since Gil's sudden failure here among the produce, she'd become aware of a need for fitness. Any time of the day, when one of those scary moments of boredom or aimlessness came over her, she'd stretch, or jog on the spot, or do jumping jacks, sometimes leap about quite wildly, until she was panting and felt her heart beating fast. As far as she could tell, though, she hadn't ever broken a sweat. Her mother had claimed she did not perspire. Just a biological quirk that ran in the women of the Hamm family.

With her arms raised above her head, Liddy turned around and gazed at the back of the trailer. (She didn't think of it as her *house*. It was always the *trailer*.) Only one window, the bathroom window, faced the backyard, if you didn't count the one in the lean-to. Which was a shame. The trees and the garden were just as pretty to look at as the prairie view, although the back view also took in the biffy and some weathered outbuildings, which some people might not like.

Gil had bought the mobile home brand-new when he'd been a young man. The farmland itself had been in the Hamm family for three generations. Gil had torn down the old house, and built a fancy deck at the front of the trailer and a lean-to at the back. Over the years, he'd replaced the soft Manitoba maples with sturdier ones, and poplars, and planted fruit trees and shrubs here and there, and had lived a safe, predictable, bachelor-farmer life on his quarter of land. Liddy had gone to stay with Gil after their mother died, because various relatives suggested she'd be lonely. It was meant to be a temporary arrangement. Liddy hadn't intended to stay with Gil in the trailer for more than a week. That had been twenty years ago. One day he'd come through the back screen door into the kitchen where she was picking over beet leaves for beet-greens soup, had taken off his cap and scratched the thin spot on the back of his head, and said, "Well, the Ford's shot and I gotta find a new combine. You still need that house in town?" Liddy remembered that she was making beet-greens soup because she usually used sorrel leaves, but the sorrel clump had been grazed off by deer, and when Gil had asked her about the house, she'd said, "If I'd stayed in town I'd still have my sorrel."

A pea pod slid off the pile. "Okay, then, time for a new pan." But instead of bending over to pick up the aluminum pan, Liddy lifted the skirt of her cool cotton dress and leaped over the row of peas. She continued towards the back of the garden, gaining momentum as she soared over each row of vegetables, raising her knees like a jump-horse, pointing the toe of her canvas runner straight down as her knee went up. The hollyhocks and cosmos and gladiola at the back were much too tall for her to clear. She turned around and repeated the exercise, ending up back at the bowl of peas. She placed her hands on her knees and then breathed hard for a few moments. Straightening up, she put her wrist against her forehead. "Why, I do believe I've gotten myself a little dewy. Did you see me flyin' over those veggies? I really had to take a stride to clear the squash and the cukes."

Again there was no answer.

Liddy looked down at the peas and then at the whole garden. It grew bigger every year. Why? She didn't need all those vegetables, wouldn't even eat all the peas she would pick today, unless peas were all she ate the whole year long. She gave some of the bounty to her cousins each fall at Thanksgiving, but the freezer in the lean-to was still half full from the last harvest.

For the first time since Gil had died, Liddy felt completely alone, even though the cicadas had resumed their patient droning in the bushes.

As if Gil might be playing a trick of levitation on her, Liddy scanned the clouds. To her satisfaction, a magnificent specimen presented itself just above the shelter belt in the western sky, tall and billowing and shiny, with facets of pure white and grey and pale yellow. No wonder Gil had decided to hitch a joyride up there.

Yet, when Liddy lowered her eyes to the earth where her feet were solidly anchored, she felt both a sense of abandonment and a creeping uneasiness.

And then it struck her: a wide black slit showed in the skirting around the trailer. She was certain she'd replaced that panel tightly after fishing out her pans earlier. She'd already visited the panel twice that morning, and she'd always replaced it tightly. "Keep out the vermin," Gil always reminded her. But now it was not quite closed. She often wondered what kind of vermin he was talking about.

In the living room, Liddy dumped the pea pods onto a carpet of newspaper. This was where she would spend the afternoon shelling them, here in this cool, dark place. As she headed back to the garden with the empty pan, she paused outside the lean-to door and, without looking at the opening under the trailer, said out loud, "Well, I must have just been careless, thinking I'd be putting things back so soon." No answer from Gil. Liddy raised her eyes to the nimbus, which was passing to the northwest. "You still riding that cloud?"

Picking the opposite side of the pea row now, facing the trailer, Liddy couldn't help but glimpse that black space from time to time She didn't pick all the peas. Her mother's pan was only half full when she hefted it to her hip and crossed the garden to the back door. She walked quickly, with only a perfunctory glance at Gil's cloud. It had sailed off into the northeast like an iceberg in an arctic sea. Moving as fast as she could within the confines of the narrow trailer, Liddy dumped the remaining peas onto the pile already there and rushed outside to throw the pan under the trailer and close up the panel. When she was done, she sat with her back to it and breathed hard. "Mama," she whispered breathlessly, "this is the second time today I've broken a sweat."

Gil, her brother, had always been with her. Where had he gone? Was it finally time? She'd expected him to leave her gradually. There'd been no warning.

In the dim room, with the light of day a mere pattern of horizontal strips on the window blinds, Liddy shelled the peas with nervous fingers. The quiet bothered her today, and she moved the green plastic bowl from her lap to the coffee table with the idea of turning the radio on in the kitchen, though she didn't usually switch it on until the afternoon, when her favourite announcer phoned people across the country to talk about happy, trivial topics, like the best vacation spots and recipes calling for rhubarb. But she needed something to cut this silence.

And still, she hesitated. Her fingers grasped the knob, but wouldn't turn it. The radio seemed like cheating, somehow. And what if Gil wasn't really gone?

Then she heard it, clear and strong through the floor of the trailer, and heard it as though she'd been expecting it: the familiar sound of the skirting panel being moved. Liddy had heard it often enough from inside the kitchen when Gil had been alive. The dead Gil did not move anything or make any noise.

The lean-to door opened. It wasn't the latch she heard, only the soft groan of the spring as it stretched.

The back door of the trailer was opposite the fridge. Liddy turned to see which of Gil's vermin had gained entrance to the house. The man in the creek had been wearing a black shirt. This man was wearing a black T-shirt, too. STURGIS was printed in big red letters across his chest. He was barely a man, though, by Liddy's estimation. Except for burrs stuck to his pants and socks, he appeared to be a fairly clean-cut boy, no pierced body parts—none that she could see, anyway.

They stared at each other for several seconds. The man was perspiring through his shirt and breathing heavily as if he'd just run a long way. Liddy knew he hadn't, knew he'd been hiding under her trailer for quite some time.

His eyes darted about the kitchen. Liddy folded her arms under her bosom. The movement startled him, and he leaped towards the counter. Liddy stiffened but didn't budge from her spot in front of the refrigerator. His arm jostled the raspberry jars. One of the twelve dropped off the edge of the counter.

Liddy heard it crack and burst on the tile floor on the other side of the peninsula. "Judas," she muttered.

With a strangled cry, the man seized the knife she'd used earlier to cut the sausage. She noticed that the knuckles clenching the knife were sharp and bloodless. At the same time, she pictured the raspberry syrup spreading on the black and white chequerboard tile, reaching for the edge of the living room carpet.

"I don't want to hurt you, lady," he said. The voice quavered, the tongue made dry sounds on the roof of his mouth. "I just want you to give me the keys to your car."

He'd been busy since she'd come in from the garden, had already found her Toyota in the garage, had determined that the keys were not in the ignition. She pictured him skulking around the yard, crouched over as he had been earlier in the creek bed. A curl of sun-bleached hair lay flat and wet against his temple. "Please just give me your car keys," he repeated.

Please?

"My brother is in the biffy back there," said Liddy. "He'll be coming in any minute. I don't know if you saw that .22 in the lean-to when you snuck in here."

"There's no one else here," said the young man. "I know you talk to yourself. It's okay by me if you talk to yourself, it sure won't make a difference in my life, but don't give me no horseshit about a brother in the toilet and a gun."

Beside Liddy on the counter next to the fridge, in a metal pie plate, lay that hunk of frozen sausage. She knew it was there without taking her eyes off the desperate intruder. If he would just look away for a second, she thought, maybe I could whack him across the temple with it. But she decided her plan wasn't feasible; after all, the sausage had been thawing for at least an hour—it was probably too soft by now to do any damage. She might just as well hit him with a pillow.

The man's eyes widened as though he'd read her thoughts. But he whispered, "The cops!"

Liddy glanced over her shoulder through her kitchen window. The man kept the knife raised but his hands trembled and his eyes flew about, seeking a hiding place.

"You'd best go under the trailer where you came from," Liddy whispered back, as though the crawl space were his home. "They'll look in here for sure."

The man had edged his way out into the back porch, his eyes on Liddy. On his way out, he grabbed an armful of old newspapers Gil had collected over the years. "I'll hear everything you say," he spat at her. "I've got matches, and if you give me away, I'll light these before they can haul my ass out from under there. This trailer will be toast by the time the fire truck gets here." Then he was gone.

A polite knock at her front door.

"Lame idea," Liddy said to herself. "Water hose lying right there." Only one officer was waiting on the deck. She'd seen him before, one of the local RCMP.

"Sorry to bother you, Miss Hamm." He stepped into the entryway and towered over her. "Just wondering if you've seen a fella running around here anywhere, or anything unusual like that." He peered into the trailer.

"Today?" Imagine him knowing her name.

The Mountie blinked and tugged at the brim of his hat. "Well, yes, today, this morning."

Liddy shook her head. "No, I can't say I have. What did this fella do? Anyone I know?"

The officer moved further into the trailer. "You haven't been inside all the time, have you? I notice you've been working in your garden."

"That's right, I was."

"Quite a mess to clean up there." He pointed at the broken jar on the tile like some sort of housekeeping inspector.

"I put it too close to the edge. It fell just before you knocked."

"We found his bike mired in the creek bed." The Mountie's thumb jerked towards the north. "My men are searching your outbuildings. Hope that's all right."

Liddy was pretty sure they needed her permission or a search warrant before they started, but she said, "Fine."

"And I'd like to search your trailer."

"All right. " It was happening just as she'd thought it would. "My, you're scaring me, Officer." Trying to appear nervous, she pinched her dress collar closed at her throat. "Is this man dangerous?"

The officer began by looking behind the living-room curtains. Liddy noticed that the puddle of raspberry juice had stopped just short of the rug. "Not many places to hide here," she said. "Unless he's a real puny criminal."

What a story she'd have to tell Gil, if he ever came back.

"I think you'd best wait outside," the officer said. "We don't know for sure if he's armed or not."

No sooner had she crossed the bit of lawn out front than a second Mountie appeared around the corner of the trailer. This one was a little shorter than the other, and stockier, strong-looking. "You don't have any other vehicles than the car in that garage there, do you?"

"No, I sold the truck after my brother passed away." Liddy could see red lights twinkling at Buff Bush and on the road beyond. There were probably cop cars all around her farm.

Then the officer said, "Would he be able to hide under your trailer?"

Liddy's hand again flew to the collar of her dress, except this time it wasn't part of the act. "Not unless he had a screwdriver in his pocket," she lied. "Or dug under there like a rat." Had her fugitive taken care to fit the skirting panel snugly into place?

The policeman kicked one of the panels.

"I think I'd know if someone had wiggled underneath there," Liddy continued. "You might want to check the biffy at the back. He'd be a sitting duck if he were hiding in there."

"We're checking all the buildings, Ma'am."

They'd started before getting her permission, even before knocking, perhaps. How had they not seen their man slip beneath the trailer only moments ago? Plain dumb luck on his part, Liddy thought.

"We'll have dogs here in a while. You'll see quite a bit of activity around here until we catch him. We'll be using the dogs to search your yard, too. Make sure you keep your doors locked. In fact, I suggest you go to town until we've got him. He could be hiding in your bushes."

Dogs! Liddy had to think for a minute. No way was she going to miss the excitement. "I'm staying put," she said. "You seem to have the place surrounded. I'll be safe in the trailer."

The Mountie frowned.

"With my doors locked," she added.

"Well, keep your eyes open. And if you see anything at all, call the police."

Liddy waved a feminine goodbye to the officers as they stode off to catch their criminal. I don't know who's dumber, cops or thieves, she thought. Under the trailer's the first place I'd have looked. Anyone can tell those panels aren't screwed on.

After lunch, imagining crickets and beetles creeping into the clothing of the terrified young man hiding under her trailer, Liddy emerged from the lean-to and scanned the farmyard. As far as she could tell, there was no one around at the moment. From the kitchen window she'd seen plenty of activity in Buff Bush, figured they probably had the dogs out there by now. It had taken a while to dawn on her that the bike the Mounties had mentioned was probably a motorcycle; he wouldn't have eluded them on a regular bicycle.

All was quiet on the farm. The cicadas buzzed in the bushes. Still, she couldn't take any chances.

As it did most of the summer, the water hose lay loosely coiled on the ground near the spiggot. Liddy opened the tap and guided the hose and stretched it along a path through the vegetables towards her flowers at the back of the garden. If anyone who knew her habits, or knew the habits of good gardeners, were watching her, they'd find it odd that she was watering plants in the full heat of the afternoon sun; Liddy always sprinkled the flowers at sunrise, so that the moisture could spend the morning humidifying the foliage and sucking down into the soil before evaporating. She took a good long time spraying the flowers, waiting for someone in a uniform to emerge from the shelter belts, warning her to stay locked in the house or interrogating her about the suspicious aberration in her watering routine.

But everything remained quiet, despite the police cars and the searchers in the creek.

Liddy rewound the hose where it always lay. She tapped on the loose panel and spoke softly. "Hey, Sturgis—you still there? All clear."

Had he escaped while she'd dozed restlessly on the sofa in her darkened living room? Was it disappointment creating the frown she felt around her eyes? "Gil?" she whispered softly. He would know what to think about it all. But she did not hear his voice. "Good riddance," was what he'd say about the missing man. But Liddy's curiosity itched under her skin, like the after-effects of strong coffee imbibed at a funeral lunch. She tried banging the skirting with her heel, but the noise startled her.

Liddy called, "Hey, Sturgis—" Then she sang. "Stand up, stand up for Jeeee-sus...."

Because she didn't know what else to do, Liddy resumed

watering the beans and carrots beneath the sun and the cloud mountains. Leaves turned silver under the cold rain.

The panel shifted. A flash of white—his eyes, followed by the black shirt. Liddy dropped the nozzle and strode over to the spiggot. "You're gonna have to skidaddle. The bloodhounds are on their way."

But the boy looked sleepy. How could he have fallen asleep with police and dogs tracking him? Liddy's hand twitched. She wanted to reach over, like a mother, and brush the lock of blond hair out of his eyes.

"I don't know what you did that got you here—" she began.

"I need your keys and something to eat," he spat at her, snapping out of his momentary stupefaction. Turning, he bent over and reached lazily under the trailer. In his hand now was the knife.

Just like a man, thought Liddy, being chased by dogs and guns and thinking about food.

"What's that word on the front of your shirt?" Liddy asked. "I know it's probably not your name."

"The keys! The keys!" He motioned towards the lean-to door.

"Well. While you were dozing under there, I threw the keys into the bushes. I know where they landed, but it would take you quite a while to find them, if ever. So you can take your chances with the dogs and go look for them, or—" and now Liddy motioned to the lean-to door "—you can come inside where you'll be safe."

"Safe?"

"I'll give you food, and I won't tell the officers you're here. But you can't have my car."

"You hid the keys inside!"

He thinks he's so smart.

"Are you planning on killing me?" Liddy asked. "Are you a killer?"

He stabbed her with his eyes. Then he said in a low, flat voice, "I could be."

Liddy inclined her head towards the porch. She walked ahead of him to show that she trusted him not to plunge the knife into her back. A stray breeze carried the faint baying of the tracker dogs. He followed her inside.

Liddy had cleaned up the raspberry mess. Her fugitive did not seem to notice, wasn't worried about things like broken jars and red stains on well-kept carpets. He stretched his arms, and the knife, up to the ceiling, and arched his back. Liddy buttered four zwieback. From the corner of her eye, she saw him put his left hand in his pocket. His fingers worked inside the pocket as though he were looking for a coin.

"I've got salami," she told him. "Or—"

"Peanut butter," he interrupted. "Have you got any peanut butter? And honey?"

Liddy moved to another cupbaord. "So what's this Sturgis?"

"Just a place," the boy mumbled. "A place I went once."

"Recently?"

"A while ago."

"Who'd you go with?"

"My dad. He was big into bikes."

"'Was?'"

"Just make those sandwiches! And you're gonna have to drive me somewhere."

"Tell me what you did."

"They think I stole something, okay? That's all you need to know."

"Stole something. Where is it, then?"

"Never mind."

And then it ocurred to Liddy: the young man spoke with an accent, an American accent. He might have jumped the border, which was only six or seven miles away.

Without asking his permission, she made the sandwiches with chokecherry jelly, the way Gil had always liked them. Once she caught a glimpse of her fugitive bending over the raspberry jars, gazing into the clear red liquid with a wistful, not hungry, expression in his eyes. "I'll loosen the lid on one of those and you can take it with you," she told him.

Why was she doing this, helping this criminal get away? Because he was threatening her with a weapon? She didn't believe he had it in him to slit her throat. What would happen if he whisked her away in her Toyota—would he dump her on the side of the road somewhere and then ride off into the sunset? Maybe she'd could go with him—the weather was nice. What would be the worst that could happen to her?

"Listen, Sturgis, maybe we should call someone."

"*Call* someone?"

"A girlfriend, or a lawyer. . . ."

He stabbed a zweiback with the butcher knife. "I'm not giving up. I found a good luck charm." He pulled the object out of his pocket. "See? Right down there." He pointed at Liddy's floor. "It was under my elbow." When he held it between his index finger and his thumb, Liddy saw its perfect shape, the shine on its bevelled surface. The arrowhead was as clean and sharp as it had been when it was first made. You don't deserve it, she wanted to say; you're on my land.

But instead she slipped the bun off the point of the knife and continued her sandwich making.

Suddenly it struck her hard: Gil was gone, replaced by this brave and stupid boy who probably didn't even shave yet, a false child, come too late. And a woman who sat unwittingly on arrowheads was a worthless woman indeed. Tears sprang to her eyes.

Then, through closed windows and thin walls, they heard the bark of a dog, just one bark, that may have been far away, but was so startling in the silence of the kitchen, it might well have been right under the window. Liddy's hands flew as she gathered up the lunch. But when she turned to face the boy, holding the paper bag of food out to him, her eyes wet, she saw that there were tears in his eyes, too, and that his Adam's apple in his skinny neck was jerking up and down above the red letters on his shirt.

"I think it's too late," she said.

He grabbed the bag and stuffed a jar of preserves into it.

"It's too late," Liddy repeated. "It would be a courageous thing to give up now and face the music."

He hovered near the door. Liddy noticed that his nose was running.

She moved towards him. "I don't know what you did, or what happened to your dad, or what Sturgis was all about," she said, "but—" She touched his arm, the knife dangled from his fingers at his knee.

And she wished he could have ridden away on a cloud to some safe haven, like Gil had, instead of on a loud motocycle into a muddy prairie slough.

She wrapped her arms around him and the bag of food, not caring that another jar might drop and shatter on her clean floor. Her gaze fell on the pan of bright peas on the living room floor. They anchored her as, once again, the German shepherd's deep-chested bellow, much closer now, penetrated the trailer's walls. In her mind, Liddy ran across vast fields, under a vast sky, chasing Gil's cloud, beseeching him to return, because she could already feel the loneliness coming on.

A PRIVATE PARADISE

"This must be some kind of miracle. Some kind of miracle."

Somekind—ofwonderful....

"Don't you think?" The man dropped to his knees and curled his body forward, touching the top of his head to the grass. Was he praying?

He raised his head and sat back on his haunches. His face was flushed, shiny. "Are you sure you're okay? No concussion or anything? What's your name?"

Was it a test? "Dana," she said. "My name's Dana."

"Dana. I'm Johnny."

Dana and Jo-o-ohnny were sweethearts....

"I don't think this can be explained any other way," he said. "I never thought I'd see one."

"See one?"

"A miracle!"

Able to take a deep breath at last, Dana turned to the man and said, "Do you go around looking for them, waiting for them?" He was behaving like the one with the concussion, hallucinating.

"Well, I think about them sometimes, just wonder if I'll recognize one when it happens."

Dana nodded. The man appeared to be about the same age as her, maybe a little younger—thirty-two or -three. He had a high forehead, a clean-shaven, sunny face, and thin, fair hair. For the first time since she'd been pulled from the pickup truck, she looked over at the wreckage several yards away in the drainage channel in which the two of them sat.

"Sorry I can't call 911," said Johnny. He took a cell phone from his pocket. "Damn thing's completely dead. You got one in your truck?"

Dana shook her head and gazed at the configuration that, only moments earlier, had been two, separate, well-behaved vehicles tooling along an empty highway in the morning prairie air. Now they were conjoined in an absurd position like two mismatched acrobats, his bulky, square delivery truck upside-down on the roof of her maroon pickup. The cab of her Ford looked like a pop can somebody had just crushed against his forehead. "I left my phone at home." She smiled at Johnny. "Can't have too many miracles on one day, can we?" She cocked her head. "But listen: my radio's still on." A melody streamed from the open window of her truck. Before the accident, she had been listening to the opera with the volume turned up. Even though the engine wasn't running now, the soprano's voice leaked through the open window and drifted across the ditchgrasses. "I suppose that's a tiny bit of miracle, eh?"

The man smiled back at her. "I guess we'll have to wait for someone to come along, then. Nearest farm is too far to walk to." He didn't comment on the music.

Maybe she was the one with the concussion. Maybe her skull was in shards beneath its thin skin. She'd heard of accident victims walking into ambulances under their own steam, apparently lucid, unharmed, only to succumb to the swelling of their brains, their skulls invisibly smashed to bits. She lifted her hand to the side of her head. Was that blood?

And then red popped out everywhere: on her fingers, on the forehead of Johnny, on the side of his vehicle—the edging around navy blue letters that spelled out DREAMCLOUD ICE CREAM PRODUCTS against a pale blue background.

"You're bleeding," Dana and Johnny said in unison. A meadowlark trilled at the edge of the field behind them.

"I didn't feel anything," said Dana. She pulled a sheaf of her straight, nut-brown hair from her shoulder and studied the blood forming a crust there.

"I think any minute now we'll start feeling pains in places we didn't even know we had," Johnny said, laughing.

"Maybe we're dead," said Dana. "Maybe this is what death is like. You sit in a ditch and wait to be picked up."

"Then we'd see our bodies inside the cabs." Johnny moved closer to her and peered at the gash on her temple. "Wouldn't we?"

"Would we?"

Moments ago they'd been strangers on a little-travelled highway between two towns, he driving behind her. Then she'd slowed down at an intersection to turn towards Gretna and he'd swerved and hit a pole, and ended up on top of her pickup in the ditch. As if in a dream, she'd heard him extricating himself from the topsy-turvy above her, and then his face had appeared at her window. "Are you all right?" he'd screamed at her, over and over. "Are you all right?" She'd reached for the crank to turn down the window, to answer him, before realizing that there was no window left in the frame. Cubes of shatterproof glass had dislodged and tumbled to the floor of the cab and to the ground. "I don't know," she'd replied.

He'd opened the door and tugged at her shoulders without checking to see if she'd sustained a spinal cord injury. She'd flopped out of the cab like a giant Raggedy Ann. "Can you move everything?" he'd then remembered to ask, after the fact.

Now they were forever bound to each other. Dana imagined rubbing the blood of her temple against the blood on his forehead.

But the man leaped to his feet with exaggerated agility and sprinted to the wreckage. "I'm pretty sure the gas tanks aren't ruptured," he called over his shoulder. Earlier, he'd started dragging her away from the crash site with urgent backwards steps because, he'd told her cheerfully, "The whole thing might blow!" But she'd insisted she could walk and followed him to what he calculated to be a safe distance. "A little further."

"Here?"

"A little further."

"Here?"

Now, he paused in front of the wreckage and stared up at his truck for a while. Then he disappeared around the other side and Dana heard nothing except the melodies of the unseen opera singer and the unseen bird.

She closed her eyes and lifted her face towards the rising sun directly in front of her. A pain shot down her neck into her shoulder blades. She straightened her back and wiggled her toes and fingers to make sure they weren't numb or paralyzed. Even if one part of her brain told her she was wiggling them, they might not really be moving. She watched her fingers flex. When she looked at her feet, she noticed that her left shoe was missing. The foot was still there, though. Why did shoes come off people's feet in car accidents? In crashes on television and in the movies, the camera always cut discreetly away from the carnage to that forlorn running shoe on the pavement. Her feet hadn't been involved in any trauma that she knew of. The shoe must have fallen off during the escape. She scanned the ditch. The grasses were not yet full height. The shoe might be hidden there somewhere. It was red, like blood, easy to find. Dana took off the other shoe. Her toes moved well.

"Here you go."

His voice beside her startled her. He held a box in his hand.

"First aid. Never been used." Johnny produced a pressure bandage from the kit and held it to her bleeding scalp. "Mine's stopped, I think."

"You didn't blow up," she said. Her hand found the pad of gauze and he pulled his hand away.

"What were you doing out on this lonely road at this hour?"

Look dooooown, look dooooown, that lonesome ro-oad. . . .

"I lost my shoe."

"You were out on the highway at six a.m. looking for a shoe?"

"No, no, it came off in the crash. It's—" Dana swept the channel with her free hand "—here, somewhere."

Dana had spent the night in Plum Coulee at the Happy Wanderer Hotel. She had intended to make it to Brandon, or maybe Neepawa. But when she'd passed the Happy Wanderer on the curve of the highway, and recalled all the good times she and Glenn had had there in the pub—the band called Red-Eye, the dancing they'd done—her Ranger had lost its gumption; the speedometer needle had slid to the left, and Dana'd found herself on the shoulder of the road late at night with a dead Ford. But, after sitting a while, it started okay, and she realized that it had quit only because her foot in its old red shoe had become weightless on the accelerator.

The new owner of the motor hotel hadn't recognized her. It had been years since she and Glenn had danced in the bar. She checked in under the name Althea Jones and spent a few hours lying on a double bed, staring at the ceiling. Now she'd been trying to reach home before Glenn finished the night shift at the canola oil factory. If they didn't make her go to the ER and wait for a doctor to tell her she was okay, she still might make it. But she wouldn't be able to hide the smashed-up truck from her husband. Had Johnny noticed the suitcases in the back of her pickup?

Johnny trotted along the trail they'd made in the grass. He looked to his right and his left as he went along, searching for the missing shoe.

"It's all right, I can—" As Dana struggled to her feet, she noticed that she was shaky and weak, and somewhat dizzy. *I'm not giving in*, she said to herself. *This will pass.* Eventually the vegetation stopped spinning and Dana felt stronger. But she was troubled by Johnny's running back and forth as if he couldn't stop. Out of the corner of her eye, she saw the lark perch on an old fencepost. She turned towards it. Then she heard a grunt and whirled back. Johnny lay on the ground. "Oh!" she cried sharply. "Oh-oh!"

Holding her knee with one hand, Dana hobbled over to where Johnny had fallen flat on his face. "Are you all right? Are you all right?"

He propped himself up on both arms and said to the grass, "I survive a smash-up with a truck and then proceed to kill myself tripping on a gopher hole." But he leapt to his feet with the same agility he'd had earlier and brushed his palms together. Dana discovered that he was about the same height as her, and she wasn't very tall. "I'm all right." He smiled at her. "See? There it is." He pointed at the ground. They both stared at the hole for a while.

Dana said, "Do you trip *on* a hole or *in* a hole?"

"Well, not *over* a hole, for sure." Johnny scratched his head. "I don't know. If you say *in*, it sounds like you're down in the hole, tripping."

Like Alice in Wonderland, Dana thought.

"I hope your leg isn't broken," he continued.

"No, I just twisted my knee somehow."

"We could have both been a lot worse off. It's a miracle."

Dana sat down again. They were closer to the wreck and she could hear the music more clearly. "Don't bother with my shoe," she said.

"Okay. You don't mind if I go look for another gopher hole, do you?" He began again to trot along the path.

Dana wondered what he was like when he hadn't just survived a smash-up.

He turned suddenly. "I like that opera stuff out here," he called. "Seems right, somehow."

I want to stay here forever....

"Oopsy-daisy!" Johnny held up the shoe.

Dana smiled at him over the heads of the grass stalks.

"Look at that!" Johnny said when he'd returned to her side. "The sole's broke in half. You can't see anything wrong if you just look casually at the shoe. But—see?" He flipped it over and bent it. "A split right across the ball of the foot." He handed her the shoe.

"I don't know how I'm going to explain this to my husband," she said.

They both turned at the sound of a vehicle coming down the highway from the south. Trees obscured their view.

"You think he'll be upset you broke your shoe in a crash?"

Dana laughed. "The sole may have been broken before the accident. No, I mean, all this." She made a slow circle in the air with the red shoe.

"Well, I imagine your husband will be just too glad that you're alive, Ma'am," Johnny replied, sounding offended. "Do you have kids?"

Dana shook her head. She wondered if she would have tried to escape if there had been children.

The approaching car had cleared the tree line. They could see and hear it deaccelerating as its driver took in the crash site.

Johnny ran up to the shoulder of the road. The car stopped abreast of him. Dana nestled into the ditchgrasses. She caught the odd word exchanged between Johnny and the driver. Soon Johnny was pointing at her and saying, "I'll stay here... 911... miracle... she's in good enough shape... take her with you."

No! She had to stall, needed time to think. She didn't recognize the car, couldn't tell who was in it. But it was bound to be someone who knew her, or knew Glenn. She slumped lower into the grass.

Johnny was beckoning to her. "I'd rather stay here," she called, pulling her hair over her eyes. "Thanks...."

Johnny hurried down the slope of the ditch. The car idled at the side of the road. The driver didn't get out. "Dana, the hospital's only about twenty miles from here. You should go get checked out. What if you go into shock or something?"

"What if *you* go into shock or something? Don't make me explain, but—I need to stay here." To the man in the car, who didn't look particularly interested in helping, she shouted, "I'm fine. I'll wait for the . . . 911 people." To Johnny, she said, "Captain has to stay with her ship."

The driver waited for Johnny's nod before putting his car into gear and resuming his journey. Dana and Johnny watched the gleam of the sun on his fender move along the ribbon of road. They were suddenly unsure what to say to each other.

He's figuring out there's more to this than has met his eye. . . .

Johnny stood with his hands on his hips and his legs apart. His eyes followed the vehicle as it rapidly became a speck on the road. He spoke at last with his back to Dana. "Boy, this sure is a lonely corner, isn't it? There isn't another living thing in sight. Seems like no one but us and that fella exist in this world. And he didn't have a phone, either."

"Can't get everything we wish for, I guess."

Johnny still had his back to her. "He was worried he'd be late for his shift over in Morden. Said he'd phone 911 from the hotel in Plum Coulee. Let's see." He glanced at his watch. "Coulee's about ten minutes away. I figure we're looking at at least twenty minutes before a cop shows, longer if there isn't one anywhere close, and even longer for an ambulance to get here from Morden. Sure are lucky nobody got seriously hurt. At least we know we're not dead."

"Or, that fella may have been Satan," Dana replied. She tugged on the elbow of his shirt. "Johnny?" The meadowlark trilled from a more distant spot.

He turned. His eyes were round. "You okay? You should have gone...."

"Yes. Johnny, what were you doing on this road? It used to be a sugar beet highway back when farmers grew sugar beets. Way out at that end is sugar beet growing land, and way out at that end is the main highway where the beet trucks took the loads to the city. Hardly anyone uses this road any more, let alone a delivery truck full of ice cream."

"That reminds me!" The man jogged away from her along the faint path in the grass. "Whole load's gonna be shot anyway!" he shouted at the sky.

Were there two secrets on this lonesome road?

Dana put on her shoe and began to pace back and forth in the ditch. She hadn't liked the feeling of dizziness and faintness she'd felt a few minutes ago, didn't want to weaken. If she forced herself to move, she could walk it off, she was sure. Her strides became longer and she flapped her arms to stimulate her blood flow.

"Should I turn off your ignition, do you think?" Johnny called from the wreckage.

"No! Keep the radio playing!" Music was the looking glass she'd slipped through.

When Johnny returned, he was carrying three colourless cardboard boxes.

"More first aid?"

He set them down in front of her and crouched to open their lids. DREAMCLOUD was stamped on each one in dark blue letters. "You could say that. I've got ice cream sandwiches, revels, and frozen yogurt butterscotch sundaes." He sat back on his haunches and smiled. "Let's celebrate."

Dana was getting a little tired of the whole miracle routine, but she chose an ice cream sandwich, even though it wasn't her favourite. She wished he'd brought a chocolate sundae; she really could have gone for a chocolate sundae.

"These sandwiches are special—mocha flavoured with almonds, and a high-quality cookie dough," Johnny explained.

It was the best one Dana had ever tasted. She told Johnny so.

With his index finger, Johnny brushed ice cream from underneath his bottom lip. "So. You got a job somewhere, Dana?"

"I work at the library part-time," she replied. "But I'm not a librarian. Not a trained one. There's this big head librarian with a university degree who comes around and tells us what to do. And in summer I work part-time at a greenhouse, selling plants."

"So which job were you heading to so early in the morning? My bet would be the greenhouse."

Dana wondered what Johnny saw when he looked at her: a worried woman with a clown mouth made of mocha-coloured cream and cookie crumbs? "We could use napkins or something, couldn't we?" she said.

He plucked tissues from his shirt pocket. "I found these on the seat of your truck. It's all there was left."

He must have seen the luggage, then. Which meant he was fishing. "I wasn't heading to any job," said Dana. "Let's say I was out here for the same reason as you were. This isn't a road either of us would normally be on."

He gestured towards her left shoulder. "You've got a daddy-long-legs there. Now hold on, hold on, I didn't mean to scare you. Some people are like that with spiders, though, aren't they? Now you've got a great big streak of chocolate on your blouse."

"Where'd it go?"

"Don't ask me. I'm sure it won't be back." Johnny looked around. "Actually, I think we've scared all the wildlife hereabouts away."

"Maybe we should get our stories straight," said Dana.

"Our stories?"

"Well, what we were both doing out *here* at this time of day is bound to come up, don't you think?"

Johnny balled up the sandwich wrapper and tossed it over his shoulder. "Me, I'm just selling ice cream."

Dana nodded at his truck upside-down on hers. "Your sales technique could use some fine-tuning."

She stood up to check the condition of her body. Some of the muscles were stiffening now, but the sustenance of the ice cream sandwich had calmed her and given her new optimism. As she gazed about the landscape, she saw that puffy clouds had popped up on the western horizon. From the south, a slight breeze was rippling the grain and the grasses. Insects hidden in the ditchplants began to buzz. She hadn't heard the meadowlark in a while. "You go first," she said. "You were coming from the city...?"

"My refrigerant's leaking," said Johnny.

"Is that bad?" asked Dana.

"Not good for the environment, I'm sure," he replied.

"It is if it kills spiders. Don't worry about something you can't do anything about, Johnny."

"Maybe there is something I can do. I'm trying to think."

But he read the look of skepticism on her face. Dabbing at his lips with the tissue, he said, "Well, I guess you'd like me to say I spent the night in a haystack with a farmer's daughter."

"Maybe. I know for a fact that you're spending the morning with a farmer's daughter. I happen to be one."

"I did have deliveries to make all over the place today. I was coming from the city." Johnny raised his head and pointed his jaw towards the southwest. "Just beyond these fields, up in the hills, maybe twenty miles away, is a special place. You've probably been there—it's called Dead Horse Creek. I don't know how it got its name. At one spot in the hills—a part you might not have been to—the creek forms a series of pools or ponds surrounded by trees and bushes and wildflowers. You walk in from a hidden little road—a track, actually—that forks off from another hidden road, and it leads to these ponds. It's the prettiest place anywhere around here."

"You got up at four a.m. to meditate at the Dead Horse Creek? Is that your story?"

"I got up at four a.m. to fish."

"To fish."

"My tackle's in the front seat of the truck. I do that once in a while in summer, when I'm making this run. This highway is a shortcut. My wife used to come along sometimes. It was our private paradise."

"But she doesn't come along any more."

A new sound blew over them with the breeze, the motor of a plane. They both turned their heads towards it.

"I hope she will again. But she's sick now. Some kind of depression. I don't tell her I've still been going. I'm afraid it'll give her something else to feel bad about. She seems to look for things to feel bad about."

"Maybe, if you talk about it, she'll want to go with you," said Dana. "Maybe she needs to be in that place."

The airplane noise intensified. Johnny nodded. "Maybe it is. What's the point of having a private paradise, anyway?"

Dana began to reflect on the paradise she and Glenn had somehow lost, her search for a new one, her night at the Happy Wanderer. But her thoughts were interrupted by the loud drone of the approaching airplane.

"It's a crop-duster," said Johnny. "Flying real low. Looks like it's gonna spray this field right here."

"He'll see the crash and wonder," said Dana.

The plane banked and swooped towards the wreckage in the ditch. They saw the face of the pilot through the cockpit window as he passed. "He'll figure we need help!" shouted Johnny. "We should signal him, let him know it's under control."

"How?"

Johnny shrugged. The plane banked and came at them again.

Dana started to wave. "How do we tell him?"

Johnny yanked her arm down. He stretched his own arms out in front of him and crossed his flattened hands rapidly one on top of the other. Then he shook his head and jabbed his index finger towards Morden. Through mirrored sunglasses, the pilot stared at them from the bubble of his cockpit. Johnny smiled at him. "Wonder if he got that."

They watched as the plane flew over their heads. The wings dipped in acknowledgement.

"Well, he got something," said Dana.

As if understanding that help was on its way, the pilot turned the craft towards the far end of the field and released a white mist over the young plants. The plane dipped and

A PRIVATE PARADISE

soared and wheeled sharply and dipped again. It was too far away now to be loud. They could still hear the music from Dana's truck accompanying the dance of the crop-duster.

"I wish I could be on that plane with him," said Dana into the quiet air.

"You know that fella?"

She shook her head. "I just wish I could have a ride like that. And then just wing away into the wild blue yonder." She turned to Johnny and laughed for no particular reason. But she knew her eyes were wet, because not too long from now, she would be unpacking her suitcases in her old bedroom in her old house. And Glenn would be there to watch her do it.

Johnny looked away as if he sensed she was having a moment.

"Yeah," he murmured. "Too bad those spray planes are all one-seaters. Anyway, talk about your environmental disaster. We'd better get out of here. I don't want that stuff on me. Just let me check on that leak."

Dana crossed the road to the ditch on the other side. This one was narrower and steeper. Thistles bloomed blue on its slopes. Here, a row of hydro poles bordered the adjacent field. Dana picked her way through the coarse vegetation and leaped over the wet ditch bottom. She sat with her back against one of the poles and waited for Johnny. Together, without speaking, like spectators at an airshow, they gazed at the crop-duster performing his aerobatics above the canola field.

"Are you gonna tell me your story?" Johnny said finally.

"I liked yours. I think it'll do just fine."

"You don't have to tell me yours."

"You stole my fishing tale." Dana stretched out her legs.

The knee was not quite as stiff now. "Everything's different on this side," she said. "We can't hear the music—"

"Well, snatches now and then."

"—or the meadowlark. And we can see only part of the wreck. Just the top half of your truck. DREAMCLOUD upside-down."

"When I saw your luggage, I thought you were going on a holiday. But I figured if that was the case, you would have said so right off."

It wasn't the words so much, but the way he'd said them; it was the intricacy of thistles, the sweet smell of ripening wild plants, the joy of the lark, the absurdity of the two trucks. Dana put her hand on Johnny's sleeve. "Can I hug you? It's kinda crazy but...."

"Well, sure, I'll even hug you back," said Johnny. "There you go now. Tension. You need to get rid of it. Yep. I'm surprised you held it in so long. Why do you think I was running around like a fool after your shoe before? If I would've sat down, I would've bawled like a six-year-old."

His shirt collar smelled like paper boxes and chlorophyll. The airplane roared as it lifted and banked, closer to them now than before. Was the pilot watching them from his glass bubble? Was he talking to someone on his radio?

"Look!" Johnny pulled away and pointed. "That was fast."

Dana squinted at the sheen of white cumulus on the horizon. Far away, tiny lights flashed red, like stray bits of glitter winking on a child's drawing. "Here they come."

"Here they come."

Dana said, "Tell me my story, Johnny."

"Okay." He didn't seem surprised, seemed to have been composing it in his mind the whole time. "Dana was bored. Dana needed an adventure. So she set out early one morning to have a collision with an ice cream truck. There, how's that?"

"They won't buy it. And it's not as good as yours."

"One morning you put that same slice of 60% whole wheat bread into the same toaster for the two millionth time and you put the same peanut butter on it, because somewhere along the line your husband said he liked that peanut butter and you took it to mean it's the only kind he'll eat, so you keep buying it, and then you flung his underwear you'd washed a couple of days ago into the dryer, the same brand of underwear he'd been wearing for fifteen years, and which you washed in special mild soap because he gets a rash from regular detergents, and then you opened every cupboard door and fridge door and freezer door and pantry door that you've got trying to decide what he might like for supper and still couldn't decide, and then you looked at your windows and thought for the two millionth time that they sure need washing but, hey, they'll just get dirty again, what's the point, and then you went to your job at the library and everyone there seemed happy and obviously never let their windows get dirty and probably had weekly meal plans taped to the inside of their obsessively tidy kitchen cupboards, and then early, early this morning, when it was still dark maybe, you got your resolve together and fired up the Ford Ranger and headed out to search far and wide for a different brand of peanut butter."

The crop-duster made its last pass. As it reached the end of the field, the pilot saluted with the wings of this plane and climbed into the blue air.

Dana waved. "What about the suitcases?"

"Full of men's underwear. You were gonna dump it all into Dead Horse Creek."

"Where I would have found you fishing."

"We were destined to meet today, Dana."

The emergency lights angled silently towards the intersection. The meadowlark, as though seeking human company, had landed unseen somewhere near them and warbled its sunny melody.

Dana looked deep into Johnny's eyes. "But what do I tell Glenn?"

Johnny didn't speak for a moment. He twisted off the blossom of a thistle and offered it to her. "You'll know when you see him coming at you with worry in his eyes."

Dana took the blue flower from him. He got to his feet and held out his hand. "Let's go back to the other side now."

They passed the three boxes, forlorn and scattered in the ditch where they'd sat earlier. Johnny started to gather them up. "No," said Dana. "Let's leave them. They can be our monument, our shrine."

He tossed the box he held back onto the pile. They stared at the configuration for a while, memorizing it, knowing that it would be a short-lived monument, soon to be marauded by stray dogs and foxes, dissolved by rain.

Dana sat down in the back of the ambulance. In giving her version of the event, she mentioned peanut butter and underwear. It was decided that she should have her head injury checked out. She waved to Johnny, who was declining treatment. He didn't see her at first. "Johnny," she called.

He raised his hand. "See you at Dead Horse Creek," he said.

Dana nodded, and it occurred to her that though she'd heard two stories today, both of them had been Johnny's. He had told her everything she needed to know about his life. What had he learned about hers?

"Do you want us to call someone, Ma'am?"

"Yes. My husband."

Doors closed. The ambulance rolled along the smooth pavement and gathered speed. Dana had a short trip across the prairie to come up with a truth for Glenn. She looked out the rear windows. The ice cream truck with the inverted lettering on its side became smaller and smaller. Anyone happening on the scene of that accident would not believe that two people had walked away from it. Johnny was right—miracles could happen.

Where was the flower he'd given her? It had slipped from her fingers without her noticing, before she'd had a chance to be pleased with it.

The thistle was probably lying beside the road now. A breeze lilting across the prairie might have nudged it into the grass. In a few days its petals would turn white and fluffy, and float away like clouds.

LAUNDRY DAY

Benno Hooge's socks hung forty to a line, twenty pairs, all black, all woven from the same blend of wool and nylon, all from The Bay store in Winnipeg. His wife, Toots, had not been allowed to buy the socks. She had tried a few times. Then, around twenty-five years ago, when he'd turned fifty, Benno had announced that he didn't like her choice of socks. And she didn't like his—they pilled in the dryer and embarrassed her in public. But Benno said they were the only kind that didn't slide down in his shoes.

"Thousands of men wear these socks," she'd told him on his fiftieth birthday, shaking the cotton-polyester socks she'd bought at the Granton Mall. "They don't slide down on all those guys, or else the stores wouldn't carry them."

"So? So?"

"So you must be deformed or something!" Toots had shouted at him. "Come to think of it, you do have funny feet, just like your father."

"So you should feel sorry for me."

They had both finally laughed over the socks. But in the end, Benno had won. "I have to stick with the old kind because my deformed feet make other ones slide down in my shoes."

Which meant that for the last twenty-five years, Toots had had to wash the socks on the gentle cycle in the machine and hang them out on the line so they wouldn't pill.

But her husband was dead. Toots stood at the sink window in her kitchen and watched the row of black commas bob in the afternoon breeze. This was the last time the forty socks would hang on the line in the backyard. They'd sat in a forlorn pile at the bottom of the hamper for over a month, the last of all the clothes she'd washed and packed up for the missions collection. His side of each closet—the one in the front hall, where his Sunday coat and his raincoat and his hats had hung, the one in the laundry room, the one in the bedroom—was vacant and bleak, pillaged by the Grim Reaper himself. It was funny, she thought again, how he had passed away right at the end of his clean sock supply, as though he'd planned it that way. He'd had a stroke on the driveway. Hadn't died on the spot, but a few days later in the hospital, where they provided socks for anyone who needed them. Which he hadn't. She pictured him gazing into his sock drawer, finding it empty, and saying to himself, "This is as good a day as any to die."

Toots had left the washing of the socks for last.

The lawn was nicely cut. Toots was glad the Franz boy had done such a good job. Everybody called the boy Manny, short for Manfred. But he was a puny child, so far not like a man at all. He could really push that mower though, Toots had to admit. His older brother, Jesse, used to mow the lawn whenever Toots and Benno went on a driving trip to Fort McMurray to see their son, Leroy, who was an engineer in the oil patch. But Jesse had quit the mowing business recently to work at the IGA, and passed it on to little Manny. Jesse had been puny at one time, too, Toots suddenly recalled. She wondered if Manny would have a job at the IGA some day, like his brother.

    The town of Granton didn't have very many back lanes, but Toots's sink window looked past the clothesline, across the yard, over the potentilla shrubs, and across an alley to the Schroeders'. Doreen Schroeder was her main neighbour. (When friends or relatives came for a visit, Toots always told them: "And see that shady place across the lane there, the one with all the bird feeders? That's where Doreen lives; she's my main neighbour.") Ralph and Doreen were a lot younger than the Hooges. They and their two young children had moved from Winnipeg into the old Nikkel house two years ago. They'd started right in with bird feeders and back-door visits. "Hogie? Hogie?" had been Doreen's response when Toots had introduced herself. "How do you spell that? Did you invent that sandwich?" Doreen had kind eyes and a lopsided smile and Toots hadn't taken offense. Doreen's friendships knew no age barriers. She paid no attention to the boundaries around her neighbours' yards, either, just yoo-hooed over the hedges and fences and barged in. Toots liked it. Benno hadn't, at first. But he got used to it. He would even wander occasionally into the Schroeders' yard when he noticed Doreen's husband working out there. Toots's younger sister, Jane, had remarked quite casually one afternoon, "You're lucky to have a neighbour like that. Some day she'll be a godsend to you and Benno."

Her off-handed prophesy had come true. After Benno collapsed on the driveway, before Leroy arrived from Fort McMurray with Muriel and the twins, Doreen had stayed at the hospital with Toots. And then, after the funeral, when everybody had left, she'd popped in a couple of times a day with food and stories about the neighbourhood. Toots could do without the lentil casseroles and the buckwheat bread, but Doreen's stories always fascinated her.

Toots gazed past the socks and across the back lane. She hadn't seen Doreen in almost two weeks, hadn't seen anyone outside for a while, either, no one tending the bird feeders or puttering in the flower beds. The neighbours next to the Schroeders had "enough playground equipment to compete with Disney," Benno told everyone who, sitting on the Hooges' patio for the first time, commented on the steel kindergarten-coloured tubing winking through the trees. It was normal not to see Ralph and Doreen's children in their own backyard. But the emptiness Toots had noticed was not due to the absence of children. Something was wrong.

She stared at the Schroeders' back deck, and then, almost as if Toots had willed it to happen, Doreen appeared. She descended the deck stairs and came towards the potentillas, where Benno had kept a space trimmed between two shrubs for Doreen to get through, though he often grumbled that it would be an invitation to trespassers. Toots always said Benno wouldn't have needed to trim the shrubs; Doreen's frequent comings and goings would have stunted the branches all on their own.

She had a height and grace Toots admired, and in summer she often wore a white T-shirt and faded ankle-length jeans and turquoise leather sandals. Her feet were always tanned in the summer. Toots could not figure out how any part of Doreen's body ever tanned; their yard was canopied by mature elm trees. Her hair was long and curly. Goldilocks, Benno called her. "Here comes Goldilocks," he'd mutter from his Muskoka chair on the patio whenever he saw her approaching.

Here came Goldilocks, as usual not looking left or right before crossing the alley, because hardly anyone ever drove there. Her hair was gathered at the top of her head with ponytail elastic.

The air was hot. The socks would dry quickly.

Doreen touched the socks as she went by; in fact, stopped beside the line and looked at the socks and grasped one in her hand as though it were a juicy apple she wanted to steal.

But she didn't take the sock, just continued on up to the back door and knocked on the window the way she always did, even though there was a doorbell button to push. Toots realized that she had been so still at the sink window that Doreen hadn't noticed her standing there, though Toots was a big woman with streaky grey-white hair.

"Warm for June, huh?" said Doreen.

"To tell you the truth, I didn't notice until I saw the tail on top of your head. I was standing at the window and...."

"Is everything all right? I haven't...."

"I was just thinking about you and then...."

"Sorry. I should have told you, but...."

"The coffee is cooled off." Toots pointed to the carafe on the stove. "I'll get some ice."

In summer, this was what they did: drank iced coffee with sugar syrup and cream out of the pilsener glasses Jane had given Toots for her birthday. If either of them was celebrating something, they'd leave out the sugar and add a drop of Kahlua or creme de cacao to the coffee. They'd sit on the Muskoka chairs and look at Doreen's yard and talk. They hadn't done that since Benno had gone. Doreen's most recent visits had consisted of problem solving: who all gets a thank-you card? *People who gave flowers or donations, or who helped in any way.* Where do you draw the line? Do you send a thank-you card to people you paid? *Sure, send the money in the card.* Should I keep all the flowers? There are so many. *Some people donate them to hospitals and old folks homes.* I'd like to keep some, but I'll hate throwing them into the trash when they've dried up—Jimmy Berg will see them when he empties the can into his truck. *Put them into your composter and spread the compost in the garden next spring. Benno loved the garden, didn't he?* I don't know which of his things to keep and which to throw away. Leroy already took what he wanted. *Start with the little things that you cherish and put them aside. Then ask yourself if any of his relatives or friends or the guys he used to work with might want tokens to remember him by.* I can't do this. I just can't. *Then do it when you're ready.*

Jane hadn't been any help, had fallen apart even more than Toots had. As she'd predicted a year earlier, it was Doreen who would be the godsend.

Doreen looked at the sympthy cards she hadn't yet seen while Toots poured the cream into the carafe. Toots picked up the jar of syrup but put it down again before adding it to the coffee. Doreen would normally be chattering away as she read each card, commenting a little irreverently on the awkward messages people had written under the verses inside. But Doreen didn't say anything, just cleared her throat from time to time. Toots wanted to ask her if she'd been sick, but decided against it. She put three ice cubes into each glass and poured coffee over the cubes. Then she grabbed the wicker tray from the top of the fridge and placed the glasses of iced coffee on it. The Kahlua bottle was in a high cupboard with other seldom-used liquors. Toots made sure the cap was tight and laid it down on the tray. In the drawer beside the fridge, she found a box of extra-long swizzle sticks and put a green stick in one glass and a yellow one in the other.

Doreen glanced up from the cards. "Oh my!" She slapped one hand to her jaw. "Are we celebrating something today? What's up?"

Toots thought for a moment. Finally she said, "It's been so long since I've done a normal thing." But she was really doing it for Doreen, because maybe Doreen was coming over less often because she didn't want to deal with mourning any more.

"Well, that's fine. Let's do something normal." At last Doreen smiled her crooked grin, and Toots knew she had done the right thing. Doreen held the door open for her and they went out onto the patio. Toots set the tray on the round cedar table. "Laundry day, I see," said Doreen.

"I guess you couldn't miss 'em." Toots tipped a few drops of Kahlua into the coffees.

"To tell you the truth, I think the socks are what called me over here today," said Doreen as she stirred with the green swizzle stick.

Toots raised her glass. "Let's have a toast."

"Okay," said Doreen. "What shall we toast?"

"I don't know."

"New beginnings? Is it too early?"

Toots glanced at the clothesline. "To the last of the socks."

But her eyes welled up and her voice broke on the word *socks*. Doreen reached for her. "No!" Toots almost shouted. "No. New beginnings. You're right."

They clinked the tall pilsener glasses. Benno always said the toast wouldn't hold if you spoke between saying the words and taking a drink. And Toots had taught Doreen, who always wanted to talk after clinking instead of taking a sip. Benno had also told Toots that in a true toast, the drinkers should drain their glasses completely, that originally toasts were made with small shots of pure liquor to be tossed back with a flourish of the body. (He had been proud of the Russian element in his ancestry, but Toots wasn't sure how much of the lore he'd dispensed in measured amounts was accurate.) "That was in the old days when women didn't drink with men," he'd said. "Ladies only took dainty little sips of their wine. And then men started to do that, too."

Toots had replied, "Men probably didn't want women to take long guzzles of alcohol."

"Men do have a protective gene."

Doreen kept stirring her coffee. The ice cubes rang like wind chimes. Toots imagined what it would sound like if the black socks hanging on the line were wind chimes. Every few weeks she could hang them out and the neighbourhood would sparkle with the music of Benno's socks, and everyone would remember him for a few hours. If there was a breeze. And as the socks dried and became lighter, the ringing of the chimes would....

"Don't say anything, you haven't taken a sip yet," said Doreen.

"What?"

"Shh! You haven't taken a sip since the toast. New beginnings, remember?"

Toots guzzled in an unladylike way.

"Well, that should seal your future," Doreen said.

Toots put the glass down and dabbed her lips with a flowery napkin. "When I was a little girl and took a swallow of something strong or spicy, I'd sputter and cough, and then my father would clap me on the back and say, 'That'll grow hair on your chest!' And then he'd laugh and laugh at the thought of a sweet little four-year-old girl with hair on her chest." She set her gaze on the socks and said, "What's new?" Usually when she asked that, she meant in the neighbourhood. Doreen always knew what was going on. "Are the Winters back yet?"

"The Winters are back from their summer vacation. I told you they went to Newfoundland. Rocks, rocks, rocks, Laura says. Abe broke his toe on a table leg in the lobby of the hotel and hobbled around for the rest of the trip."

"What was he doing barefoot in the lobby of the hotel?"

"He was wearing sandals, or flip-flops or something."

Toots had never heard of flip-flops until Doreen had moved into town. "I thought it was always cold in Newfoundland. Why was he wearing sandals? He doesn't wear sandals, does he?"

Doreen shrugged.

"Funny he didn't break his toe on one of those rocks. That would have made more sense."

"Anyway," Doreen continued, "they took a ferry to Cape Breton Island, and a reporter on the ferry was interviewing the passengers for an article she was writing for a travel magazine in the States. She interviewed Abe and Laura."

"What did she want to know?"

"Laura said she told her that they had taken a lot of ferries on their vacations, and this was the best trip they'd ever had."

"Really?"

"Laura told me it wasn't true, but she thought she might have a better chance of being quoted if she was very positive and descriptive. The reporter had no idea when the article would be in the magazine, so now Laura wants to subscribe to it so she can see if she's in it."

Toots raised her feet onto the low stool in front of her chair. "Did she tell that reporter that her daughter stabbed a boy in a knife fight? She should have told him that, then she would have had a good chance of being in the article."

Doreen smiled. "Maybe she could send the reporter a note. 'Oh, and by the way....'"

Granton didn't have much violence. When Jennifer Winter had stabbed Ricky Voth on the parking lot between the ice cream bar and the chicken grill, it was big news, even though she'd used a pocket knife and he'd been defending himself with a screwdriver.

Doreen asked, "Have you taken the rest of the boxes to the Starvation Army yet?"

Toots shook her head. "I thought I'd wait until the socks were washed."

"How many are there again?" She asked that question almost every time she happened to drop in on washday.

"Forty, still forty."

"Pairs or socks?"

"Socks. Twenty pair."

"And do you darn?"

"Never darn. Can't darn a modern sock. Throw them away."

"And buy another pair."

"He went and bought another pair." As though he couldn't live with any fewer than forty socks. "Oh, he wanted me to darn. But I gave it up when I was still in my twenties." Toots stirred her ice cubes. "What about Rhonda?"

"Rhonda's lawyer is on holiday. He's not touching her case until he gets back."

Rhonda Lavoie wanted to sue her dentist for lacerating her tongue during a tooth extraction. She said the damage was taking a long time to heal and was preventing her from eating. But everyone who knew Rhonda knew that she was obsessed with her weight, and that this was just a convenient excuse to walk around looking like a skeleton. "Well, that's very handy for them both, isn't it?" said Toots. "She has an excuse to starve herself for another three weeks, and by the time he gets back, her tongue will be healed and he doesn't have to be bothered with such a silly case."

Doreen nodded. Annie Plett, who lived on one side of the Hooges, ambled along the lane in her Fortrel duster and her Velcro shoes. (Toots herself preferred slacks and loose shirts and Reeboks.) Annie had brought Toots store-bought cookies the day after Benno had died. Her husband had died on their farm many years ago and she had moved to town, into the tiny bungalow next door. "I don't bake any more," she'd explained to Toots the day after Benno died, handing her a plastic plate with the cookies arranged on them as though she had baked them. "It's my arthritis." Her hands looked like the Japanese bonzai trees Toots had once seen at a flower show in the city.

Every day in summer Annie Plett went for a walk along the alley. She was on her way home now. "I see you've got Benno's socks out today," she called, as though referring to a litter of kittens.

"The last time," Toots called back, hoping that Annie wouldn't come into the yard.

Annie stood on the other side of the potentillas with her gnarled fists on her hips. "Did you hear they found a bug in our water?"

"Really?"

"What bug? What water?" said Doreen.

"Our drinking water!" Annie waved at a gnat hovering around her ear. "Some kind of parasite or something. It was on the news this morning. Boil your water." She set off down the lane again. "Boil your water!" she tossed over her shoulder one more time.

Toots lifted her glass. "Well, this is boiled," she said.

"Are there exactly forty socks on your line now?" said Doreen.

"What?"

"Exactly twenty pairs? Now?" Doreen pointed to the washline with her swizzle stick.

"Doreen, I hate to ask, is there something wrong? You seem...."

Doreen didn't respond right away, but frowned into her iced coffee.

Toots put her glass down and stood up, in one motion. "Let's go for a ride."

"A ride?"

"I want to show you a place."

"I'll get my purse."

"You don't need your wallet where we're going. And I'll drive." Toots was proud that she still drove everywhere, even to the city, and drove well, when many women her age had either quit driving or doddered along the streets of town like half-blind, deaf old dogs.

"Well, I like surprises," said Doreen.

"You need one today, I think. Are your children coming home for lunch?" Toots knew they usually ate lunch in school.

Doreen shook her head, and the women went into the garage.

The Chrysler's interior had just been shampooed. Klassen from the dealership had phoned on Tuesday and offered to pick it up for servicing and its annual steam-cleaning. *The widows' special*, was Toots's response. She pushed the button on the garage wall that automatically opened the big door. Behind her, she could hear the splat-splat of Doreen's sandals on the cement floor. Once Toots had backed the steel-coloured car out onto the driveway (straight as an arrow), she pushed the button that automatically closed the door again. "Never leave your garage door open when you're gone, they say," she told Doreen. "An invitation to burglars."

Then Doreen asked, "Are you keeping the car?"

Toots sat up taller in her seat. "What do you mean? Why wouldn't I? I'm a good driver!"

"No, no, I know that. I just thought you might trade it in for a smaller one, that's all."

Toots had thought about it. Klassen had suggested getting a compact. Said he had a buyer that very moment for the big Chrysler. But this had been Benno's car. She couldn't throw it out the way she had his clothing and his shaver and his eleven baseball caps. Something had to stay, didn't it?

The women headed south out of town on the main highway, but soon turned east onto a gravel road. A light rain during the night had stifled the dust. Toots talked about the crops they passed, the way Benno would have, and made comments about the farmyards. Doreen knew the names of some of the people who lived on the farms, but she didn't know their histories the way Toots did. So now it was Toots's turn to tell stories. Funny that she knew more about these far-flung strangers than about her own neighbourhood. It was because Benno had been an insurance salesman for a short time. He'd seen the inside of most of the farm homes all around Granton.

"Those people who live in that old house have a son who's a lunatic," Toots explained to Doreen. "He never stops talking. They have to lock him in the barn a few hours every day so they can get some peace and quiet."

"Doesn't seem right to do that to a child," said Doreen.

"He's forty-three."

"Oh. I'm not sure that makes it okay."

"He doesn't mind. He talks to the cats and the pigeons. They like it."

"Is he autistic?"

"Maybe that's what it is."

After about ten minutes of going east, Toots turned south again onto another road, this one not gravel, but just plain dirt, with no ditches on the sides to drain the water off the fields, and then onto a long driveway that led to an arrangement of trees surrounded by young green wheat. Toots stopped the Chrysler in the shade. "Here we are."

When they opened the car doors, the heat took their breath away. A glassy pond was sheltered beneath the trees they'd parked under. Behind the pond, forming an L-shaped line, more trees towered over what had once been a farmyard.

Aside from a derelict granary squatting in the wheat field, no buildings remained.

"This is where I met Benno," said Toots.

"Here?" said Doreen. "In the middle of nowhere?"

"It wasn't the middle of nowhere then. This was my aunt and uncle's farm once. I spent a lot of time here when I was growing up. Come."

Toots led Doreen around the pond to the long row of cottonwoods behind it. Green flies landed on the women and decorated their clothing with brilliant, iridescent colour. Chirring and whistling and clucking echoed in the enclosed pond. High grass lay between the pond and the line of trees. The women waded through it, their open hands skimming the tops of the budding stalks. The air was cooler under the roof of leaves. Here and there, fallen limbs lay across the women's path. Toots found a place in the shelter belt where two stumps were separated by only a sapling. She gestured to one stump and sat down on the other. They faced not the pond but the open prairie, which at this time of year was more or less level with half-tall grain.

"This is a perfect picture, isn't it?" breathed Doreen.

She didn't look directly at Toots, but with one glance Toots could tell that Doreen's face had lost that earlier tightness, that her mouth had turned up at the corners and that her eyes had softened. They had both needed to get away, from socks, from bird feeders. "That farm way over there—" Toots pointed, "—that's where Benno lived. He had six older brothers. When I used to come to my aunt and uncle's for—"

"Aunt and Uncle who?" Doreen interrupted. "What were their names?"

"Aunt Mary and Uncle Peter. I used to come here every year for summer holidays. Benno—"

"Summer holidays? Where did you live?"

"Oh, we lived in town, my sisters and parents and I, but in those days it wasn't unusual for kids to go to a nearby farm for the summer. Actually, we had to work while we were here, help out with the chores, and weed, and do canning, and—"

"Cheap labour."

"Oh no, we loved it. There was a big old barn to play in and an old horse to ride. And there was Benno. He used to come over in the evenings and on Sundays and play with us, right here in the poplar trees." Toots tore a leaf from a twig sprouting low on the trunk beside her. "Look at these leaves, Doreen. These leaves are so beautiful, like smooth leather. There were a lot more trees here when the place belonged to my Uncle Peter, different kinds of trees. And Benno had still other kinds at his farm. I made scrapbooks of pressed leaves, but I don't know what happened to them. Every once in a while I think of the scrapbooks and I come here to feel these." She rubbed the leaf gently between the palms of her hands. Doreen did the same.

"What happened to the six brothers?" Doreen asked. "You'd think at least one of them would have married a sister of yours. Didn't any of them come here to play, too?"

"Benno was an afterthought. His next brother was seven years older than him, almost an adult when I first got to know Benno. He's still alive, that brother, in a nursing home in BC."

They sat quietly for a while and listened to the busy pond. "Blackbirds," Toots said.

Doreen nodded.

"We should have brought our coffees."

Doreen nodded again.

"How did you meet your Ralph?" Toots was certain that he was what they had come here to talk about.

"Oh, well, Ralph and I...."

"High school sweethearts?"

On a distant road a pickup truck appeared, floating above the half-tall grain, silent, gleaming under the bright sun.

"Yes, we were," said Doreen. She fanned herself with the poplar leaf.

"And?"

Doreen's arm dropped. The hand and the leaf hung limply at her ankle. "I guess it's time to tell you who I really am."

"Who you really are? You're not really Doreen Schroeder?"

"Eva Agnes Marie Hooge, let me introduce myself." Doreen straightened up and thrust out her arm as if to shake hands with an invisible person in front of her. "I'm Doreen Sandra Loewen Schroeder."

Toots and Benno had asked Doreen about her maiden name, and her family, when they'd first met in the lane between them. She told them she was a city girl and an only child. When they'd pressed her (because they knew Loewens in the city), she said her mother had been a single parent. They hadn't questioned her further. Toots's reply now was cautious. "Aah—your middle name is Sandra."

"You probably remember my mother Mary. Everybody else here does."

"Remember her?"

"She lived in Granton, a long time ago." Doreen's voice trailed off. She gazed steadily across the field of grain.

"Mary Loewen," said Toots.

"Mary Loewen."

Toots spoke softly. "Mary Alone?"

Doreen nodded. "Yes. Yes. Mary Alone."

Mary Alone was Doreen's mother?

Toots nodded. "I remember her. She was a—" Toots fumbled for the right word. "Well, she was sort of between a chiropractor and a ... what do you call them?"

"A masseuse."

"Yes, exactly—a masseuse. Mary Alone was your mother?"

"Surprise!"

Not yet fall, but a leaf of poplar let loose of its tree. Toots, whose eyes had lifted to the clouds, watched it spiral earthwards past fully clothed limbs to land in the long grass. "Well, she was very gifted, lots of men and women went to her with their aches and pains, and she fixed them."

The truck came along the road that passed the poplar grove.

"Oh, yeah, she fixed them." Doreen was angry now. "Especially the men. One of them got her pregnant, and she had *me*. Apparently my father is someone here in town."

Toots didn't know what to say. She picked up the fallen leaf and started a tear in it. Mary Alone had lived in Granton thirty or forty years ago. She'd had a reputation of being a loose woman. Testimonials of her magic touch spread by word of mouth. She had no licence to be a chiropractor or practise massage, hadn't advertised. Rumours spread that some men went to her house for more than therapeutic massage. Some people had called her the town whore. Benno himself had occasionally visited Mary Alone, when his back bothered him, for what he called "a correction." When Toots had heard the gossip about her, she had suggested to her husband that he not see her any more. Benno had agreed, and, as far as she knew, he had not gone back. Toots had no idea when Mary Alone had left Granton; the woman had simply faded away.

The truck coming along the road slowed down as it passed.

Curious about my car being on this yard, Toots thought. Out loud she said, "I sometimes wondered what happened to your mother. You just found this out now?"

Doreen nodded. "Ralph and I were in the pub one night a while back. A bunch of guys at the next table—older guys—started talking about this Mary Alone, this Mary Loewen that used to give massages. They were making fun of her and saying terrible things about her. When I was a kid, people used to come to our apartment for massages."

"In the city."

"She did them in the dining room with me watching. There wasn't any—funny stuff. But that's how I knew, when we were in the pub, that their Mary Alone was my mom Mary Loewen. I'd never heard her called that before."

"But—it's probably all lies, gossip!"

"My mother won't tell me who my dad is. Was."

Toots looked at Doreen hard. "Is your mother still alive?"

Doreen nodded. "She's seventy. Has an apartment at a seniors' home in the city. I asked her if she had lived in Granton at one time. She told me she had. And then she said, 'You've heard, haven't you? I was afraid you'd eventually hear all those lies.'"

Doreen stared down at her feet. "We have to get outta here, for the sake of the kids."

Silence fell between the women. A dog in a nearby ditch caught their eye, a dark silhouette trotting with his nose to the ground. Blackbirds hovered and clattered in the air above. Toots should have known. She chided herself for not having known. Not that there were problems at the Schroeders, but that a second bad thing was going to happen after Benno died. And now that the second bad thing had happened, there would be a third. Bad things always happened in threes. Everybody knew that.

Finally Toots said, "Did you ask her about your dad?"

Doreen shrugged. "She just repeated what she's always told me: 'He's a family man, a nice man. A grandfather by now.' He could be a great-grandfather, maybe. Or even dead. 'We don't want to upset the applecart,' Mom would say."

"EXCUSE ME!"

The blackbirds stopped their chatter. Toots dropped the poplar leaf. A red-faced man stood in the grass between the pond and the row of trees the women sat in. He had a round face and a receding hairline with puffs of dry brown hair above his ears. He wore a navy work shirt that matched his pants, and those high leather workboots Benno used to call shit-kickers.

"This is private property," he said in a loud voice.

Toots stood up. "Are you the owner of this land now?"

"What do you mean *now*? We've had this land for years and years. And we don't like trespassers. You townies think this is a nice spot for a picnic, littering up the place. Well, it isn't."

Now Doreen stood up. "We're not having a picnic."

"I don't care," the man said in his shit-kicking way. "I'm just saying, it's private property. If you want to sit in the trees and recite poetry, get permission first."

Doreen looked at Toots in bewilderment. "Did he say *poetry*?"

"Do you remember the people you bought this land from? Pete and Mary Buhler?" Toots waited for the man to reply. She wanted to find out just how much he really knew about the heritage of the land he owned.

"No, and it doesn't matter. Just keep in mind that you're—"

"I know, trespassers." Toots took a step towards the irate man. "Just you keep in mind that this was my parents' farm—"

Doreen gave Toots a sidelong glance.

"—before you bought it at your ridiculous price and forced them off and burned down their house and barn. I'm just paying respects to their memory." Toots put her arm around Doreen. "I'm reminding my daughter here where her roots are."

Doreen smiled at the farmer.

"Everybody's got a story like that," the man muttered.

"Exactly. Keep that in mind. Some day you'll be the one with a story."

The man turned and started to walk away. "Well, make sure you—" He didn't seem quite sure of what to say. "—don't stay too long," he fumbled. He walked a few feet. Then he turned back and wagged his finger at them. "Don't go galloping around in the wheat. And don't smoke!" He headed for his truck, one of those big, flashy, silver things that reminded Toots of a spaceship. "Set the whole damn place on fire...." His voice trailed after him into the cab. As he stepped up onto the running board, Toots saw bands of red and grey wool showing above the top of his boot. With that petulant boot, he gunned the engine.

"Do you know him?" whispered Doreen, even though he couldn't have heard her above the roar of the motor.

Toots shrugged. "No," she replied. "But I'm pretty sure he's one of the Krahns who live a couple of miles that way. He has that Krahn look."

Doreen gave Toots one of her lopsided grins. "You lied to him, Mummy. Your parents didn't live here. Did they?"

"They could have," said Toots.

The women stood and watched the truck glide up the driveway and onto the road, and then speed back in the direction it had come from. Was this scolding the third bad thing?

"He's one of those people who looks for trouble all the day long, isn't he?" said Doreen.

The women did not return to their seats on the poplar stumps. They stood there in the tall grass and watched the truck and its anger recede.

Then Toots said, "Doreen, I'm sorry. But don't let this get between you and your mom. Those men in the pub, that was all silly gossip."

What if it hadn't been? What if Mary Alone really had seduced men who came to that small back room of her small house. What if Benno...?

The idea came as such a shock to Toots that she felt faint, had to take a step back to steady herself.

"We're thinking of moving away," said Doreen. "Back to the city."

Toots studied Doreen's profile, looking for familiar features she might have not have noticed before. She edged a little further away so she could take in the younger woman's whole body. "But that's where you came from," Toots reminded her. "You wanted to get away from there when you came here." She couldn't hide the tremor in her voice.

"It doesn't feel good here any more."

"People your age don't remember about your mother. Hardly anyone talks about her any more; it's not important." Toots hesitated. Then, "You don't take after your mother, do you? I mean, your face...."

Doreen laughed. "No. The one thing she always said about

my father was that I look exactly like him. So, you can imagine how I'll be staring at all the older men on the streets of Granton from now on."

Toots raised her hand and smoothed back the hair that the breeze had scattered across her brow and temples.

"Ralph has a job offer—manager of a landscaping business."

Benno could have been a manager. He'd worked for a long time at the same plant Ralph had worked for when he arrived in Granton. Benno had been content as a supervisor. It was all he'd ever wanted to be. "I'm not interested in wearing a suit to work and sitting in an office all day," he'd told Toots whenever the bosses offered him a new position. "I like what I'm doing." The company gave shares to the workers. When Benno had retired at sixty-five, he'd cashed in his shares, and he and Toots had lived comfortably. Toots had often wished that Benno would take the manager's job. He'd been a manager type of man. But mostly, she had just wanted to take that one step up into a different segment of Granton society, the one where you dressed up for cocktail parties, sat with the other managers' wives at the company picnics and the Christmas banquet, or in a luxury box at a hockey game in the city. But though Benno had been a good manager in his personal life, he'd also been a common man, one the workers on the plant floor respected and liked, and Benno said he would feel like a traitor if he abandoned them.

"So you're all leaving. When?"

"We don't know for sure if we are leaving. If we do, fall some time, I guess." Doreen pulled at a stalk of grass. "On the other hand, it could take till Christmas." She stared into the distance, over the young green fields, as though she could see Christmas on the other side.

Now I'm going to grow old, thought Toots. The idea made

her smile. She pictured herself in the company of all the women she knew, the ones around her age, who, in her mind, had grown old too easily. Without Doreen, her one young friend—not a relative, a true friend—she would get a hump on her back and bother the doctors every week and complain about draughts. In a year or two, she would move into the nursing home, maybe next door to Mary Alone, and make simple-minded doo-dads out of plastic and synthetic wool at a big table in a whitewashed room. If only Benno....

Toots twisted her face away from Doreen as she felt tears spill over and melt into the corners of her mouth.

Doreen took Toots's hand between her two and rubbed, the way they had rubbed the poplar leaves a few minutes ago, a lifetime ago.

Toots wiped her cheeks with the cuff of her cotton blouse. "If you go, make sure you sell," she said, "to a nice young person like yourself, somebody who lights up the neighbourhood."

Doreen gave Toots's shoulder a pat and then said, "About those socks, Agnes Marie."

"Socks?"

"Benno's twenty pairs of black socks, swingin' back there in the breeze."

"Yes, yes...."

"You said Benno had exactly forty socks."

Toots nodded. Far away, the shiny truck still glistened as it raced under the climbing sun towards more trouble.

"And you hung exactly forty socks on your line today."

"Yes, yes...."

"So—what did you bury him in? I mean, was he barefoot in his shoes?"

"Barefoot in his shoes?"

"Was he?"

Toots shook her head. "I think I did something bad." And now the tears poured, almost as much as they had when Toots had stood at the coffee machine at the hospital and cried as the brown liquid spattered into the paper cup. She'd felt as if her tears were filling that cup, except that it would not have been big enough to hold them all. A nurse had led her to a little crying room at the end of the hall.

"I bought new socks," she said to Doreen.

"Well, that's all right. It's all right to buy new socks for a—"

"For a corpse."

"—for your husband."

"No, I had to tell myself it was just his body, he wasn't my husband any more. I went to the mall to get a funeral dress. My daughter-in-law took me. And—I still can't figure out why—I went into the men's store and bought new socks. Except, not the kind he liked, I got the kind that won't pill in the clothes dryer, the ones that he says always slide down in his shoes!"

Doreen slung one arm across Toots's shoulders.

"And then I gave them to the undertaker to put on Benno. I could have changed my mind and given him the ones Benno was wearing when he collapsed. He'd only worn them a few hours. I almost did change my mind. But...."

"The socks don't matter."

"As if socks would ever pill in heaven's dryers."

"The socks don't matter," Doreen said again. "They won't slide down in his shoes. It's not like he's walking anywhere."

Toots blinked at Doreen. "What do you mean, not walking anywhere?"

"Well, do you think?"

Toots gazed back out into the prairie. The pickup truck had disappeared. She shrugged. "Who knows? I just know that when I get there, the first thing I'll do is see what Benno has on his feet."

The birds had long resumed their clicking and whistling. Other vehicles appeared on the roads that crossed the land in a grid. The dirt and gravel had dried up by now, so that the tires spewed streamers of dust behind them. It was nearly noon, everybody was going home for lunch, bachelor farmers were going to cafés in town.

As the women moved lazily through the grass towards the Chrysler waiting beside the pond, Toots said, "I noticed that that man, that Krahn, he had high socks in those boots. Didn't look like they'd slide down at all."

"You know something?" said Doreen. "I think I read somewhere that they don't put socks and shoes on—dead bodies."

"Really?"

"Shoes take up too much room in the coffin or something. Or they make it too heavy. You don't see the bottom half of a person in a coffin."

Toots tried to remember if she'd emptied the loose change out of the pockets of Benno's burial suit. She said, "But I gave the undertaker socks and shoes!"

"But did he ask you to?"

Toots stood beside her car and looked over the roof at Doreen on the other side. "I don't know. Leroy was there by then and he just came to me one morning and said, 'Dad's burial clothes,' and I jumped up and got his things together, and then Leroy said, 'No hurry, I'll take them to the funeral home this afternoon,' and then Muriel asked me if I had a dress and I said no and we went to the mall and...."

"Maybe everybody in heaven is barefoot."

"But what would the undertaker have done with Benno's shoes?" Toots wondered out loud as she got into the car.

"Some sort of morticians' black market," answered Doreen. "We should check what they're wearing on *their* feet."

"I think I'd better count the socks on the line."

Toots took a different route home, the way Benno used to when they went for rides in the country, somehow always finding unfamiliar roads to explore. This time they didn't go by the lunatic's house. Toots continued her stories about the residents of the farms they passed, and couldn't imagine why she hadn't done this more often with Doreen. Now Doreen was moving on, and Toots had no idea with whom she might share those stories. She'd been abandoned again, this time on a splendid morning in June.

Most of the farmyards were dead under the heat of the noonday sun. Nothing moved, not even dogs. Each farm seemed to be posing, like the cover of a book, for the tale that unravelled in the Chrysler.

Toots said, "Quite a few people live in Granton but work in the city. Maybe Ralph could drive up and back every day for years and years. Lots of people do that, you know, have done it for a long, long time. Maybe he can even carpool!"

"The job isn't the main reason we—I—want to move, you know that."

But there was hope. Toots needed to keep that hope alive, even though the third bad thing still niggled at her. What was the time limit on the third bad thing happening, anyway?

The trip to the country was almost over. Toots could hardly bear it. She switched on the car radio. Where were the stations that played lively music, the old music that she and

Benno and their friends used to dance to when Benno had belonged to the Optimists Club? She leaned towards the radio and found the SEARCH button. The car dipped onto the shoulder of the gravel road and dug into a soft mass of stones. The sound of it under the tires drowned out the music Toots's SEARCH had landed on.

"Whoa!" shouted Doreen.

They careened back and forth as Toots tried to control the bucking Chrysler.

"Whoa!" Doreen cried again. She was leaning back, Toots could see out of the corner of her eye, and gripping the armrest with one slender, brown hand.

They weren't going very fast. Still, Toots didn't want to land Doreen in the ditch. "Don't over-steer," Benno had warned her on ice in winter and gravel in summer. "Over-steering is the main cause of accidents in these kinds of conditions."

With a final sideways flip of its tail, the car found its way back to the smoother centre of the road. Toots slowed it down to a crawl and, without saying anything to her companion, continued her search for the right music.

A horn blared behind them, sending them both shooting towards the roof. Not daring even to look in the rear-view mirror, Toots eased the Chrysler to the side of the road. A silver spaceship slid by. The red- and round-faced man behind the wheel scowled at them and shook his finger at them for the second time that day.

"Well, now we're in his bad books for sure," said Doreen. "He must think we're real bad town trash. I've got a good mind to go back there and gallop around in his wheat."

"Next time," Toots laughed. "Let's go again in a week or two and do exactly that."

"Deal."

"Anyway, he can go scratch himself." Toots had found a station that played rock 'n' roll. Without asking for Doreen's permission, she turned the volume up high. At once Doreen began bouncing in her seat and singing. "Do you LUHV ME-E, do you really love me, do you LUHV ME-E, really love me. . . ." Her ponytail flicked from one side of her head to the other. She clapped her hands and snapped her fingers, and Toots laughed and kept time by beating her palm on the steering wheel of the Chrysler. And Toots discovered that you could survive and laugh and move on in your life, just as she would have to do without her man. She re-entered Granton as though it was a town she hadn't been to for a long time.

The figure of Doreen dissolved into the mottled shade of her backyard. Toots stood on the well-cut lawn near the potentillas and watched her go. These days were numbered. Her eyes followed Doreen into the house, and then gazed beyond the house, beyond the streets of Granton, across the strong, burgeoning fields of wheat into that place where future and memory mingle, the place where Benno and Mary Alone now lived, having moved on in their own ways. Without raising her eyes, without bothering with the clothespins, Toots reached up and began to pull the socks off the line into a cradling arm.

RAPE FLOWER TEA HOUSE

The tea house sat across from a railroad track, with the street in-between, on a rambling property full of lilac bushes and caragana hedges and clumps of crooked maples. Next door, Vernon Koop's roosters crowed just any old time of day. Occasionally they even scrambed to the top of the fence and frightened the tea house guests, who liked to sit on the deck in summer with their iced drinks and their hot biscuits and raspberry preserves. The house itself was almost a hundred years old. The clapboard storey and a half had an enclosed veranda running along one side. Part of the second floor had been transformed into an apartment. Esther and Juney rented it out on a casual basis. The tea house was called The Yellow Blossom because in summer the open prairie on the other side of the track often bloomed golden in canola or mustard or sunflowers. Sometimes the farmer who owned the field had grain on it, or flax, which bloomed blue, or beans, which had no flowers to speak of. But in ten years, there had been a lot of yellow. Juney had wanted to call the tea house Sunshine Blossom, but Esther was stuck on the word yellow. "Listen," she told Juney. "*Yellow Blossom Tea House.* Sheer poetry, isn't it?"

"Not so long ago," Juney had pointed out, "canola used to be called rapeseed. Why don't we name the joint the Rape Flower Tea House?" Esther had been unofficially in charge of the project. She usually got her way.

Juney bought a golden retriever and named him Sunny. Every once in a while she took Sunny along to the tea house and tied him up under the trees so the dog could watch the guests coming and going. The two women decorated the rooms in a floral theme. In summer they brought in fresh-cut flowers from the extravagant gardens they tended right on the property. Juney loved art; she'd invited local artists to fill the walls with their paintings and the sideboards with their sculptures.

One morning in early summer, Juney tossed chunks of rhubarb onto a slab of dough on a large oblong pan in the tea house kitchen. Another slab of dough lay on the counter. The oven was already heating up the room. An old air conditioner stuck in one of the wood-frame windows had already been roaring for hours. On the stove, two cauldrons of ham stock spouted steam towards a ventilation fan in the ceiling. Juney asked Esther, "Did Vernon bring the eggs yesterday? I need one for the wash on this crust."

Esther was mixing the biscuit batter in another part of the kitchen. "They were on the stoop when I got here. With a note." She unfolded a full sheet of paper. "Here: "'Quit shaking your broom at my roosters,'" Esther read. "'They are sensitive. Please be a good neighbour.'" She squashed the note in a floury fist. "I've a good mind to go shake my broom at Vernon. Nobble some common sense into him." The rocking of her bowl made a nobbling sound on the countertop, as though she were whacking Vernon's skull with a broom handle. The women seldom saw or spoke with Vernon. They put a cheque for the eggs on his doorstep once a month. Every now and again he left them a cautionary message. Few people in town ever spoke with Vernon, though he could be seen tending his livestock by anyone who cared to look over the fence. Because neither his house, nor the tea house, was quite inside the town limits, he was allowed to raise animals on his yard. "And he typed it this time. On a computer, I think. Did you shake the broom at the roosters, Juney?"

Juney could hear the laugh behind Esther's question. "Well, maybe I did. One of them was sitting right there above Lorna's head yesterday while she was eating her lemon crumble. I guess I'll have to write Vernon a note. Explain to him for the zillionth time what a rooster crapping in the wrong place could mean for our business."

"You might be right," said Esther. "Maybe an aptly worded note would have more effect than talking to him."

"Or shaking a broom."

"After all, he only communicates with us in writing. On a computer now."

"Still badly spelled." Juney glanced at the little clock on the counter. Nearly nine-thirty.

"Bus Day today," Esther reminded her.

"Eleven o'clock," Juney replied. Once a week in the summertime, a tour guide from the city escorted a busful of day-trippers out to the tea house. Today was also the day Brenda and Claudette would be coming home.

Esther slung her sticky biscuit batter onto a floured board. "Nancy called just before you came. Big group, she says."

"Well, that's all right. It's a nice day, we'll get a lot of walk-ins, too, I expect. I hope Liz brings us some of her chives." Liz had been hired to pitch in during busy times.

The front door slammed. A face with a moustache appeared in the pass-through near where Esther was working. "Hi girls!" the man called in a voice louder than necessary. Ervin Rosenfeld always seemed to Juney to be drunk. Obviously it was too early to be intoxicated, but he always spoke as though addressing a large crowd. His skin glistened with a beery sweat. Since he'd retired from his job a month ago, he'd fallen into the habit of dropping around the tea house in the morning, and then again later in the afternoon just before closing. Now he came into the kitchen and swatted Esther on her butt the way he did every morning.

She slapped him with the tea towel that was always draped over her shoulder when she was baking. "You here to beg for cinnamon buns again?"

"You've got the buns part right," Ervin crooned, shamelessly massaging her rump.

Both women had been widows when they'd started the Yellow Blossom Tea House, youngish widows whose husbands had died only weeks apart in a palliative care ward. They'd become friends while staying with their husbands at the hospital, but it had taken another few years for them to hit on the idea of the tea house. Juney had been content with widowhood and running a business, and so had Esther, for the most part. But after Ervin Rosenfeld had arrived on the scene two months ago, it hadn't taken long for Juney to figure out that he and Esther were falling in love. Ervin hadn't ever been married, or so he said. He'd come from Saskatchewan about ten years back and had dated several women in town; a ladykiller, people called him. Esther didn't seem to care about his reputation.

Having sprinkled sugar and cinnamon and fragments of candied orange peel over the rhubarb, Juney began to cover the pan with the second sheet of pastry. Ervin's lanky arm slid around her shoulders. "How's my little geisha girl this morning?" he breathed into her ear with his chalky breath. Juney's finger pierced a corner of the pastry.

Ervin had started calling Juney *geisha girl* after he overheard a customer talking to Juney one afternoon. "Isn't anyone here Japanese?" the woman had brayed as Juney served her a quiche-and-salad special. The woman put a strong accent on the last syllable of the word. "I thought for sure this'd be a Japa-nese place, but I don't see even a hint of Japanese, and I know what Japa-nese looks like. Maybe you should do it up with paper fans and sushi." While Ervin eavesdopped nearby, Juney had patiently explained the origin of the tea house name, but it only seemed to disappoint the guest.

"Look what you made me do!" Juney waggled her finger at Ervin through the hole in the dough.

"Me fix-y paist-ly?" he simpered in a falsetto voice.

Juney applied a sharp elbow to his ribs. Ervin mistook this for good-natured horseplay and pretended he'd been stabbed with a knife. He fell to his knees, clutching his side and groaning. Esther gave him a gentle kick in the thigh. "Get out of here, bum," she laughed, and handed him one of yesterday's cinnamon rolls. At the pastry board, Juney repaired the dough and fumed in silence. The thought of Esther and Ervin in bed together turned her stomach.

As though reading her thoughts, Ervin asked Esther, "Did you make the reservation?"

Esther's quick glance at Juney was as sharp as Juney's elbow had been in Ervin's ribs. "Did I tell you, Juney?" said Esther as she cut the biscuits with the rim of a teacup. Ervin lounged against the oversized refrigerator with his bun. "We're going to the lake next week. *Early* in the week, for two or three days."

Juney clenched her teeth. So they were going away again, leaving the managing and the baking to her and whoever Esther found to substitute for herself. This was the third time the couple had gone away together in two months. Ervin resented the time Esther had to spend at her business. Juney had noticed that the previous month's accounts, which were Esther's responsibility, still hadn't been done. The writing was on the wall.

The front door clicked open and shut. Liz scooted by the pass-through and hung her sweater on the hall-tree in the corner. The trio in the kitchen heard the rustling of plastic bags.

"I've asked Dolores to help you here again, Juney," Esther continued. "She's going to let me know tonight. We're only going to be gone three days at the most, and one of those days we're closed anyway, and no bus tours."

With a small knife and short, jerky motions, Juney slashed her pastry so the steam could escape when the fruit started to cook inside the big, flat pie. The only holidays the two women had ever taken in the past, aside from a day off here and there, were when the tea house was closed for two weeks after Christmas, and a week in early spring.

To avoid Ervin, who still hadn't left, Liz entered the kitchen from the dining room, carrying two white bags. She was younger than Esther and Juney, a tall, slim woman with makeup and straight dark hair. Today she was wearing her yellow sundress and black open-toed pumps.

"Bus today," Juney told her. "Big group."

"I brought the chives for the potato salad," said Liz. "And sorrel for the soup." She flung the bags onto the counter instead of going to the fridge where Ervin was devouring his bun. Liz had her own big garden and a husband and three children and managed to juggle it all with her job at the tea house. "What's the plate today?"

"Sausage rolls with potato salad," Esther replied.

Footsteps sounded on the staircase that came down one side of the exterior of the house from the second floor. Ervin asked, "Isn't your lodger moving out today?" Crumbs dribbled from his lips. He tried to catch them with his free hand.

"Yup. Why don't you go help him with his luggage?" suggested Esther. "He hauled piles of books and stuff up there when he came." Ervin gave her one last squeeze and bounded out of the kitchen. "And tell him to come in for a cinnamon bun!" The current tenant in the upstairs suite was a young man who had been hired to teach at the school in town for the coming fall. He'd planned to spend a few weeks learning the ropes at the school and looking for a more permanent residence. Over the top of the window air conditioner, Juney could see Ervin pumping the teacher's hand and yapping at him in that good-time-Charlie way of his. He even pulled a cigar out of his pocket and offered it to the man, but Juney saw him shake his head as though Ervin had offered him poison. They opened the trunk of the teacher's car. As Juney brushed the egg wash over the top crust of her pie, she heard the heavy tread of the men on the exterior staircase.

Liz asked, "Anyone moving into the suite once he's gone?"

Juney said nothing. Esther started with, "Wellll...."

"It's not for sure yet," Juney said. She had asked Esther if it would be all right if her daughter and grandchild took the upstairs room for a while. Esther hadn't been very cooperative about it, because, she said, they had agreed they would not rent it out to one guest for more than two weeks at a time; after all, it was supposed to be for people visiting the town, sort of a bed-and-breakfast type thing, not someone's home. And, though Esther hadn't put it in so many words, not a haven for welfare cases; Juney could hear it in her voice. And today Brenda and her little girl, Claudette, would be arriving from Thunder Bay, where they had lived with the baby's father until he had abandoned them and run off to who knows where. Thunder Bay was not very far away, but Brenda had made little contact with her mother the years she was there. The loser boyfriend had held her and the child hostage.

Juney had moved into the smallest bungalow in town some years after Sam had died; she hadn't imagined that she would ever be sharing it again with her daughter, never mind a lively three-year-old and a high-spirited dog. She hadn't expected her only child to come home again. Under different circumstances—a larger house, more money, a leisurely retirement—Juney would have relished the thought of caring for Brenda and Caludette, of becoming a family once more; the company of a canine went only so far. But she'd settled into the tiny house, the life of a single woman, and was enjoying, for the first time, a career of sorts. As much as she loved her family, especially Claudette, Juney couldn't help but worry that they would tie her down.

Brenda was willing to work for her keep, had asked Juney over the phone if she could have a job at the tea house, had almost insisted on it. But Juney doubted that Brenda would fit in. And what would they do with Claudette? Take her along to the tea house, Brenda had said, between you and me we could check on her, it'll be fine. But Juney knew the child would need constant supervision. We've already hired for the summer, Juney had told Brenda, we can't just fire Liz. If you want to be a waitress, there are other places in town. But then I'd have to find daycare for Claudette, Brenda had pointed out. And then Juney had said, we'll see.

Juney tried to picture replacing the trim and tailored Liz with the bulky, loud-mouthed, copper-haired Brenda. Esther wouldn't go for it. But then, what was Esther doing, letting that pig Ervin into their lives? Would having Brenda here be any different? And, for the first time, Juney actually began to relish the thought of letting Brenda live upstairs and work part-time at the Yellow Blossom. Her daughter was a good cook; maybe she could sub for Esther in the kitchen when Esther and Ervin indulged in those romantic getaways of theirs.

The morning train lumbered past, on its way to pick up wheat in the next town. Ninety years ago, a steam locomotive would have chugged by the clapboard house, pulling boxcars full of grain and lumber, and, in those days, furniture and hardware and dry goods. Even nowadays the train still towed that odd caboose behind it, like somebody's little house. What if Esther did quit the tea house? Juney imagined herself packing a bag and hopping onto the narrow porch at the back and settling into the caboose and just going along wherever it went, living the rest of her life in the company of strong, simple men, feeding them soup and warm pies on cold winter days.

Esther wrapped the biscuit dough around baked sausages while Liz chopped potatoes for the sorrel soup. Juney began pulling trays of pastries out of the upright freezer that stood next to the fridge: dream cake, peppermint brownies, bienenstich. And now that the rhubarb pie was in the oven, Juney would make a mousse from fresh cream and raspberries. It was ten o'clock. The little old ladies from the tour bus would be hungry by eleven-thirty. And they loved sweets.

Just before eleven, Ervin stuck his head into the pass-through again. "Hi girls! Your lodger's coming back for lunch. He went to sign a lease at one of those fourplexes on Garden Grove Road. Need any help here?"

"Sweep the patio," said Esther. "And open the umbrellas." She liked giving orders, and Ervin liked taking them. Juney wondered who was in charge when Esther and Ervin made love; maybe neither, or maybe they took turns. She had to avert her thoughts from their sex life, because she remembered that it turned her stomach.

Tea was served in three rooms: the windowed veranda, and the rooms that had once been the parlour and dining room of the old dwelling. The narrow veranda had six tables along the windows. The parlour had five tables, and the dining room had two big tables for larger groups. The more elderly daytrippers seldom chose to eat on the patio; they worried about the bugs, the heat, the wind. Forty people would be on the bus today, and, once the local trade came in a bit later, the little house would be bulging. From eleven till eleven-thirty, the bus ladies would tour the yard and the gardens and admire the artwork. Then Esther and Liz and Juney would take their orders: the plate, or soup and cheese and a fresh roll. Juney would pour the beverages while Esther scooped the soup. Liz would carry out the drinks and start with the food, and Juney would join her while Esther finished filling the food orders. By noon, everyone would have been served, and then the local trade would start trickling in. Then Esther would go out and take their orders while Juney dished out the desserts and coffee for Liz to deliver to the bus ladies. The three women had the routine down pat. But it wasn't all clockwork. There were always fusspots in the group, demanding something altogether different from what was on the menu, because they had allergies, or they were vegetarians, or they just didn't like what was being served. Then Esther would stand in the middle of the kitchen for a few minutes, improvising. She always came up with something. The fusspots didn't have any problems with the desserts, though; they'd wolf down anything. On bus tour days, Dolores popped in around twelve-thirty to start manning the till. Since day-trippers hardly ever left tips, Esther had cajoled the tour company into skimming off a percentage of its take as a gratuity for the Yellow Blossom Tea House.

Ervin came in with perspiration on his forehead and a dead stogie between his lips. "I found a chicken struttin' around on your patio," he chuckled, and sagged into a chair at a small table in one corner of the kitchen. The women sometimes sat there when they had a break in the middle of the afternoon.

Esther glared at him as though he were the chicken. "What did you do with it?"

"I chased it with the broom," Ervin replied. "All the way to the back of the yard. Caught him a few good whacks to his rear."

"If it was a *him*, it's a rooster," muttered Juney. She slipped into the veranda room to make sure all the tables had vases of pansies and nasturtiums. Behind her, she heard Esther tell Ervin to wash his hands.

From the veranda window, Juney could see the back of the train. It had stopped on the other side of a long row of poplars just south of the tea house. The train was hidden from her view, except for the caboose. As she caressed one of the nosegays, she heard a familiar rumble on the street. "Bus is here," she called over her shoulder. Esther let out a little shriek, but Juney knew it wasn't a response to the bus trundling towards the house.

The blue and grey bus turned off the street and lurched over the potholes to the grass parking area beside a lilac hedge. The door of the bus was on the opposite side from where Juney was, and she liked to watch the passengers come around the front of the bus and traverse the lawn in pairs and threes. Except for a sprinkling of middle-aged women, most of the day-trippers were seniors. They often held onto each other as they walked. The ones with canes or walkers fell behind the spry ones who strode on ahead of the pack. Sometimes daughters accompanied their mothers on these outings, so there were always a few younger ones in the group. Today three men were on the bus. Even if they didn't know one another, the men with their wives would probably sit together at the same table, had probably sat in a pack on the bus, too. In the kitchen Esther had begun to bark out the last-minute checklist.

And suddenly, there was Brenda, nearly six feet tall and heavily built, in front of the bus. She was sauntering along with the passengers, holding Claudette's hand, looking at the ground through her sunglasses. Because of the sunglasses, and because she'd dyed her hair an even brighter shade of red, Juney might not have recognized her if it hadn't been for her distinctive build. And she seemed to be holding a conversation with one of the old ladies who flung her cane out in front of her foot at every step. But why would Brenda and Claudette have come on the tour bus? It didn't make any sense. They couldn't have come on the bus. The stooped woman glanced at Brenda every few seconds as though engrossed in a story Brenda was telling her. Juney leaned forward and scanned the yard for a car that might have brought her daughter to the Yellow Blossom Tea House. Not that she would have recognized her daughter's car. She wasn't even sure if Brenda had one.

Brenda had always been somewhat of a stranger to Juney and Sam. No, not always, not when she'd been a baby. But as she'd grown, she had floated further and further away from them, like a child drifting alone out into the ocean. They'd decided it was the phantom grandpa effect.

For all intents and purposes, Juney had not had a father. He'd died shortly after her birth. She possessed only one photograph of him: the head and shoulders of a young man. No other photos existed that she knew of. The man had shown up in town one day, looking for work. Someone had taken him in as a boarder, and he'd ended up marrying Juney's mother. He'd been young when he'd fallen from the scaffolding of a grain elevator he'd been helping to build.

Juney knew little about her father's personality or his stature. He might have been a big man, or might have become one, had he lived longer. The black and white photo told her nothing of his colouring, but when Brenda had been born,

Juney's mother told told her that he'd had coppery hair. The way he'd come into her mother's life could indicate that he'd been aimless, the way Brenda was. So whenever their daughter did something that was uncharacteristic of themselves, Juney and Sam would say, "Must be the phantom grandpa."

It was only lately that Juney had begun to wonder about her phantom father's genes inside *her*, this desire to escape in the caboose of a train from her old life and all the people in it. She had begun to think more and more that, had her father lived, he would have eventually left her mother to continue his restless trek. Juney had not tried delving into his ancestry. His family name hadn't been that common; how hard would it be to uncover his history? "He came from the Rockies," her mother had said. Juney imagined he was working his way east. What would he have done when he arrived at the edge of the continent?

"Juney, the tea!" Esther shouted from the kitchen.

In summer, iced tea was more popular than hot tea. The cold tea was homemade, had chilled all night, in fact. But Juney still needed to squeeze the lemons, stir the juice into the tea, and cut other lemons for decorating the glasses. "I'll be.... I have to.... Be right there!" she yelled back at Esther.

But then Juney ran outside to greet her daughter and grandchild, and to find out how they had so magically appeared.

The lemons were too slippery, the skin too thick, the knife not sharp enough. The slices didn't want to straddle the edges of the tumblers today. Esther spooned potato salad onto transparent plates while Liz went along behind her, garnishing each dish with cucumber and yellow cheese. The patrons washed into the eating rooms like a south wind. Voices hummed and crackled and Juney dropped ice cubes into the waiting tumblers. Halfway through, she ran to the front door and peered through the window at the patio where Brenda and Claudette sat beneath an umbrella and watched the tourists wandering among the delphiniums. The petite, blonde Claudette spoke to a doll she held on the table in front of her; Juney could see her lips moving. It turned out that Brenda and the little girl had come in their own car, which was parked on the far side of the yard. The bulky tour bus hid it from view.

Juney hadn't cried until she'd embraced her daughter, and then little Claudette, felt the realities of their bodies through their clothes, the texture of their hair brushing her forehead. And when she'd looked into Brenda's eyes, Juney saw tears shining in them, too.

There'd been no time to talk. Juney had suggested they wait on the patio.

Can't I just move our stuff up to the apartment now? Brenda had asked.

Someone's still in there, Juney had half-lied. You can stay at my house for a while, she'd blurted out, then hurried back inside the tea house.

Esther left the kitchen to seat three women who were not part of the tour. While she was gone, Juney put extra cheese and an extra sausage roll onto one of the plates and carried it and two glasses of iced tea out to the patio. By then, Ervin had happened by, was even sitting at the table with Brenda, who would have told him immediately what she was doing there, so chatty she was. He was grinning at her through that bushy moustache of his.

"Why didn't you tell me you had such a beautiful daughter?" he boomed at Juney when she set the food down. "These girls are gorgeous." He gestured at Brenda and Claudette with his dead cigar.

And that's when Juney knew for certain that they couldn't live at the Yellow Blossom. Ervin liked his women extra large, Juney had overheard Esther telling Dolores once.

To Brenda she said, "This is Esther's friend, Ervin Rosenfeld." To him: "You're scaring the guests. Get off the patio." It was the first time she'd spoken that directly to Ervin, though she did not look him in the eye when she said it. She stood still and waited for him to leave.

He eased out of his chair. As he walked away, he threw over his shoulder, "Catch ya later."

Brenda followed his retreat with her eyes.

"I'll pay for your lunch," Juney told Brenda. "You know where my house key is—"

"No, I don't!"

"What? Of course you do, it's under that little—"

"Oh yeah. I remember."

"Under that little what, Mummy?"

Juney patted Claudette's arm. "I'll see you there at five."

The new teacher came up the path. He liked the patio, had often sat in the bright, hot sun to eat. Now he settled at a table beside Brenda and Claudette's and looked at them through his wraparounds. He rested one arm along the back of an empty chair. This was trouble, too, Juney thought; he'll tell Brenda he just moved out of the suite and she'll have her things up there in a flash. "I think Esther said these tables are reserved today," she chirped at the man without considering how easy it would be to be caught in that lie. "Would you mind eating with Ervin in the kitchen?"

Juney couldn't see his eyes through his sunglasses. "Sure," he said. But he left the patio as slowly as Ervin had.

"He's the one who's living in the suite," she explained to Brenda. "He'll be teaching here in the fall."

Her daughter looked at her, but Juney couldn't see what was going on behind those dark shades, either.

Liz was flying by the time Juney returned to the house. Most of the tourists were inside now. Ervin and the teacher sat at the kitchen table, deep in conversation. Esther hissed at Juney as she flitted past, "Where have you been?"

"You know how hard it is to get away when people start asking you questions about the flowers," Juney said as she grabbed an order pad and a pen from the top of the fridge.

"What were you doing out there in the first place, are there customers out there?"

Juney nodded. "I had to chase Ervin away from them," she whispered. "I don't think a big hairy man with a cigar should be fraternizing with the customers." *I should have gone after him with the broom, like Vernon's rooster,* she thought. Esther stared at her for a moment. Then they both left the kitchen to help Liz take orders.

We have a lovely fresh sorrel soup today, with a lovely homemade butterhorn roll and some lovely old cheddar. Or you could have the plate, which has a mild sausage encased in a light biscuit pastry and a lovely old-fashioned potato salad. And can I interest you in anything to drink? The coffee is just brewing and we have some lovely iced tea, made the old-fashioned way....

Over and over again. Except Juney didn't use the word

lovely much, hearing it swirl around the room from the lips of Esther and Liz.

Juney managed to catch the next walk-ins, and persuaded them to sit on the patio. One more group and the three tables would all be occupied, at least for a little while, and her lie would be erased. Ervin and the teacher would be served last. By the time they left the kitchen, Brenda would be gone.

"Isn't that your girl out there?" Esther ladled soup into deep bowls stacked beside the range. "I thought you said she'd be here next week."

"She's early. I've hardly had time to talk to her myself."

"She's not expecting to move into the apartment today, is she?"

Juney could hear the warning in Esther's voice. "No. I told her to stay with me for a while."

"Good."

"I guess you'd like Ervin to live up there," Juney whispered. "He keeps hinting about it." Her second lie of the day and it was not quite noon.

"What?"

Liz came in for a tray of drinks. Juney followed her out of the kitchen with another tray.

Round and round they went, laden with food, cheerful but curt with the patrons who wanted to yap about the history of the tea house. Each table was provided with a pamphlet giving the whole history of the place, describing how Esther's great-aunt Nora had left it to her, how it had stood empty for years before the two widows had hit on the plan for a restaurant. Esther had even included pictures and a description of the slow renovation of the house, and details about the perennial gardens. Juney had wanted her to mention the chickens next door, but Esther said if Vernon ever died or moved away or stopped keeping chickens, the pamphlets would be out of date. Juney's sole contribution to the pamphlet was a drawing she'd made herself of the house right after the reconstruction was finished, back when she and Esther had both been unattached and eager and full of energy and good humour, when they'd still had a sparkle in their eye.

Esther and Juney and Liz took the dessert platters around. The women at the tables squealed with pleasure and sinned against their diets.

By two o'clock, the hubbub had subsided. Brenda and Claudette had left for Juney's house; Liz and Dolores were gone for the day; the teacher had said his goodbyes; Ervin had disappeared as he usually did at that time. The washing up was finished. Juney grabbed a hoe from the tool shed at the bottom of the yard and began working in the flower beds. Hardly anyone came to the tea house between two and three. They'd be busy again between three and five with the afternoon crowd. Esther and Juney handled that stretch alone because they served only tea biscuits and desserts. The day was warm and calm and lazy, and honeybees had begun to gather nectar from the showy blooms in the gardens. Juney had toyed with the idea of dashing home to help Brenda and Claudette rearrange the tiny second bedroom, but decided against it in the end. More than ever today, she needed this free time in the afternoon, when she could spend a quiet hour with the bees and the finches while others rearranged her life.

Esther, still in her apron, took a notion to tour the gardens while Juney hoed. She strolled casually among the roses with her arms folded beneath her breasts and stopped here and there to snap a deadhead from its stem. She moved closer and closer to Juney, who continued chopping at the soil, and finally said, "Well, I guess I'll go in and make that cake. Kids' birthday party tomorrow, remember?"

Juney nodded. Meatballs, noodle salad, funny cookies, chocolate milk.

"So what are you going to do about Brenda?"

"I don't know," Juney replied. "We'll have to talk it out."

"Was she disappointed about not living here?"

Juney shrugged. "She still thinks she will, probably. We have to talk it out."

"I hope you understand, *she* understands."

Juney bent over to pull out a thistle that had been missed the last time. Its sharp spines pierced her fingers.

"Juney—I'm thinking of getting married again."

"That's nice. Who's the lucky fella?" Juney tried to rub the thorns out of her skin.

"Well, obviously...."

"Has he asked you?"

"No, but...."

"Doesn't seem like the marrying type."

"This is the real thing, though."

"I see."

"Just wanted you to be prepared. I mean, it may happen on our holiday next week."

"You're getting married next week?"

"Of course not. But he might ask me."

"If you think so." Juney resumed her weeding.

"You don't like Ervin, do you?"

Esther said it in the same tone of voice she'd used when

she'd told Juney she was going to make the birthday cake, which suggested that she didn't really care if Juney liked Ervin or not.

"It's hard to imagine the two of you as a match, is all," Juney replied.

"We have an awful lot of fun together."

"Oh, so you're marrying him for fun."

"Oh, Juney...."

"I'm just saying, there's no need for holy matrimony, is there? Just go out and have your *fun*, and let it ride."

"I'd like to live with him."

"No need for that, either."

"Well, I'll make my own decision."

"Of course you will, Esther. Don't ask for my permission."

Esther said nothing, just gazed at a rose bush.

"Go make your cake, girl." Juney waved her away.

Esther retreated along the path that led back to the house. "And are you paying for your little getaway *again*?" Juney called after her.

Before Esther had reached the door, one of Vernon's roosters clambered to the top of the low fence between the two properties and crowed in triumph.

"Scat!" Juney shouted. "I'll cock-a-doodle-doo you, you stinky old bugger!" Juney aimed the sharp end of her hoe at him. Esther watched from the porch.

"Juney, no!"

But Juney ran at the bird with her makeshift lance in front of her and in a second had knocked him off his perch amid a ruffling of feathers and anxious squawking among the hens on the other side.

Esther shook her head and slammed the door behind her.

Well, if Vernon's around, Juney thought, there'll be hell to pay. And I'm up for a good fight right now.

Juney wondered if it was time to tell Brenda about Juney and Sam. Juney and Sam. The life of the party. Jiving at the Lions Club dances, swaying and singing around the old piano on New Year's Eve, organizing the fundraiser fish-fries. A fun-loving pair in an elite social circle. They had a party room in their basement and more patio lights in their backyard than any other in town.

Juney had put the fantasy aside a long time ago. It's what she wished people would say about her and Sam, would have said, when he was still well. She imagined an author writing a history of the town and interviewing everybody about their favourite people, and everybody saying, Juney and Sam. She'd never wished for wealth or influence. Juney had always simply wanted to be one half of a hot couple.

When Sam had died—even before, when he'd been diagnosed as terminal—she'd abandoned her dream. She couldn't be hot on her own. Neither she nor Sam really had the right stuff. The truth was, they were a quiet, inhibited pair. They went to the Lions Club dances and the rest of it, all right. But they weren't quite brave enough to join the group singing around the piano. The most Juney had ever done at the fish-fries was operate the cash box while Sam hustled the beer. They were accepted, even liked, but not popular. Sam had been taken away from Juney before they'd begun to glitter.

Even though Juney knew it was a mistake, Esther was starting over. Juney had found a kind of respect and even celebrity as half-owner of the Yellow Blossom Tea House. But she knew deep down that it was Esther's swagger and bluster that entertained the patrons. Once Esther decided to leave the Yellow Blossom for good—and Juney had no doubt that that day would soon come—the popularity of the tea house would wane. Juney could picture it: herself as a grey-haired hag drowsing at the cash desk while spiders spun webs from her forehead to the dusty Tiffany fixture overhead. People would drive by, shake their heads, and cluck their tongues. "Used to be a good place way back. Too bad Juney couldn't make a go of it. If only Esther hadn't gotten married...." So much lay with Esther.

Now the only fantasy Juney could conjure up was to run away with a bunch of rough men and bake pies and play the odd game of twenty-one while the train rolled on and on along two never-converging rails. She wanted to abandon Esther before Esther could abandon her.

Those were the things she must tell her daughter.

A lump of paper popped over the fence into the tea house garden. It bounced on the flagstone sidewalk and rolled behind a rose bush. Juney walked over to it and snagged the wad with her hoe. I SAW THAT, it said. Apparently Vernon had run into his house and typed it on his computer. In the past, he'd scribbled his notes on tags ripped from feed sacks. Juney stepped onto one of the benches in front of the fence and searched for Vernon with her eyes. His overalls were just disappearing into the small red chicken barn. She crumpled up the scrap of paper and threw it after him.

Tires on gravel announced a customer. Juney turned to see who'd come for early tea—or late lunch. The women were Americans. You could always tell the American women by their accents and clothes and hair and jewellery. And in this case, the licence plate on the car. She admired the confidence in their voices, their ready laughter. But Juney also knew she could not be them. She went back to her hoeing and ignored them. Esther would take care of the tea.

But she had scarcely resumed her weeding when she again heard the crunch of tires on the parking area near the house. She sighed and, without looking to see who it was, headed for the main building. Esther would be wanting her inside now.

Ervin Rosenfeld stood in front of the tea house door. He watched her approach among the flowers and she could see that he was leering at her. She set one foot on the porch step. "I love a woman in an apron," he said.

"And I love a man who stays out of my way."

Ervin's large lips turned up in a larger grin. Not that Juney actually looked at him. She didn't have to, to sense that ugly mouth squirming into its lecherous shape.

Since it had been only Ervin Rosenfeld arriving earlier than usual in the second afternoon car, Esther didn't need Juney for serving. Juney decided to start the next day's soup: basil chicken with fresh vegetables and lemon thyme. The extra freezer in the basement was always filled with soup stocks the women made whenever they had spare time. While the broth was thawing on the stove she would wash the pea pods and lemon thyme she'd picked earlier that morning in the tea house garden, and then chop the young carrots Esther had found at the farmers' market the day before. Her mother had taught her that the first carrot you pulled had to be eaten raw. These still had their tops attached, just the way Juney remembered her mother's, except that her mother would have dug them from her own garden. Juney had a garden, too, but her carrots were far from ready for digging. They would have to be thinned first.

Katrina. Mother of June, who was named for June Allyson, who Katrina saw in movies at the theater in a little American town called Cherry Creek, just across the border. In fact, Juney's second name was Allyson. Most people didn't bat an eyelash when they read or heard her whole name, didn't have a clue who June Allyson was. While Brenda had been growing up, Juney had pointed June Allyson out whenever the actress's face would appear on the television screen. "Your grandma loved that woman," Juney would say. "She named me after her." It didn't seem to mean much to Brenda. We should watch a June Allyson movie together some time, Juney thought as she gnawed the carrot down to the fat core near its stem. Find out what that lady was like. It would be a place to start. It would establish the touchstone that would connect the three generations.

But together with the raw carrot, the memories of soup, the anticipation of that touchstone, came the pungent yearning to cast herself adrift in a vast landscape and keep moving. Like a thunderbolt, it struck Juney, transforming the carrot in her mouth into a nugget of hard truth: a destiny. To continue her father's life, to continue his journey. Brenda had only gone to Thunder Bay and back again. It was up to Juney to do it right.

But as she carved up the vegetables, she thought, I'll never leave this town. I'm too much of a coward.

The telephone rang. Esther, passing through, snatched at the receiver.

"It's Brenda," Esther told Juney. The Yankee women's voices echoed in the empty dining room. Just before taking the receiver from Esther's impatient hand, Juney noticed the hoe; she'd brought it into the tea room after her encounter with Ervin on the porch. There it was, leaning against the wall near the telephone.

"Hello?"

"Mom, it's me."

"What's up?"

"I talked to Tammy. I called her parents."

"Yes?"

"Did you know she's divorced?"

"I suppose I did—separated, anyway."

"Why didn't you tell me?"

"I've hardly talked to you at all in the last two years."

"Mom, Tammy's my best friend."

"Then why didn't she tell you herself?"

"She was up in Fort McMurray."

"Well, it's not the Antarctic."

"I'm just surprised. She's here in town and in a real bad mood."

"Well, keep out of her way, then."

"It just really surprised me."

"Brenda, are you calling me at work to tell me you're steamed because I didn't tell you Tammy got divorced in Fort McMurray?"

"Well.... No. I—there's a bunch of girls getting together—tonight—with Tammy—and—"

"—you want me to babysit." Juney was not quite able to keep a certain tone out of her voice.

"I'll put Claudette to bed before I go. I just thought if you were going to be home anyway...."

"That's not it.... I need to— Look, I'll be home in a couple of hours. I'll see you then, okay?" Juney hung up the phone.

Her fingers grasped the handle of the garden hoe. Where would she find a June Allyson movie on such short notice?

"Are all the paintings for sale?" The voice at Juney's elbow startled her so that she almost dropped the hoe. Although the phone was in a private part of the tea house, one of the American women had wandered in and was asking about the art.

"Just the ones with prices on them," Juney replied. Where was Esther?

"The one I want doesn't have a price on it." The woman showed her teeth with a broad smile.

"Then it isn't for sale." Juney tried to usher the woman out of the kitchen.

"Couldn't you call him?" The woman was really smiling and drawling now, and the sequins on her short-sleeved sweater sparkled extra bright.

"Call who?"

"The artist!"

"Sorry," said Juney. "He lives in Fort McMurray. He just went through a messy divorce and doesn't want to be bothered."

Esther was in the dining room, yakking with the other American. Juney could hear them now. "Your tea must almost be ready," said Juney to the sequined one, gesturing towards the tables. "Have you considered sitting out on the patio?" she added.

Juney turned back to the kitchen. Through the rear window she saw the hulk of a man on the other side of the caragana bushes behind the house. His body blocked the light passing through the branches. All she could see was a shape. Ervin was trimming the shrubs with a pair of old hedge clippers. She imagined the sound they'd be making, the metallic snapping of the twin blades as they bit into the soft wood. Sam had been an almost obsessive hedge trimmer. Juney had found his constant puttering among the lilacs and catoneasters irritating. Now she would have given anything to hear him, through an open kitchen window, clipping away, whistling in that bemused way of his. Instead, it was Ervin Rosenfeld. And the window was closed because the air conditioner was on.

Trembling maple leaves began to dapple the sunlight on the west side of the tea house. Soup began to simmer on the stove. The last of the guests lingered over their coffees and teas. The kitchen no longer needed to be cooled, what with the shade of the trees and the busy time being over.

Juney turned off the air conditioner and lingered beside the kitchen table next to the window. The hoe was still in her hand. She rested her cheek against the wood handle. The chatter of the women in the next room camouflaged the snipping of Ervin's shears.

Juney stood there for several minutes. Her thoughts meandered aimlessly as her eyes followed the slow-moving form of the man on the other side of the hedge. If only Esther could see him for who he was.

Juney thought about how little she'd had to do with Claudette these past few years; about Sunny, and what a good companion the dog had become—not as good as a husband, but better than Brenda, in some ways; about the aromas of the soup cooking on the stove; and about Sam, and what their lives together would be like now if he were still here: probably very much the same as before. But if Juney had known about death, that Sam would die, she would have been more contented with what they had, with the way they were. They would have been happy. Brenda and Caludette would have been part of their happiness.

She imagined walking out of the kitchen, hoe in hand, and leaving the tea house. The path of wood shavings would lead her to the backyard, an area that had not changed much since Esther's cousins had played there. It was the only place on the boundary between the tea house property and Vernon's that did not have a fence or buildings dividing them. As she walked along the path, Ervin's tuneless humming became louder, and a flicker of movement off to the side told her that Vernon Koop was lurking behind a couple of maples at the edge of his yard.

Juney saw herself continuing across the lawn. She parted the caraganas and stepped into the glow of sunlit canola blossoms. Ervin was facing away from her, bent over the lower branches, still humming something that might have been "Waltzing Mathilda," blurred by the stogie in his mouth and snipped into fragments by the clippers. Looking past him, Juney saw the train resting on the spur of track that ran next to the poplar row.

Ervin moved slowly along the caragana hedge. Juney said nothing; she stood behind him and clawed at pigweed with her hoe. Then he straightened up and turned. As soon as he saw her, she slipped back through the shrubbery and onto the bit of lawn at the rear of the tea house. Ervin Rosenfeld followed. She waited.

"Did you want something?" he called.

"Not really," Juney replied from the middle of the patch of lawn. She dropped the hoe and folded her hands in front of her skirt.

Ervin Rosenfeld said, "I wish we were friends, Juney." He took a step towards her. "We really should try to get along better, don't you think?"

Juney nodded. Esther would be cleaning up the tables inside. Was Vernon still hiding behind his maple trees, eavesdropping? Juney did not care if he was.

Ervin took another step forward. The shears hung from one hand. With the other he flung his stogie into the shrubs. "I don't know why you don't like me. Maybe it's something I said to you once that I can take back. Or maybe it's something I can change."

Juney shifted her body so she could look past the house, between it and the hedge, to the railroad track. "You're a very different man from my husband, Ervin. Very different. You're crude and gauche and too—macho. Such a flirt. I'm not used to a man like you."

He grinned at the flattery. "You might get used to it. Esther did."

"I might. I might not."

"How about a truce, anyway?" He thrust a hairy paw at her.

"Maybe I should relax more."

"That's it!" The man did not try to disguise his eagerness. "Try a little flirting yourself. Get a new fella for yourself." He was close enough now to touch her. By this time Esther might be puttering around in the kitchen, perhaps even looking for Juney, looking for Ervin.

Juney raised one hand and reached out. She locked her eyes into his.

Ervin Rosenfeld clasped her hand with his large one. She was surprised to find it soft and supple, not unlike Sam's.

"I'm just naturally a kisser, Juney," Ervin said. "I'm very affectionate."

But he hugged her first. Wrapped his bulk around her thinness, pulled her chest against his. She smelled sweat and cheap cologne and sour cigar. She felt the hedge clippers pressing on her buttocks.

From within this embrace, as she waited for the kiss, Juney gazed past the ear of Ervin Rosenfeld to the caboose almost hidden by caraganas and poplars. Was it moving now, moving on to the next place? Yes, she could hear the rumble of the engine further on down the track. Out of the corner of her eye, Juney saw the window where she had been sitting only minutes earlier, listening to the babbling of the Americans and the bubbling of the soup on the stove. At any moment, Esther might look out that window.

The caboose melted into the prairie. Juney felt the shears slide down her skirt as Ervin dropped them onto the grass. His hands slithered over the silkiness of her clothes. She waited for the kiss, and for Esther's face to appear at the window. All she'd have to do was catch a glimpse of Ervin through the tea house window. . . .

Standing there at the kitchen table, very still, still leaning on the hoe, Juney felt a smile forming on her lips. A soft laugh escaped from her throat. The rooster crowed in Vernon Koop's barnyard, probably from the top of the tea house fence.

The chatter of the American women ebbed into the foyer and out the front door. Goodbyes were exchanged. Esther's voice was there.

Juney heard footsteps come through the kitchen, then stop. Without turning away from the window, Juney pictured Esther behind her: her face would be glistening with the perspiration of the day's work, her eyes alight with love and yearning for her man.

"You still here?" asked Esther.

Through the trees, the yellow blossoms glowed in the sun of late afternoon.

"Yes," Juney answered. "I'm still here."